THROUGH DIFFERENT EYES

THROUGH DIFFERENT EYES

KAREN CHARLESON

Garry Thomas Morse, Editor

EDITIONS

Cover design by Doowah Design.
Carved paddle design on cover used with the kind permission of Robin Rorick Haida Art. More of Robin Rorick's artwork can be seen at www.robinrorick.com
Photo of Karen Charleson by UVic Photo Services.

This book was printed on Ancient Forest Friendly paper.
Printed and bound in Canada by Hignell Book Printing Inc.

We acknowledge the support of the Canada Council for the Arts and the Manitoba Arts Council for our publishing program.

Library and Archives Canada Cataloguing in Publication

Charleson, Karen, 1957-, author
        Through different eyes / Karen Charleson.

Issued in print and electronic formats.
ISBN 978-1-77324-006-0 (softcover).
--ISBN 978-1-77324-007-7 (EPUB)

        I. Title.

PS8605.H3697T47 2017   C813'.6   C2017-904690-X
                                               C2017-904691-8

Signature Editions
P.O. Box 206, RPO Corydon, Winnipeg, Manitoba, R3M 3S7
www.signature-editions.com

For my children:
Lelaina, Layla, Steve, Estella, Mariah, and Joshua

ONE

It was those stupid white girls in Port Hope. They had started the whole thing with their whispering, their giggling, and their never-ending streams of innuendo. They were like hungry seagulls ever vigilant for a handout. They had spotted Michael immediately when he returned to Kitsum that spring. It was not that they cared or even noticed that he was there for his mother's funeral. They did not really know anything about him. They just saw another new guy to ogle and speculate over. Brenda Joe knew all that but she chose to overlook their behaviour. She supposed that there was nothing better for girls to do in Port Hope than to fantasize.

In 1985, Brenda was in the last months of Grade 10. Weekdays, she bused to Port Hope Secondary, and then back to what was legally known as Kitsum Indian Reserve Number One. Sarah was her constant companion. They were the same age and in the same grade, and that seemed to matter a lot at the Port Hope high school. The two girls had been in the same class ever since they had both started kindergarten in the old trailer that served as the preschool at Kitsum Elementary. They had never been especially good friends. All through the elementary grades, Sarah had mostly stuck close to her older sister and a couple of other kids Brenda did not know that well. Their families were what people in Kitsum called "Holy Rollers." They talked a lot about going to church events and Bible study meetings. Summertimes, a bunch of the Kitsum kids went to the Bible camps that they organized.

Brenda's dad, however, had always been adamant. He called the camps "brainwashing." One year she had begged for weeks to be allowed to attend because her best friend Marcie was going but her father never let her go. He took her and her brother out on his boat instead. It was a nine- or ten-day fishing trip, that one. By the time the *Pacific Queen* was tied up again in Kitsum Harbour, Bible camp was long over.

Brenda always sat with Sarah on the school bus because they were the only two girls left from the group that had started off in the old trailer. During lunch hour, she sat with Sarah and the Kitsum students who remained in the classroom that was partly used as a cafeteria. They ate the fish, egg, or meat sandwiches made with homemade bread that their mothers invariably sent with them. Their moms did not think they should eat junk food from the corner store. Nor did they believe their daughters when they told them what the other kids did. The girls discussed community events in Kitsum and the current gossip of the day. Sometimes, they even talked about what they imagined was going on in Port Hope.

When her best friend had still been attending school, lunchtimes had been different. There were no awkward lulls in the conversation, then. There was no quiet staring out the windows at Port Hope students who always seemed to have more to do and more places to go. The time had sped by because there were endless things to talk and laugh over. Brenda had not needed to hunt for extra excitement. If Marcie had been there in Grade 10, Brenda would not have even considered hanging out with those Port Hope girls.

By the early spring, Brenda had begun to earn her own money from babysitting. After finishing her food from home, she would often head over to K & M's Convenience for a cup of hot chocolate or a handful of penny candy. Brenda felt more important, being able to buy what she wanted like the Hope students.

The Port Hope girls hung around in three very distinct groups. One group consisted of the cool girls. They were the ones who played school volleyball and basketball and somehow were also selected to cheerlead for the boys' teams. They possessed large stockpiles of stylish new clothes and their parents owned the newest trucks and biggest houses. Brenda saw little point to even talking to them. The second group of girls was made up entirely of the ones who partied a lot. They smoked in the downstairs washroom and outside in the student parking lot. They bragged loudly about going out with older guys and getting into bars. Naturally, they could not get into the beer parlour at the Port Hope Hotel because everyone there knew everyone else and exactly how old they were, but the hotels in Campbell River and Port Hardy were fair game.

The third group of girls was not as tight-knit as the other two groups; it was a group made up by default. Hope girls who did not fit into the other two groups ended up there. If Brenda had to give that group a name, she would have called them something like the "In-betweens." The Kitsum students were not part of any of these groups. The Hope kids treated them as though they were their own group. Oddly, the teachers did, too.

A couple of the "In-between" girls who occasionally acknowledged Brenda's existence liked to hang around K & M's. One noon hour, Brenda ventured there, and they called her over to sit with them on one of the benches that was pushed up against the store's stucco-covered outer wall. She had sat tentatively on the edge of the painted wooden plank, but the girls had not appeared to notice her nervousness. Beth told her that she liked her jacket and offered her potato chips from the bag she had just opened. They seemed genuinely friendly. Brenda could not help but feel flattered by the attention.

Tracy and Beth were not big-time partiers and they were not quite as cool as the cool girls. Their fathers, like many Port Hope men, worked in the woods. Yet these were not the daughters of fallers or foremen. Tracy and Beth's dads almost certainly performed less glamorous tasks such as bucking or cutting up the fallen trees and loading the huge trucks. For Brenda, this knowledge was next to hereditary. Life in Port Hope was reflected in similar logging towns and camps on the North Island.

Brenda discovered very quickly that Tracy and Beth's favourite topic of conversation was guys. Which guy was the best looking? Which guy had the nicest hair, the coolest truck, or the most stylish clothes? Which guy had they spotted watching them? Which guy was just waiting to ask one of them out? Obviously, they had noticed Michael Clydesdale when he turned up in Hope. He was a good-looking guy, no doubt about it. Beth and Tracy soon bombarded Brenda with questions: Did he have a girlfriend? How long was he staying around? Where did he hang out? Other than his name, Brenda did not know much. She could point out some of his relatives, but Tracy and Beth were not interested in looking at *them*.

Tracy was the first one to suggest that Brenda should "try" for Michael. Actually, she voiced an idea that was already taking shape in Brenda's mind. Tracy and Beth told all kinds of stories about their own experiences with older men. Sometimes it sounded like they were in a race with one another to see who could pile up the most. Their parents did not seem to care how much they ran around. Brenda knew that if she had even attempted any of the stuff that Beth and Tracy bragged about, her parents would have grounded her for months, and lectured her until her head exploded. Brenda could not admit to Tracy and Beth that she had never had a real boyfriend. She had fooled around some at a couple of basketball tournaments at home and in Campbell River. She was far too embarrassed to tell her new friends about the one time she had actually had sex with a boy. The only soul she had ever told was Marcie. Only a fool would have done what she had done: lose her virginity to a basketball player from the Mainland who was only visiting Kitsum for a weekend of ball. A couple of strained phone calls, and that was that — she never heard from him again.

Full up with Tracy and Beth's talk, Brenda felt that she needed to make the effort to flirt with guys again. The more she thought about it, the more she agreed that Michael really was not such a bad choice. He was not related to her, which in Kitsum was an important consideration. He looked like he took care of himself. He was not a friend of her brother's, or worse still, her parents. He was not a teenage boy. He was older, and compared to guys her own age, he seemed solid. Yes, he was already a man. Also, she wanted to impress her new friends, and not with the short story that was really hers. She needed something better, something that was more grown-up.

Word soon reached her that Michael worked on the construction crew in the new subdivision. A road looping around the top of the village had been pushed through a couple of years earlier. It overlooked the entire span of Kitsum Harbour and opened up areas for building along the upper middle section of mountainside. The first eight houses were close to being completed, and four more homes were in the early stages of construction. New home owners were counting down the weeks until they could move in. The loop road was open, but it was often blocked by the builders' trucks and supplies. The only people stirring in the new subdivision were the construction workers, and many of them were not even from Kitsum.

Instead of walking straight home when the school bus dropped her and her brother off beside the Kitsum Band Office, Brenda began taking a longer route home. She needed the extra exercise after sitting around all day, or so she had told her brother. Junior had only shrugged; he preferred walking home with his friends anyway. Brenda would walk by the building sites extra slowly and find excuses to linger nearby. She did dumb things like stop to retie her shoelaces or straighten her books. She also pretended to be astonished by the progress of each new house.

Brenda guessed that she was one of a handful of people who Michael saw go by all day. Maybe that was the reason he had noticed her right away. At sixteen years of age, Brenda chose to believe that Michael was enchanted by how pretty she looked, and by the way her chestnut hair caught the sunlight and shimmered like ocean waves on a bright, calm day. She thought that he was impressed by her animated gestures and feigned desire to learn everything she could about the new houses. His fascination was easy for her to imagine. Brenda carried every crumb back to Beth and Tracy at lunch hour. The way Michael stared at her, smiled at her, spoke to her.

Once Brenda started spending her entire lunch hours with Tracy and Beth, Sarah became a little colder towards her, a little less willing to chat on the bus. The distance from Kitsum to Port Hope was only about fifteen or twenty kilometres if you measured it in a straight line, but the gravel logging road that connected the two places consisted mainly of switchbacks that more than doubled the distance. Potholes and rough, rocky sections forced all vehicles to slow to crawling speed. When the forestry company had extended the road from Hope into Kitsum in 1975, the company representatives had promised to keep it maintained. As soon as the logging was finished, though, it was the men from Kitsum who were out after the big winter storms, unclogging drainage ditches and culverts, and cutting fallen trees off the road. There was no way to drive safely from Hope to Kitsum in under forty-five minutes. Brenda had all but abandoned Sarah at school, but to her credit, Sarah remained relatively friendly to her on those long daily bus rides.

Brenda enjoyed the attention from Michael, and she enjoyed the admiration that earned her from Beth and Tracy. As a result, she felt attractive, popular, confident, and grown-up. By the time school let out in late June, she had invented an entire romantic relationship out of a bunch of waves and smiles. Of course, there had been a few short conversations, and the one occasion when Michael had happened to drive by her in Port Hope and had stopped to give her a ride home from school. The more she entertained Beth and Tracy with her exploits, the more a relationship between her and Michael became reality. Their grins and gasps only fed the fire. By the end of the school year, Brenda was determined to have him as her actual boyfriend. An older guy, a good-looking guy to boot, a man who drove a truck and worked hard and treated her decently. Yes, Michael was perfect. This would impress everyone. All of the Kitsum girls and even the cool girls from Hope; they would all have to show her some respect.

By early July, Brenda had worked out a summertime routine. Mornings and early afternoons, she helped her mother around the house. There was always cleaning or laundry to do. In addition, there was often fish to be cut up or put into the smokehouse. Her mother was too grateful for the unexpected help to question Brenda too closely. Brenda felt vaguely guilty, recognizing that her helpfulness had put her mother off her guard. But the tactic to gain more leeway was working. Brenda kept it up.

Later those afternoons, Brenda told her mother that she was going to the lake or to Marcie's. More often than not, she would head straight for the construction sites. Most days, she timed her mountainside trips so that she had about half an hour to loiter before Michael got off work. That way she was readily available to walk along the new loop road with him at the end of his day or to catch a ride part of the way back in his truck. Once the new road met what people were beginning to call "Old Top Road," Michael would continue along down toward the old village and she would bid him a dramatic farewell before heading home.

Michael had never actually invited her, but he had told her where he lived when she had asked him. He had a room at his uncle's house. Downstairs, he had added. He had no desire to go upstairs where his Uncles Fred and Murray and his Auntie Ethel lived. When the elder Clydesdales partied there, he just turned his radio on, locked his door with a latch, and stayed in his room. No one bothered him there. Brenda calculated that he had carefully told her these details for a reason. If he had not wanted her to visit, he would have simply said that he lived with his uncles and aunt. That would have been the perfect brush-off. Everyone in

Kitsum knew that the Clydesdale house was a notorious party place. She would have been too afraid to look for him there.

That summer, Brenda went to the community hall every evening. Basketball generally started around nine o'clock and lasted until the doors were locked at midnight. Junior was on the Kitsum Intermediate basketball team, and he played every night with his teammates and a variety of older players. This was the first summer since they were small that Brenda could remember her brother not going fishing with their father. He had a job with the Kitsum Band that year as one of two youth recreation workers.

Brenda had no trouble tagging along. Most of the teenagers and young adults went to the hall every evening anyway. This was more fun than just sitting at home. Given that the basketball games ran so late, their mother would not allow their younger brother and sisters to go with them. Her only rule was that Brenda and Junior had to be back home by midnight. She had initially tried to make it eleven o'clock but Junior had convinced her that he would still be in the middle of a game by then.

For the first week or so, Brenda stuck around. Then one evening when Junior was playing ball, Brenda left early. It was normal for people to wander in and out of the hall. Even if Junior had noticed her gone, he would have assumed that she was just outside or hanging around on the beach below with other teenagers. The Clydesdale house was in the old part of the village, not too far away. Brenda walked quickly to Mo George's store. Mo sold pop, chips, and candy out of a small addition he had built onto his house. His wife sold bread, and occasionally pies and cakes. Still not sure that she would not chicken out and turn back towards the hall, Brenda committed herself to a pop that she was too nervous to open and drink.

There was a tangle of berry bushes and young alder trees next to Mo's where an old shed had once housed a generator that was used before Kitsum got hydro. She struggled her way through the new growth, almost tripping a few times over garbage and junk discarded in the bushes. Then she emerged, intact, very close to the Clydesdale house. Only the thought of someone seeing her rummaging around so far away from her own home at this time of night kept her moving. Before she could change her mind, she was knocking softly on the basement door. If Murray or Fred or Ethel answered, she would tell them that she was looking for Junior. That sounded better than saying she was looking for her boyfriend.

Michael was the one to open the basement door. He was surprised; that was all. She wanted him to be thrilled or at least moderately pleased to see her, but she settled for the raised eyebrows and tilted head. She had to ask him to invite her inside. Then he seemed to think that she had wanted to see his uncle or aunt. "They're drinking up there, you know," he warned.

Brenda forced herself to laugh lightly. She could hear the country music blasting from an open upstairs window. "You don't drink with them?"

Michael shook his head and muttered something about not enjoying the old alcoholic crowd. She ignored the bitterness she heard in his words.

"Just thought I'd drop by and say hi," she managed. "I was at the hall. Kind of boring there, the same old faces, the same old games every night."

The basement between the outside door and his bedroom door was a disaster. Old clothes, damp newspapers and decaying cardboard boxes, tools and fishing gear, tin cans and bottles; they all seemed to mingle in haphazard heaps that threatened to topple if bumped the wrong way, provided they had not already toppled. As she looked around, he could not hide his embarrassment.

Michael's room was a sharp contrast. It was small and sparsely furnished. Brenda saw a single bed, neatly made and covered by a slightly faded green blanket. She saw an old dresser on top of which sat a small radio. She heard the sounds of an urban rock station. Beside the radio was a trio of paperback books. A yellow plastic crate, serving as a table for an alarm clock and flashlight, was pushed up next to the bed. Not one picture or photo adorned any of the walls. There was no sign of the disorder beyond the door, but there was not much sign of life either. She did not know what she had expected to find in his bedroom. Perhaps some indication of who he was, of what he liked or cared about. Instead, his room seemed institutional, almost how she imagined a prison cell or military barracks to be. Michael sat on the bare cement floor while she perched on the edge of the bed.

Brenda was wearing faded skin-tight jeans and a sleeveless rose-coloured blouse. She had left her hair down, without ponytail or barrettes, and it cascaded down her back. She knew that she looked good. Even so, Michael was reluctant to do more than steal the odd glance at her. He asked her a few questions about school and what she was doing for the summer. That was all. When the silence between them grew too thick, she got up and left. She replayed the scene over and over again as she walked back to the hall and home. She figured that he was just shy or that he was just being respectful.

Brenda visited Michael at his room exactly four times that summer. Most nights, she could not manage to get away from the others at the hall. Teenagers hung around in clumps. It was unusual to see anyone sneaking off by themselves. The worst times were when she thought she had gotten away, and one of the girls would catch up and walk with her. Once she made it all the way to the Clydesdale house only to find people sitting outside. There was no way she could walk by them without being noticed, and worse, questioned. As if to frustrate her plans further, her mother decided to occasionally let Thomas go with her and Junior to the hall. Tom had been begging to be allowed ever since school let out. Junior told their mother it would be fine, that he and Brenda would keep an eye out for their younger brother. Brenda fumed.

The second time that Brenda was able to successfully make her way to the Clydesdale house, the place stood ominously dark and quiet. She knocked on the basement door and she clearly heard the echo. Michael answered the door. Once again, he invited her inside with reluctance. She wondered if he was ashamed of where he stayed, and if that was the reason he discouraged visitors. She had brought him a pop from the store, but he told her that he never touched the stuff.

Brenda had expected the second visit to be easier than the first. She was wrong. Being alone together in the basement room seemed even more awkward. Michael was mostly silent. Her disappointment soon began to show. Then he broke the silence. "Look, I had a long day at work. I'm pretty tired, okay?" She had left a few minutes later.

It took nearly two weeks for Brenda to convince herself to visit Michael again. Maybe this guy was just not interested in her. She had to know for sure. She forced herself to take an afternoon walk by the construction site. Michael returned her smiles and waves, just like he had before. Perhaps there was something there after all. Something to work with. When she had crossed the unfinished road and had looked up at the second storey where he was working, she had seen how fully and completely he smiled. Yes, his whole face had lit up. She knew that she had made him happy. More encouragement on her part could move things along. With a vague sense of determination, she made more trips to the worksite.

The summer holidays were already winding down. Brenda would be returning to school soon and what would she have to show for the summer? Not much, that was for sure. Yes, she could add some juicy details to her sneak visits to the Clydesdale house, but what had really happened? There was still no boyfriend to show for her efforts. The days were already getting shorter. One night after nine o'clock when it was already dark, Brenda walked from the hall to Michael's. She stood at the basement door for a while, thinking that she could hear faint music. Then she knocked. No one answered. She knocked again and still no one answered. She was forced to retreat.

A few days later, on a Sunday evening, Brenda returned to the Clydesdale house. If Michael did not answer the door this time, she swore to herself that she would never visit again. *Never.* She was about to give up when Michael opened the basement door. He did not seem surprised to see her. Straightaway, he stepped aside in the doorway and gestured for her to come in. He kissed her as soon as she was inside his room. Then instead of sitting on the floor, he sat beside her on the bed. After all of her planning and fantasizing, Brenda expected to be more prepared, more ready. Instead, she found that she did not know what to do. She was so nervous that she froze. She could no longer speak.

In one way she had no idea of what she was doing, of what was going on; in another, she knew exactly. She felt unable to move, and yet there she was, moving her mouth, her arms, her back, her shoulders. The only thing that made sense to her, that felt like a necessity, was holding and touching this man who was still a stranger to her. He did not say a word. He did not have to say anything. She felt like this could go on forever, that all she had ever wanted was to be wordless like this, to be making and hearing voice through her body alone.

Afterwards, things changed quickly. Michael seemed angry; she felt that very clearly and wished she could not. He turned away from her on the narrow bed and sat up, facing the wall. He still did not speak, and she could not bring herself to make a sound. Michael was being very deliberate with this action, or non-action. Minutes went by. He was waiting for her to go. She picked her clothes up from the floor, dressed, and made her way home through the darkness.

After what was essentially a humiliation, what had ever made her go back? She no longer even dared to visit the construction site. After how he had treated her, how could she have returned? She did not know; that was the thing. Brenda had become obsessed by what she could not figure out. Somehow she had got things wrong and was misreading the situation. No matter how much she tried, she still could not figure it out. Once more, she told herself. She would give Michael—this idea she had of Michael and Brenda—one more chance.

If she was somewhat unsure of his anger the first time, she did not doubt it the second time. She had to undress before he would even go near her. She could feel his scorn in every touch. When she was leaving he stood up and kissed her gently on the cheek. Then he lay back down and pulled the single blanket over himself, once again facing away from her. She understood that he was saying goodbye. She did not even turn around when she let herself out. She already knew that she would not be back.

TWO

From where Nona sat at her kitchen table, she had an uninterrupted view of the front and the southern side of the Joe house. From her sturdy wooden chair, she could see directly into their living room. Her son had warned her once again on the phone only the evening before about becoming too involved — too preoccupied, he had said — with the comings and goings of Martin Joe and his family. She could not help looking out her own window, could she? Nona had told Charlie many times as he was growing up that her neighbour was her close relative, and therefore, their close relative. Martin's father and her mother had the same grandmother. They were *that* close. It was only proper for Nona to keep an eye out for her own family. Charlie really did not grasp that part.

As she drank her morning coffee, Nona watched all the Joe children leave for school. A few minutes later, she saw Martin come through the kitchen porch door and down the same three short steps. Martin, she assumed, was on his way down to the Kitsum dock and the fishermen's floats. Commercial fishing for chum (or dog salmon, as the fish were more commonly known to locals) was due to begin soon. There was nowhere else he would have been going but to his boat, the *Pacific Queen*. Martin had been a commercial fisherman for most of his life. In the days before a fishing opening, he would head down to the floats every morning to work on his boat like all the other fishermen. Nona's late husband had followed the exact same routine, and she still kept up with the fishing news.

Something was afoot in the Joe household. Nona finished her second cup of coffee. It was an unusual movement that had caught her attention. What was going on with Ruby? Through her neighbour's front picture window, Nona could see things flying through the air. At first, she thought that Ruby was shaking out the brightly coloured couch covers and pounding dust from the thick cushions and rug. But no, that was not it. Lamps and books and chairs were not hurled across the living room when anyone cleaned. Nona lowered the volume on the radio. She was sure that she could make out the sounds of banging, of things hitting walls, and *that*—that was most definitely the sound of breaking glass.

There was no other possible explanation. Someone must have told. That must have been what happened. Things had been okay at the Joe house after sunup. Not anymore. It was no secret; everyone in Kitsum probably knew by now. Everyone that was, except Ruby. Why would anyone tell her? Some people had no common sense.

Nona's cousin had phoned her the night before. Nona did not consider it anything to brag about, but Carolyn had called to say that Charmayne was home. So her daughter was back and showing off. Nona had nearly snorted in response. What was it this time? Her new car, her new clothes, her husband's new job? Charmayne always had something. If she was really so happy living in Vancouver, Charmayne would have stayed there. If she was really satisfied with life with her husband, she would not show up in Kitsum every few months to cause nothing but trouble. Martin Joe was only the latest on a long list of married men for whom she had created a scandal.

The door across the street slammed hard. There was Ruby, stomping the short walkway to the road. Even from a distance, Nona could see that her face was red. Her light jacket was only partly pulled up over her shoulders. Her usually neat hair hung wildly over her shoulders. Ruby was not a big woman—she was indeed quite short and slender—but the way she charged toward the road made her appear a lot larger. The woman looked livid. She headed straight past Nona's open window without so much as glancing upward, and stormed on down the trail that led to the southern end of the village.

Martin would be home soon and what would he find? Poor man, working all morning on his boat so that he could do well for his family, only to come home to an empty house. Not just an empty house, she corrected herself, but a house that his wife had trashed. Every man makes mistakes. Nona wished that she could step in and do something for her cousin, maybe redirect him to her house for a decent lunch. But right away, Martin would have known that something was wrong. He always ate at home.

Carolyn had filled her in about Charmayne's current visit. Nona was supposed to be envious that Carolyn had a child who visited her mother so often. When was the last time Charlie came home? Carolyn had asked innocently enough, as though she did not know very well that Charlie had not been back since the spring. Nona had almost worked out a way to hang up on her cousin when Carolyn changed her tone. In a voice quieter than the one she normally used, she had begun: "Sometimes I don't know what to do about Charmayne."

"What do you mean?"

Carolyn had spoken vaguely about Charmayne and "her men," only to pass it all off as a bit of fun for her. After all, there was not much to do in Kitsum. Before Nona could feel her blood boil again, Carolyn had dropped her voice even lower.

"But the latest…I could not believe the latest. I mean, I always thought he was faithful to Ruby. I mean, I know he got into some trouble when he was younger, but that was ages ago. He's on the straight and narrow nowadays, you know. I mean, I did not think he would do that. Not anymore."

Nona had to be sure of what she was hearing. "Who?"

"Martin," Carolyn had breathed. "Charmayne was with him on the weekend. Martin. She told me herself. I guess she was having a few drinks with a couple of her friends at Dan's place. Anyways, Martin stopped by, looking for Dan's boy. He needed another deckhand for the dog salmon opening. Only Dan and his son had gone to Campbell River. I guess Dan's daughter told Martin that they'd be back soon and offered him a beer while he waited.

Charmayne was surprised when he joined them. Martin ended up talking to Charmayne, and so it went. She didn't have to spell it all out for me. Ruby is going to be so pissed."

Carolyn had emphasized the "pissed," letting the "ss" sit behind her teeth for that extra instant. Nona had wanted to say a thing or two to her about Charmayne. There was a lot she could have said, too. Instead she had merely asked when Charmayne was going home. Carolyn could read into questions as well as anyone.

"Charmayne is leaving on Saturday." The conversation ended there.

It had taken Carolyn many years to get back at Ruby, but she had finally done it. Nona had sat for a long time thinking about what had happened. Even smart, capable men like Martin who knew the ways of the world could still be damned fools around young women. Especially one who looked so much like the young girl who had wanted him so badly all those years ago. Nona remembered the fishing season when Carolyn herself had all but chased Martin around Kitsum. She remembered the young woman's string of invented excuses to go down to the floats when Martin had been a deckhand for his father. In those days, he could often be found working on the old *Kitsum Pride* when he was off school. Back then, Carolyn had told anyone who would listen that Martin liked her. Nona had never bought it though, no matter what tales Carolyn had told her and everyone else. In fact, Martin's mother had complained to Nona that Carolyn was always hanging around. She had openly told Nona that it was Ruby Smith—and only Ruby Smith—who interested her son.

Maybe Martin regretted never taking Carolyn up on her offers long ago. Maybe he just wanted to feel young again, even for a little while. Nona was suddenly angry at herself for even thinking such things. For all she knew, Charmayne might have spiked his beer. Nona would not put anything past that woman. Charmayne had been nursed on her mother's desire for revenge against Ruby. The second that Martin accepted that beer, her scheming must have begun. She would have come up with a plan to get him alone with her. Yes, Nona was convinced that Charmayne had somehow manipulated her relative.

Martin was walking towards his house. He looked like he had not a worry in the world. The chaos inside his home would be the first shock. Nona held her breath. A few minutes later she could see the man standing in the middle of his living room. She watched him turn one way and then the other. After surveying the damage, it would not take him long to realize what had happened.

Nona wanted Martin to give up waiting for his wife and to get back to his boat. The dog salmon opening was coming up fast. It was one of his last chances to fish before winter. Even so, Martin stayed put. Then the younger kids arrived home from Kitsum Elementary. It was clear that Thomas had firm instructions to wait for his sisters because the three of them always arrived home together. Ruby had done a good job there. The kids were well behaved. As a neighbour, Nona had no problems from them. The Joe children would not be found among those kids out at all hours, yelling, swearing, throwing stones, wrecking things.

About an hour later, Brenda and Martin Junior returned home from the high school. There was still no sign of Ruby. Brenda was old enough to cook dinner. The family would be fine, Nona told herself, and took a step away from the window. She had best make her own supper, even if it was only a fried egg and a piece of toast. Charlie would not have been impressed to learn that she had spent most of her day staring at the Joe house and summing up their situation. She could almost hear him: "What good does that do anybody?"

Sometimes she wished that she and Harry had had more children. It had taken her over two years to get pregnant with Charlie. A few years later, there had been a miscarriage. The doctor in Port Hope had not even been able to tell her if it had been a boy or a girl. It was too early to know, he had said, but she had not believed it. After that, she was never able to become pregnant again. Then Dr. Wensicott—the one who did not seem to know anything — had told her to "just keep trying." What kind of advice was that from a doctor? She still suspected him of being a closet alcoholic. People said that you could smell the booze on him when he was called into the tiny hospital on an emergency. A useless know-nothing, that's what Nona thought of him.

Harry had never complained. He had never made her feel bad. He had never acted as though anything were wrong. He had also taken Charlie down to the boat and out fishing every chance he got. If Nona could see Ruby right now, she would tell her to thank her lucky stars for a husband like Martin and those children of hers. Every man makes mistakes. Ruby had it good. Martin was always straight back home after any fishing trip. Nona had noticed their truckloads of groceries and the kids in their new winter jackets. No, Ruby had certainly never gone without.

The next morning, Nona was pretty sure that Ruby was still not home. After the kids headed off for school, Nona waited for Martin to leave for his boat. There had to be so much work left to getting the *Queen* ready, but there was still no sign of Martin making a move. By mid-morning, Nona was stiff from sitting in her kitchen chair. Her knees seemed to freeze up these days whenever she kept them in the same position for too long. She got up and walked around her small kitchen until she could feel her legs loosening up. She had best get busy with her own cleaning. Watching out for Martin and Ruby would have to wait.

Two full days passed before Ruby came home. By that time, Martin had finally left for his boat. Shortly afterward, Nona saw that Ruby was still wearing the same blue jeans and pale red jacket that she had worn three days earlier. She walked ever so slowly towards her own house. No light went on in the living room or kitchen. In fact, there were no signs of Ruby even being home for the rest of the morning or afternoon. No one — not Martin, Thomas, Rebecca, or Millie — went home for lunch either. Ruby did not leave again though; Nona was pretty sure of that. The prodigal wife had probably gone straight to bed.

Ruby must have gone on a bender. Though she was not a regular drinker, there were stories about her drinking in the past, just like there were stories about Martin's drinking in the past. Yes, there were always stories if you went back far enough. Even back then, Nona could have counted on the fingers of one hand how many times she had heard anything about either of them. Ruby was probably sicker than a dog. Word had already spread around Kitsum that Ruby had been drinking at the Clydesdale house. Sure, Ethel Clydesdale was her relative, but even so, what a place for her to go!

Then life seemed to return to normal. The next morning, Martin was seen walking towards the floats. Brenda and Junior sauntered down the road in the opposite direction toward the high school bus stop. Tom, Becky, and Millie piled out of the kitchen door after everyone else had left, also on their way to school. Then Nona could see Ruby's familiar shape passing behind the kitchen window.

Later on, she heard Martin talking to one of his fishing buddies on the marine radio that she still used. He would be leaving for the fishing grounds after lunch. Ruby would have her radio on across the street too; Nona knew that she would have heard. That was what you did when you were married to a fisherman: you listened to the radio to find out what he was doing, if he was catching fish, and when he would be home. That was exactly what she had done when Harry was alive and fishing.

Soon enough, it was time for bed. She had already stayed up a lot later than she had intended. However, her neighbour stayed up in her living room, and the kids stayed up with her. It was nearly ten o'clock when the car pulled up in the driveway. By the light of their porch, Nona recognized Monica, Ruby's younger sister. She wondered if Ruby had called for her, although that seemed unlikely. She could not imagine Ruby asking anyone — even her sister — for help with this one. She would have had to give her the gory details, and Ruby was far too proud to do that. Monica's arrival must have been sheer coincidence.

Nona had always had a soft spot for Monica. The girl had been just a teenager when she came to live with Ruby and Martin. Her and Ruby's parents had died in that horrible truck accident on the way to Port Hope from Campbell River. Thomas had owned a truck before most folks in Kitsum. He had parked it at the Chinese restaurant in Port Hope whenever they were home. People said that he used to give the restaurant owners fish for watching it. He was another good fisherman—Thomas. Nona remembered that his boat used to be called the *North Sea*.

Monica had done well for herself. When it was time for her to graduate at the new high school in Port Hope, she was already a bit of a local celebrity. A story about her was even in the Hope newspaper on account of her winning an important university scholarship. The Port Hope school made a big deal out of that, using her as their Kitsum success story. They had included Kitsum students to increase their enrolment numbers and get the high school built, although they would never admit it. Instead, they used Monica as proof of how good their school was for Kitsum.

Monica was special though; there was no doubt about that. Not many Kitsum kids had done as well as she had. She had enrolled at university in Vancouver and came home on the holidays. Monica had also come for Harry's funeral; that was what mattered to Nona. She had come to the house and had sat with Nona and Charlie and Harry's family. She had even helped with feeding everyone and keeping things tidy. Monica was younger than Charlie, but Nona had always thought that the two of them would have made a good couple. Though by the time Monica was going to university, it was too late. Charlie had fallen head over heels for Molly, a woman his own age from Hartley Bay—way up the coast. She had taken Charlie away from Kitsum, and for Nona, that was awfully hard to get over.

Nona went to her bedroom, still lost in thought. Yes, life would have been very different if Charlie and Monica had married. However, before she had even put her head to her pillow, she realized her foolishness. To wish away her precious grandchildren;

what was the matter with her? She was overtired from staying up too late. Maybe she had made too many assumptions about the Joes. They would do okay without her holding vigil. She would bake bread in the morning and clean her house. Then she would get back to her own business and see if Charlie and Molly and the children were still coming for a visit.

THREE

Monica had left the apartment while Saul was still asleep. She had not even dared to take a shower or turn on the overhead kitchen lights or do much of anything that would have risked waking him and beginning another dragged-out conversation. This day, she had only wanted to get to work, put in her hours, and be on her way home to Kitsum. Arriving at the office before seven meant putting in an extra two hours before most of the others arrived. Those hours — plus the overtime she had gathered in the previous weeks — were more than enough to excuse her from the job for the time that she needed to make her long trek back home.

Monica had been in the Membership Branch at the Department of Indian Affairs for nearly three years. She had worked her ass off to complete an anthropology degree, only to end up in the maze of a downtown Vancouver office building, another flunky in a labyrinthine bureaucracy completing tasks and reports that were largely useless. Saul had advised her that the job was merely a stepping stone. It was an entry point, he had explained, a place from which she could "springboard" to another position where she could make a difference. Monica had once believed him. His coaching had got her through the first two years.

The trip to Kitsum involved a two-hour ferry ride to the Island, followed by another two hours on the highway to Campbell River. That was only the first part of the trip. From Campbell River, there was a minimum four-hour drive with the second half on unpaved logging roads. A late-morning ferry would put her back in Kitsum after dark. She figured that the roads would still be good though.

It had not snowed yet that fall. Saul—ever practical Saul—had wanted her to wait until the Christmas holidays. Then she could stay for more than the weekend and really make the most out of all that travelling time. Once again, his logic was flawless. Monica did not have the energy to explain to him that Christmas was too far away. Saul had not appreciated her reasons for leaving early; he had only noted that she was skipping out of the conference they had planned to attend together. She had packed her overnight bag without another word.

The drive always took longer than she planned. She made one stop to use a gas station washroom and then another to pick up fresh fruit and vegetables and treats for her nephews and nieces. She had not intended to take a long time, but the sky was already darkening when she reached the cut-off from the highway. From that point on, the way turned into a mostly single-lane gravel road that made its own convoluted journey through the mountain passes across the island to the western coast. Within ten or fifteen minutes of slow travelling on that logging road, blackness had surrounded her. This was nothing like driving at night in Vancouver. Here darkness meant the complete absence of light. She no longer felt like she was even inside her vehicle. She was crawling along the road with only her meagre headlights separating her from an infinity of blackness.

It was impossible to count or individually identify all of the switchbacks. She imagined, rather than saw, the road clinging to towering walls of rock—sheer cliffs that fell into voids of apparent nothingness. In the vastness of the dark, whole mountains and entire forested valleys were simply absent. The pouring rivers at the bottoms of the cliffs, the canyons and narrow carved valleys, the boulders and discarded tree trunks, the gnarled root mazes that had slid down mountainsides shaved of their forest coverings; they were all gone. She knew their presence solely from memory. The anticipated two-hour drive from the blacktop highway stretched into three, then nearly four, hours. Around every corner she was expecting her car's high beams to pick up the Welcome to Port Hope sign that the town had hired some laid-off logger to create with a chainsaw. Gravel and loose stones struck the bottom of her car. Through her partially open window, she awaited the first faint taste of salt in the air.

They had found her and Ruby's parents along one of these stretches. September, it had been. Over ten years ago already. Their truck was flattened, bent nearly beyond recognition amidst the boulders and debris only metres above the rapids on the Tasgish River. The big storms with the really heavy rains had arrived early that year. The river had been raging. Only a helicopter and rescue unit could pry the old red pickup from between the rocks so that it could be lifted with the bodies of her parents still inside — out of the canyon and over the last mountain to the scrapyard in Port Hope.

The road never failed to remind her. Her mother and father had been forced off the road by a loaded logging truck. The skid marks — where the huge truck tried to stop — had been long erased, but she could still see them clearly. It had been for her that they had made the trip out. She was their youngest, the one who was attending high school in Campbell River. They had been driving home after dropping her off at the start of another school year.

When Monica had all but given up waiting for it, suddenly the Welcome sign was there, looming just above her. She stepped on the brakes to look at it. There was a painted mountain scene with snow and a glacier trailing down to a blue-green sea. Beneath "Welcome to Port Hope" someone had printed, in identical but smaller letters, "and Kitsum."

Port Hope residents liked to consider themselves a town, but that label was quite a stretch. Well under a thousand people lived there. As far as Monica knew, Port Hope remained the incorporated village that it had become when she was a kid in the early 1960s. She remembered hearing her parents talking about it. The road that Coast Forest Products had forced through the mountains is what did it. Once the loggers could drive their own trucks in and out, they were no longer content to stay secluded in a logging camp for weeks on end. They brought their wives and girlfriends to visit and soon the company was bringing in trailers for family housing. Before the loggers had moved in — people in Kitsum still talked about those not-so-long-ago times — Hope had been a straggly collection of fishing families. There had been no road to the highway and no connection to Campbell River then — just a freight boat that arrived once every few weeks when weather permitted.

Coast Forest Products kept extending their network of logging roads into new areas. When they started logging the Kitsum River Valley they pushed a connecting road from Port Hope into Kitsum. It took a matter of months for people in Kitsum to substitute their daylong boat trips into Port Hope — to visit the post office, the grocery store, the hospital, and liquor store — for an hour's drive in a truck. Learning to drive and getting vehicles were the only things that slowed the process down from one of days to one of months. A few years after the road was put in, BC Hydro and BC Tel extended their lines into Kitsum. In the span of a small handful of years, Kitsum became a cog — albeit a very small one — in the wheels of the twentieth century.

As soon as Monica spotted the gas station lights at the entrance to Port Hope, she flicked on her turn signal. Her car was still the only vehicle on the road, but she had learned to drive in the city, and those habits were firmly ingrained. After that journey through the darkness, she needed, much more than she needed the washroom or another cup of stale coffee, to announce her successful arrival to some living soul.

Beneath the brightness of the station lights, Daniel Smith was looking up from filling his truck's gas tank at the antiquated pump. Monica released and stretched her cramped legs one at a time from her small car. She zippered her thin jacket against the night air that always felt colder at home than in Vancouver. "Uncle Dan," she called.

"Monica," the elderly man answered slowly with intent. There was not a trace of surprise in his voice or on his face. Her uncle could have seen her only yesterday or, heck, even earlier that morning, the way he reacted. It was always like this, Monica thought, like she had never left or been away for any length of time.

Pushing open the convenience store door, Monica came face to face with Daniel's wife, Linda. In other circumstances, or if they had not found themselves so close to one another, the two women probably would not have hugged. As it was, staring one another in the eye, within touching distance, and with Daniel only steps away, they had little choice.

"How've you been?" Monica was first to speak. "I've just gotten in. Just now." She was still excited. Arrival was always a victory of sorts.

"Oh," the older woman responded. "You've come to see Ruby, then?"

"Yes, yes." Monica watched Linda's cheeks jiggling ever so slightly. She had gained weight since the last time Monica had been home.

"Good luck, dear." Linda patted Monica none too gently on the shoulder and squeezed by her to exit the open door. "Wish Ruby the best from Dan and me. If she needs anything, tell her to let us know."

Linda spoke as if someone had died. Was that it? Monica panicked for a brief moment. Had someone passed away? She had been gone from Kitsum for enough years to no longer have the patience for the meandering, wait-and-eventually-find-out style of conversation that most of her relatives used. She followed Linda back outside.

"Hey, what's going on?"

"You didn't hear, then?" Lowering her voice so that Monica had to bend closer to catch all her words, Linda continued, "Ruby's been having some trouble with Martin. Everyone thought that he was way past all of that, but he must have figured he could get away with it again. Running around like *that*."

By the time Daniel had returned from paying for the gas, Monica had a full enough picture of what had happened. Or what might have happened, she corrected herself. Linda was not exactly a person known for her accuracy. Still, Monica had heard the stories—from her own mother—about those times Martin had "gone haywire" when he and Ruby were still a young couple. Monica remembered it to be around the time that Brenda and Junior were still small, but before Tom and her younger nieces were born. He had been the talk of Kitsum then, her older sister's husband. But not for long, she remembered. There had been maybe a month, she was guessing now, the first time, and then another month maybe a year or so later. But after that, there was nothing. Martin and Ruby settled down. They were happy. Those times were put into the background and they had faded away.

Monica drove as fast as the potholed road to Kitsum would allow her. She had considered Ruby's house to be her own home for many years now. Ruby and Martin had taken her in when their parents died. There had been no question about it. Ruby was a dozen years older than Monica. She had been married to Martin for what had seemed already a long time when the accident happened. Thomas was a baby then; Junior was starting kindergarten; Brenda was in elementary school. She remembered Brenda with absolute clarity. Her niece had been ecstatic and enthusiastic as only a six-year-old could be. The prospect of sharing her bedroom with her Auntie Monica had been a dream come true. Monica now realized that Brenda was one of only a few shining lights for her during what otherwise had been a very dark and depressed period.

Once Monica was inside the old familiar kitchen door, there was no longer any time for her to think, worry, or recollect. Here, her nieces and nephews were talking and smiling and laughing. It was Monica's first trip back since the previous spring and there was endless news. Ruby had kept supper as Monica knew that she would. It was food from home too: smoked dog salmon with baked potatoes. Nothing she had eaten in the city could compare to this.

Ruby was quieter than usual, but with Becky and Millie and even Thomas chattering, there was no way to speak directly to her. Monica merely ate and listened, as Junior and Brenda joined in, taking turns at sharing a whole barrage of information. Her sister stood, leaning into the cupboards beside the stove, waiting for the kettle to boil. She looked tired, more tired than Monica could remember seeing her. Stress lines etched her face. Monica silently cursed Martin. It was his fault. He was the one who had done this to her sister.

Normally, the kids would have stayed up as late as possible. Monica's coming home was a special occasion and that would have given them a perfect excuse. Ruby would have had to threaten them to get them into bed. This night though, the suggestion of going to sleep came from Brenda, and her brothers and sisters went straight to their rooms without a word of complaint. Sensitive kids, Monica thought, and not for the first time. They knew very well that she and their mother needed to talk. They wanted their mother happy again.

In contrast to her children, Ruby seemed to be avoiding the upcoming conversation. In the kitchen that had become ominously quiet, Monica sipped tea with her sister and listened to the clock ticking its seconds away. "I have a huge headache," Ruby apologized. "I'm pretty beat."

It was a futile attempt at avoidance that both sisters recognized immediately. Even if Monica had not run into Daniel and Linda, and even if Linda had not told her the gossip, she would have sensed that something was wrong. Ruby barely looked at her. Each time their eyes met, Ruby averted hers. She inspected the turquoise mugs on the table; she looked over and over again at the stove and the countertops, at the closed door and the open curtained windows, anything to avoid looking at Monica.

"I saw Daniel and Linda in Hope," Monica started. She was only home for two days. Sunday morning, she would have to leave early in order to make it back to Vancouver that night. It had been a struggle just to get most of Thursday and Friday off. She wanted to get this talking over with and move on to the usual life at home that she so missed. "You know Linda and her gossip. Doesn't take much to get her going."

Ruby let out a long sigh. "Well…what did Linda tell you?"

"Some story about Martin." Monica watched her sister's shoulders tighten an additional notch. "About Martin fooling around with Charmayne. Anyways, Linda said that she was worried about you, and if there was anything she could do, just say the word."

Ruby snorted. "Linda's going to help. That's good to know." Her voice betrayed her anger. Monica waited.

"I don't know, Mon," Ruby eventually said, slowly shaking her head. "I don't have a clue what I am supposed to do. It was only a few days ago. I was still finishing my coffee after the kids had all left for school and Martin had gone down to the boat. The phone rang, and suddenly everything was different. It was like the solid ground that I had been standing on went all crooked and jagged and I could barely keep myself standing."

Monica waited for her sister to continue.

"God, he must have been fooling around with Charmayne at Dan's house. Of all places! Dan and Linda and Danny Jr.—they were in Campbell River playing bingo. Their regular thing. Her nephew and daughter stay with them too. I guess they had a bunch of their friends over. Martin claims he didn't know that Danny Jr. was out, that he had only stopped by to ask him to deckhand for the opening, and that was how he ended up 'having a beer' with the guys. Like he does that. Just 'has a beer' with people half his age."

Monica did not dare say a word. She poured herself more tea and waited for Ruby.

"I was waiting at home like a fool. Wondering when he didn't come home for supper. I thought he was just working on the boat like always. Then it gets dark and I still think he's working on the boat. Even when it was really late, I sat up and still figured that he was on the *Queen*. I was even worried about him, for Chrissakes. Worried that he was having a hard time fixing something. I almost called him on the radio.

"Instead I just waited. That's me—dumb, dumb, dumb. All bloody night, I waited. He finally calls me at something like five in the morning, tells me that he must have fallen asleep on the *Queen*. Christ, he never does that, so I knew that was bullshit. But what choice did I have? I made myself believe it.

"I can't stand this, Mon. I thought I could when I came back home. I made up my mind to come back for the kids, you know? Did Linda tell you that too? That I was gone for three days?" Ruby looked accusingly at her younger sister, as though blaming her for whatever Linda had said. Monica only slowly shook her head no.

"Now he's out fishing like nothing's happened. I'm left here to just carry on. Like always. Like he never did anything. I can't do this again, Mon. I can't…" Even though Ruby hid her face with her hands, Monica could still see the tears. Her whole body trembled. Monica tiptoed behind her older sister and began to rub her back and shoulders. Up and down and around in circles. She rubbed until her fingers felt like they were eroding into dust.

Gradually, Ruby calmed down. She wiped her face with the sleeves of the too-large sweater she was wearing. When she finally lifted her head, she stared directly at Monica. "I'll be okay now," she said. "At least for a while. I'm sorry. It's not your fault. You didn't come home for this. To listen to all my crap."

"Sure I did," Monica responded immediately. "That's what families are for, eh? I know you're tough. You've always been the tough one. Maybe it's my turn."

"Yeah, that's me all right, Mon. Tough and dependable, so everyone can treat me like shit. So Martin can just forget about me like some old sock. Good old Ruby. Do whatever the hell you want to her, and she'll be tough. She'll just keep on going.

"You know, Monica, what I cannot believe is that he would do this to me now. Now, after all these years. I haven't worried about him, you know, for a long time. And I thought things were good, really good. Maybe I was just complacent, or too lazy, thinking things were never going to change. I was already feeling superior to all those other women who have to worry about their husbands.

Now I feel like an idiot. A fool to not have seen what was right in front of me. What if I've been a fool all this time?"

"Ssshh…Ruby. That's crazy. You know that's not true. Martin has always loved you. He's not one of those men that chase around after different women. He never really has been, and he never will be. If he'd ever fooled around before, don't you think we would have heard? When he drank and partied long ago, you found out about that right away. Look what happened this time, eh? It wouldn't have been different before. Man, Ruby, you know better than I do that a person can't get away with anything around here."

"What if he's just gotten tired of me?" Ruby's voice was small.

"That's ridiculous, and you know it! It had to have been just a stupid mistake. Think about it. Charmayne must have set him up."

New tears were leaking from Ruby's eyes. The phone rang. Ruby vigorously shook her head so Monica rose to answer it. Sure enough, she heard Martin's voice asking for his wife. Ruby continued to shake her head no.

"Uuhh…she's pretty tired, Martin. I don't think she's up to talking right now," Monica managed. She was a little surprised that her brother-in-law let what sounded like a feeble excuse go without comment.

"Tell her I'll be home as soon as we're done fishing. Probably by next weekend."

"Yeah, I'll tell her."

"Monica," he added. "I'm glad you're there."

"Me too."

She repeated the brief conversation word for word to Ruby. "That man loves you," she finished.

"Sometimes I hate the fucking bastard," Ruby declared. It was rare for Monica to hear her sister swearing. The children, and sometimes she still included herself in that category, were not allowed to use "that kind of language" in the house.

"Remember, Rube, when Mom and Dad died…you and Martin took me in right away. You put up with all the haywire stuff I did. Remember how terrible I was? I got drunk every chance I could.

Got kicked out of school and you and Martin had to go there and convince them to let me back in. You used to give me all those talks and lectures, and I just would not listen. But Martin, he never said too much. He never really got mad at me. He just kept picking me up, ordering me home, and cleaning up my mess. I think he understood that I was just waiting for him to get good and angry, so I could use that as an excuse to take off. But he never did. Not even close. I used to punch him, kick him, swear at him when he picked me up. I'll bet he never even told you that. He'd just calmly stand there, tell me to get home and go to bed. You remember that time, Rube?"

"Yeah, I remember."

"It's like he waited me out. Until I sort of settled down. And he's never, I mean never, even hinted at or joked about all the crap I put him through."

"Yeah, Mon. He's a saint. A saint who fucks around with sluts like Charmayne."

"Yeah," Monica lowered her voice. "I never told you what I did. You heard me swearing at Martin. You pretended not to, but you heard it. Christ, I was loud enough. I used to…Ruby, I was sixteen. I hated Kitsum so bad. I hated you too for making me stay. I guess I blamed home and everyone for Mom and Dad. I thought that if I could only get away, I could quit thinking about them all the time. I couldn't quit blaming everyone; it was either that or take all the blame myself.

"But Rube, I used to totally come on to Martin. I'd plan it, for heaven's sake. I'd deliberately party as far from here as I could. At house parties in Port Hope when that was possible. But I'd make sure that you guys had some kind of hint as to where I was. Like I'd casually mention to Brenda where I'd be. Did you ever wonder how Martin always found me? I'd drink, sure, but some of the time anyways, not so much as to not know what I was doing. I used to hit on Martin, big time. It was my ticket out of Kitsum — to get him to fool around with me. Even a little bit. Once I had him, I figured that I could leave anytime I goddamned chose. But

Rube, as hard as I tried, I never got him. Not even close. Christ, I undressed in the bloody car, crawled all over him when he was trying to drive, and still he brought me straight home. And sent me to bed like a little kid. Every single time.

"You remember how I finally stopped partying and going out all the time, when I finally agreed to do Grade 12 in the new school in Port Hope? It was mostly because I was too embarrassed to have Martin pick me up and ignore me anymore."

"Yeah, I kind of figured that." Ruby sighed.

"You mean he told you?" Monica was genuinely surprised. "I never thought that he would."

"No, he didn't tell me. Didn't say a bloody word. And I didn't ask. You just weren't as sneaky or clever as you thought. You know, Monica, I was never worried about you and Martin. You were still a kid. Martin…he was trying to be a father to you."

"That wouldn't have stopped a lot of guys."

"Martin isn't most guys. What the hell was he doing with Charmayne?"

"I don't know, Ruby…I don't know."

Monica did not notice the living room that evening. After she and Ruby had finished talking in the kitchen, she had headed straight for the covers that Ruby had arranged for her on the couch. The lights in the room were off; only the low wattage bulb in the hall provided a bit of illumination. She was exhausted by the trip and by the talking; she fell asleep almost immediately. It was only when she opened her eyes to the morning sun that Monica saw how much had changed. Gone was the entire wall full of family photos, including her graduation photographs. Gone were Ruby's carefully tended plants, and the colourfully shaded table lamps. The book shelf that was once brimming to overflowing with books and mementos and a hodgepodge of keepsakes now looked conspicuously empty. A pair of glass coffee tables had been replaced by a single worn, wooden one. Martin's armchair was still in its usual spot, but covered by a crocheted blanket. The couch she had just slept on was not the same couch that had been in the living room the last time she was home. Monica had only failed to notice the night before because of the sheets. Whatever had gone on here, Monica shuddered, it might be better for her not to know all the details.

Her visit, as she knew it would be, was too short. Saul had been right about that. A weekend, even a "long" weekend, was not enough time to travel back and forth to Kitsum and have anything like a relaxing stay. It was all a rush, an effort to compress everything into too small a space. Still, she was glad that she had come. Had there been something in Ruby's voice that had alerted her on the telephone? Her sister had sounded tired, but Monica had believed her when she had said that she was just too busy to talk. Ruby was an active woman, always on the go with one task or another. She was bound to feel worn out occasionally. Brenda had also sounded fine — maybe a little more excited than usual — and she had repeated what her mother had said, that they were all well and that things were fine. Maybe though, Monica considered, she had heard something, some tone or implied meaning from Ruby or Brenda that gave her trip home an urgency it might not have otherwise possessed. All Monica could really say for sure was that after talking so briefly to the pair of them on the phone the previous week, she had made up her mind to visit. Not wait as Saul suggested, but to visit as soon as possible.

She did not know if what she had said to Ruby had helped or not. Her sister did not return to the subject, but she seemed if not happier then at least a little less sad when Monica sat down with her for morning coffee. By suppertime, Ruby actually laughed a few times. Monica resolved to not only get back for Christmas, but to get back as early as possible and to stay until after New Year's. Saul usually scheduled things over the holidays; he booked events that meant they could stay in Kitsum for only part of the vacation. This year he could do whatever he planned to do without her. She was coming home and she was staying home.

FOUR

By the middle of the fall, Brenda was afraid that she might be pregnant. In her fantasy world, she was waiting until she was absolutely certain to tell Michael. In her real, everyday world, mostly she worried about telling her mother. The thought of revealing anything to her father was too horrible to even contemplate. She would wait to be sure. This was what she told herself each morning as she forced herself awake.

In the beginning, Brenda did not even know what her mother and father had fought about. They had all been at school. She and Junior had returned home to find the house a huge mess and her father alone with their youngest brother and sisters. She knew immediately that whatever the problem was, it had to have been major for her mom to smash up the house and take off. Her mother had left like that only once before. That was when Brenda was maybe six or seven years old. She had missed most of the reasons that time too. She remembered though that she and her brothers had stayed at their grandparents' place for a couple of nights. She had overheard her Grandma Susan talking when her voice got a little too loud and she was supposed to be asleep. Brenda always remembered that: it was the first time she had ever heard the word "carousing." Grandma Susan had said that her father was busy drinking and carousing.

This time it was Sarah who told her on the bus ride home. She used the word "adultery" and Brenda wanted to laugh. It was too ridiculous. Sarah had to be mistaken. Brenda was certain, but only for a little while. Her mom stayed away for a full three days. Brenda got stuck not only having to go to school, but also having to cook and take care of the kids. To make matters worse, her mother went nowhere else but to the Clydesdales. Fred Clydesdale's wife, Ethel, was somehow her cousin. What if she had said something to her mother? What had the woman seen or heard? Brenda could hardly keep her mind straight, worrying about what her mother might or might not hear or think. Then she got angry at herself for worrying and that made her even angrier at the whole situation. She decided that it would serve her mother right if she snuck over to visit Michael downstairs while her mother partied upstairs. That, however, was just another fantasy. There was no way that she had that kind of nerve.

The more she thought about Sarah's words and the more closely she watched her dad, the more she gave up any certainty she had initially possessed. Her father looked beaten. He no longer held his head up like he normally did and he seemed to have developed the unusual habit of holding his chin against his chest. Still, he did not go down to the *Queen*. He said next to nothing. And her mother, she stayed away. The more Brenda thought about it, the more convinced she became that there was no way that her mother had left for anything other than something very big—something like what Sarah had mentioned. But Charmayne of all people? Maybe Sarah had that part wrong.

After three long days, her mother returned to the house. She was hungover as hell—that was plain to see—but she was home. Her father went fishing. Auntie Monica showed up and ordinary life resumed. Brenda knew that her mother and Monica talked when they were all in bed; there was no way for her to hear any of it. Neither of them said a word to any of the "kids," and Brenda was too preoccupied to bother with detective work.

Monica's visits were usually a highlight for Brenda. They had grown up so close together, and her aunt was always like an older sister. Even after Monica had gone off to university in Vancouver, every time she came home on holidays and for the summers, she was back in her "own" bed in the small upstairs room that they had shared for ages. The nighttime stories would flow back and forth. If there was anyone she could talk to about Michael, it was Monica. She waited for the chance, for a moment when Monica was not caught up in making Ruby feel better. It never came. The weekend was too short. Brenda would have to wait for the Christmas holidays.

Her mother was better after her sister left—still crankier and more irritable than usual, but better. Mostly, Brenda thought, she just looked tired and worn out. Brenda held onto her suspicions. She had already missed two periods. Most mornings, it took every ounce of her energy to drag herself out of bed for school. Some days, she just did not have the gumption. She would snap harshly at her mother instead; she would say that she was sick until her mother finally gave up trying to get her up and left her alone. Falling back asleep, she sometimes half-believed herself. Maybe she really was sick. Lots of kids in Port Hope had the flu; that could be what was upsetting her stomach over the past weeks.

School became a nightmare. Either she could not concentrate in her classes because she felt too nauseous, or she was so sleepy that she could barely keep her eyes open. Her lunchtime friends, Tracy and Beth, had vanished. Tracy had quite literally disappeared from Port Hope. Beth told her, the one time she actually spoke to her at the beginning of the school year, that Tracy's parents had split up and that Tracy had moved with her mom to Campbell River. For her part, Beth was now going out with some young logger. Brenda noticed that she now hung around with the partiers. Looking at her, Brenda guessed that was where Beth had wanted to be all along. Brenda did not bother to go to K & M's Convenience anymore; she just sat with Sarah and waited for the school day to end.

At the beginning of the school year, she had made up her mind never to see Michael again. She had stuck to that resolve for over a month. As the days had gone by, she had actually started to feel better about her decision. She thought of the man less and less. Everything seemed less exciting, but she had almost accepted that too. She would get through her remaining high school years and move away for college or university. Then she would put this chapter in her life far behind her.

The growing suspicion that she was pregnant changed everything. Instead of planning for future adventures, Brenda found herself sinking into confusion and worry about an outcome she could not even imagine. The only lifeline she had was fantasy.

There had to be a romantic scenario. Michael would recognize how much she meant to him, and what a wonderful life they could have together. He would hold her in his arms and profess his love. Then he would explain why he had been afraid to show his feelings earlier. Maybe he had been afraid that she did not feel the same way. Except there was nothing like that at all. As much as she tried to deny it, Brenda strongly suspected that Michael was avoiding her. When she had finally gathered the confidence to walk by the construction site, he had moved to a part of a house that she could not see from the road. The second and last time, he had simply pretended that he did not see her.

By December, her parents had pretty much returned to the daily routine that she and her siblings considered normal. Brenda could tell though that her mother remained slightly distracted. Too often Ruby was looking off into space with a dazed expression on her face, or staring straight at her daughter without really seeing her. It reminded Brenda of old Nona across the street, always looking out at them coming and going. At least Nona had an excuse. Like her mother said, the old lady was all alone since her husband had passed away and her son had moved up the coast. Ruby had no such reason. Then as if to make up for her occasional inattentiveness, her mother began to ask questions. They were the same questions, asked just about every other day. Was she feeling all right? Was everything okay at school?

The only person Brenda talked to about her suspicions was Marcie. Her friend had been through something like this when she had her son, Gabriel. One morning when she knew Marcie's parents were gone, Brenda went to her friend's house instead of catching the school bus. She told Junior that she suddenly did not feel well and was heading back home. She had taken plenty of not entirely truthful sick days lately, but this was the first time she had ever actually "skipped" school. She ended up spending most of the morning asleep on Marcie's couch. In the afternoon, she played with Gabe. Then Marcie made popcorn and together they watched soap operas on television.

It was the second one that they watched. Neither one of them said anything aloud, but at one point, Brenda looked over at Marcie and nodded meaningfully. The woman in *All Our Tomorrows* was pregnant. She was scared to tell her boyfriend because she suspected he had another girlfriend. In fact, the more she worried about it, the more certain she became that she was not the only one the guy was seeing. She was trying to build up her resolve and determination to become a single mother.

"How old you figure she is?" Marcie asked during a commercial.

"At least twenty-five. No, more like thirty," Brenda replied.

Marcie smiled. Then she added, "Nice house, too."

Obviously, the white women on these shows did not live with their parents, and they were not on social assistance. Marcie and Brenda did not need to say anything about the contrasting lifestyle. They had grown up seeing that every time they turned on the television.

They continued to watch though. Maybe the woman on the screen would catch up to that dastardly so-called boyfriend. Maybe he would finally stop avoiding her calls and have it out with her.

Brenda asked Marcie to give Michael a message from her. Instead of agreeing, Marcie only protested and gave out excuses. She hardly knew Michael Clydesdale; she could not get out of the house too much with Gabriel; she would not be able to find him. Brenda soon realized what was behind Marcie's hesitation. Her friend was not refusing to do her a favour—she was trying to protect her. She did not believe that anything Michael had to say was going to be good, and she did not want to return to her best friend with bad news.

No one from school phoned the house. Brenda knew that according to school policy, if a student was absent without notice, a phone call was supposed to be made to the parents. She had heard other students from Kitsum say that the school did not bother checking on the Indian kids, but she had not believed it. Plenty of people did not have phones in Kitsum, she had thought, and maybe that was why the school could not reach them. She cursed her own naivety. She was no longer a good student—she was probably failing most of her classes—why would the school bother with her? Why would they care enough to phone?

FIVE

Monica left Vancouver by herself in mid-December. She did not know if she would go back. When she had initially decided to leave the Department of Indian Affairs, she had thought that she would look for something different in the city. Then Saul had dropped his bombshell. He had been offered a position at Carleton University in Ottawa. The excitement had flushed his face and made his grey eyes twinkle. She heard the enthusiasm in his voice and realized in a moment just how desperately he wanted the job. An "opportunity," he had called it, slowly enunciating each syllable of the word. He did not know then that she had already decided to quit her job. He told her that it would be easy to arrange a transfer for herself, a move within the Department that would put her in their Ottawa offices. She listened to him energetically making plans and saw that he fully expected her to go with him, to automatically bend her life to suit his own.

Monica had lived with Saul for nearly five years. They were not married. She had been twenty-two years old and working on the last year of her degree when they had met. He had been a teaching assistant for her fourth-year ethnography class. He had been older than most of her classmates, in his late twenties. He had appeared tall and distinguished looking to her, a grad student on his way to finishing his doctorate. It was a doctorate that, the first time they spoke after class, he told her he had nearly completed. Nearly, Monica allowed herself to think sarcastically now, because that degree had taken Saul another three full years to finish. In the meantime, she had given up on grad school for herself and had taken the DIA job.

It was strange how Ruby and Martin's troubles had affected her. They had not caused her to become disillusioned or cynical about relationships. Ruby and Martin had weathered a really turbulent time, and their relationship had survived their troubles. Monica continued to view their marriage as a model of loving commitment. When Monica looked at her own relationship with Saul in comparison, she could not help but find it lacking. What she and Saul had was insignificant—almost negligible—compared to what Ruby and Martin had. Was this, she began to ask herself, really what she was willing to settle for?

The offer to teach and do research in Ottawa would be great for Saul's career. Monica could see that readily. For her, however, it was an unexpected opportunity of a different sort. It did not take her too much thinking to come to the realization that she could simply choose not to move with him. She could stay. She did not discuss this with Saul; she did not phone and discuss the matter with Ruby. Instead, she let herself stew. She vowed to think everything through and make her final decision over the Christmas holidays.

Saul wanted—needed, he said—to go to Ottawa before Christmas and look for an apartment. "See how perfectly this all works out." He had said this to her before explaining his plan for them to visit his parents in Toronto.

"You go ahead," she had assured him. "Ruby needs me. I'm going to Kitsum."

She was not being entirely truthful, but Saul was too excited by his own possibilities to delve into what she was doing. He did not even appear to be all that disappointed. He told her that he would be sad to spend Christmas without her and suggested that Monica return to Vancouver for New Year's instead. They would pack and arrange for things to be moved.

"I'm staying in Kitsum for the whole holiday," she had responded.

Saul had promptly dropped the subject. Monica knew that no matter what she said about remaining in Kitsum, he still expected her to be in Vancouver by the end of December. A few years earlier, she would have confronted him about what she saw as his thoughtlessness, but now, she could not even be bothered.

Not once had she indicated to Saul that she was willing to move. Nevertheless, he had started packing. He had actually begun to query her about saving this or saving that. In the end, under the guise of helping, she had collected the few things she considered to really be hers: photographs and gifts from Ruby and the kids, a few old mementos from her mother and father, a handful of books and school materials. She packed those into a pair of sturdy boxes that she would take to Kitsum for storage. She packed two suitcases, a bin of clothes, and another bin full of shoes, boots, gloves, and hats. What clothing of hers was left over, she brought to the Salvation Army drop box.

She should have voiced her feelings to Saul by now. He had already made one cross-country trip to formally accept his position and "introduce himself." Had he ever seriously considered not taking it? Had he ever intended to really listen to her? The answer was probably no to both questions, but still the man deserved some indication that she was contemplating not accompanying him. Somehow she could not find the words or the time. In the end, she just loaded her things into the back seat of her car and left for home.

The second Monica arrived, she embraced Ruby fiercely. She was relieved to see that her sister was really well and that things were okay again between her and Martin. After a self-doubting drive from Campbell River, her family's genuine happiness reassured her that she had done the right thing in coming home. Here she could finally put aside her worries until she was ready to think through them clearly; she could relegate that which she was unsure about back to a Vancouver that felt very far away.

She noticed that Brenda was quieter and less enthusiastic than usual. Her niece seemed to have developed a slouch and had put on weight. Monica remembered Brenda as a young child proudly copying her mother's straight-backed style of walking and standing. Monica had teased her about it, although she had also begun to use the word "elegant" to describe both her sister and her niece. In spite of being short, Ruby and Brenda maintained a stature that even taller people could not emulate. Maybe, Monica thought now, it was the extra weight that was making Brenda slouch and feel less energized.

Over the late dinner that Ruby served her that first evening back home, Monica noticed her sister looking hard at her eldest daughter. Something was up there. Ruby had also seen a change in Brenda. She was worried. On her October trip home, Monica had found no time at all for her niece. It had become a sort of tradition between them that each visit Monica would take Brenda out to do something, just the two of them. This was something that had evolved as Monica spent longer and longer periods away and as Brenda grew into a teenager. If Brenda was annoyed with her for neglecting their time together the last time she was home, that was easily remedied.

It was Brenda and Junior's third-last day of school before the holiday. Monica parked in front of the high school and waited to pick Brenda up. Port Hope Secondary had aged considerably since she had been in Grade 12 there. That had been the first year that the school was open — 1977, it must have been. Then, everything was still shining new. On this grey day, however, the small two-storey building did not look like it had seen fresh paint since the decade-past grand opening. Even the once shining letters of the PHSS sign looked faded and forlorn, as though they had lost interest in themselves. The parking lot looked recently paved though, and was filling up. The vehicle selection consisted entirely of brand new pickup trucks on the one hand, and trucks that looked as though they might rust through at any moment on the other. There did not appear to be any middle ground whatsoever. The only students who lived any distance away were the Kitsum kids, and as far as Monica knew they all still took the school bus. It had to be the Hope kids and teachers who were now driving the short distances between their homes and the school.

Monica kept her eyes glued to the front doors. The rain and wind kept her from rolling down her car window, but she heard the shrill bell anyway. Students immediately began to stream out of the doors. White students first, she saw. Things really had not changed. Towards the back of the pack, Monica spotted some of the Kitsum kids. They were still a solid bunch, Monica noted, but they were mostly younger girls and boys. But there—before she had a chance to second-guess her decision to make the meeting a surprise—were Brenda and Junior amid a handful of older students. Most students she no longer recognized. She likely knew their parents, she realized. When had she joined the older generation?

She need not have worried about Brenda or Junior spotting her. Her small car was, after all, the only one out front and it was parked directly in front of the school bus. Monica saw her niece's face brighten as she rushed directly towards her. Junior waved, but went straight to the bus. Monica smiled briefly into her rear-view mirror. Maybe it was so obvious that she and Brenda needed to talk that the whole family expected it.

"Hey you," Monica laughed as Brenda opened the passenger door. "Want a ride?"

Brenda laughed in return and fell into the vehicle. "Don't mind if I do," she replied. Just like that, things were back to normal.

The cold had reddened Brenda's cheeks and the north wind coming out of the inlet had blown the hair from her face. Her thick winter jacket was zippered up to the top, protecting her neck. Ruby and Monica had teased Brenda a lot when she was small about being forever worried about her neck getting cold. Every Christmas, one of them was sure to give her a scarf for a present. Such a little thing—having her jacket zippered up to the top—reassured Monica. This was the same happy Brenda she had known and cared for and loved since she was born.

They were sitting at a booth in the Port Hope Hotel Café. It was like old times. This was another in a long line of occasions on which Monica and Brenda could treat themselves, and share their news, their gossip, and their thoughts on everything from Ruby's latest rearrangement of the kitchen cupboards to who was running in upcoming Kitsum Band Council elections to the most recently released movies in Vancouver.

"Same old, same old, No-Hope Hotel," Monica said. She never forgot to use the local nickname. Looking around the mostly empty dining room, she saw that the booth seats were still covered in heavy orange plastic. The walls were still painted a dull yellow. Giant photos of loaded logging trucks in homemade picture frames were still the primary decorations.

"The hotel's got new managers again," Brenda informed her. "Look, there are three or four new items on the menu."

The joke was not really funny, but they both laughed anyway.

Monica would not remember exactly what they ordered, but what she would recall in vivid detail was the instant when Brenda took off her heavy jacket. That was when she really knew what had changed with Brenda. She wore a loose baggy sweater of some sort, but the sweater clung in unplanned places. Only Monica's shock kept her from immediately blurting out the questions that immediately filled her mind.

"So," she began with some difficulty. "What's up?"

Brenda had to have been waiting to tell someone. She talked only a little about school and Junior and basketball. Within minutes what she really had to say came out in a flood. She was pregnant; she knew that she could not hide it much longer. Monica could not bring herself to tell her niece that she was not hiding it very well at the moment. She was in love, Brenda told Monica, in love with Michael Clydesdale, and she had been seeing him since the spring.

Monica scrambled to place the name. She recognized the familiar Kitsum family name, but when she tried to think of someone Brenda's age, someone who was also a high school student, she drew a blank. The only Michael Clydesdale she could recall was well past high school age. He had to be at least in his early twenties. He was the late Cindy Clydesdale's son. The Clydesdales were not an overly large family. There was no other "Michael" that she knew. It had to be him. What was Brenda thinking?

Monica had to consciously work to maintain her composure. To do otherwise would only upset her niece even more. She was the older aunt now; she knew she had to say what needed to be said.

"You need to tell your mom and dad. Soon."

"I can't."

"You have to, Brenda."

"I can't. I just can't."

Monica felt forced to be sterner than she would have liked. "Don't you think that your mom has been worrying about you?" She could hear herself almost lecturing, but she continued anyway. "She knows there's something happening with you. Give her some credit, Bren. She must have her own suspicions. She's just not sure what to believe. Your mom needs to know what is really going on."

Only the fact that they were in the Hope Hotel prevented Brenda from completely dissolving into sobs. She finally nodded her agreement and made an effort to sit up a little straighter.

More than anything, Monica wanted to console Brenda. She wanted to hold her and protect her, to shield her from any harm or unpleasantness. She was still a child in so many ways; she should not have to deal with something this big, this heavy. A large part of Monica simply could not believe it. Brenda was going to be a mother; it seemed impossible. What the girl had told her about her relationship with this Clydesdale fellow did not sound good. No matter how Brenda glossed it up, it really did not sound like much of a relationship at all. The fact that Brenda had not even told him yet about being pregnant spoke volumes.

She tried as best she could to hide her feelings from her niece, but the more Monica thought about Brenda's news, the angrier she became. She was angry at her niece for foolishly getting herself into this mess. She was even more furious at this Michael person. He was older; he should have known better. It was that simple. How could he take advantage of her niece like that? It was not right.

Compounding her outrage was a rapidly growing realization that she could do nothing about the situation. Her young niece was going to have a baby. She had absolutely no control over the situation. She had no real advice, answers, or solutions to offer. For a moment, she let herself imagine that she was back in the city. There were options in the city. Life was different there. The women she knew and associated with — they knew how to handle things. They would consider possibilities like adoption or abortion. In fact, they *expected* choices.

Monica gazed down at the faded flowers bordering the Port Hope Hotel paper placemat. She would not even speak about such options in Kitsum. Why? She thought hard. Monica did not think she had ever heard anyone from home — not Ruby, not her mother, not any of her girlfriends — talk specifically about abortion. No one had ever told her that it was bad. Yet somehow, she felt guilty for even allowing herself to think about it.

Brenda was sixteen years old and pregnant. On the long, slow drive back to Kitsum, Monica tried to concentrate on that fact, although it was a lot to take in all at once. Monica was twenty-seven years old and did not even seem to have the prospect of becoming pregnant ahead of her. Ruby had married Martin when she was barely twenty-one. What was Monica doing with her life? She could not keep thoughts of herself from mixing with thoughts of Brenda. Rather than talking, Monica patted her niece's hand now and then. "It will be all right," she found herself saying over and over again. She knew that she was trying to convince herself as much as Brenda.

SIX

Once Brenda had told Monica, waiting until it was time to tell her parents became sheer torment. The news loomed over her like a massive cloud threatening to let loose its impending downpour. This was true now; there was no taking anything back. Monica had promised to be with her, but her aunt had been firm about her having to do the talking and the explaining herself. The evening at home passed excruciatingly slowly, just as time always seems to pass when one is waiting for something momentous. Junior eventually left for basketball. Thomas tried to convince his mother to let him stay up an extra half hour and Brenda almost screamed at him to just go to bed like Becky and Millie.

When all the kids were finally gone, and her mother and father were sitting quietly in the living room in front of the television, Brenda suddenly wished that at least one of her brothers or sisters was still downstairs. Her mother and father seemed to await Brenda and Monica. She wanted to run. "Did you tell them already?" Brenda whispered accusingly to Monica in the kitchen.

"Of course not," Monica answered. Brenda wished that she had.

She walked into the living room so slowly that she almost doubted that she was even moving. The air seemed as thick as the salt water that surrounded her when she dove off the dock and had to kick and stroke to lift herself up, up, up to the surface. The living room was the same living room she had known her whole life, but tonight it was a foreign place. If Monica had not been so close behind her, Brenda would have turned and fled. Instead, she somehow made it to the small couch.

Sitting there on that ugly couch, she was able to regain a smidgen of confidence. They had gotten that old sofa from their grandparents after Ruby had wrecked the other one. It was some small consolation. Her parents were not perfect either.

Neither her mother nor her father looked up. They kept their eyes on the screen. Surely they knew that something was coming. Brenda no longer watched TV with them in the evenings; she had avoided sitting with them for months. Monica nudged her arm; she motioned with her head for Brenda to begin.

"Brenda has something to tell you," Monica said.

Brenda glared at her aunt. Now her parents were obviously paying attention; any pretense of watching television was instantly forgotten. Her face was burning hot. There was no way out. In what felt like a single breath, looking down at her own feet, she told them. "I'm pregnant. I think over three months. I'm sorry. The father is Michael Clydesdale, but he doesn't know. I'm sorry."

The words were the ones she had rehearsed. They were all that she could manage. They were the bare facts, the ones she figured that they would demand. Even without looking up at her parents she knew exactly how they were reacting. She knew that her mother, who must have suspected something, was crying. Brenda imagined that she would have hung onto hopes that her suspicions were not true, and that this was not the news she was going to hear. While her mother cried quietly into her hands, her father would be sitting frozen in his chair, staring blankly at the television screen. Her father must be furious. There was absolutely no doubt. Brenda knew that he would not have suspected at all. She was still his baby girl. He was completely and utterly blindsided. She knew that he would sit and stare for a very long time.

Monica rubbed her back and held her hand. Brenda barely felt her aunt's touch. No one spoke. When she could not stand the silence any longer, she pulled away from Monica and fled to her room.

It felt like hours had passed before her mother and Monica came upstairs. They knocked, but did not wait for an answer to enter her room. She had left the door unlocked. Only the small lamp at her bedside was on; its orange shade gave the entire room the look of twilight on a clear winter's day. Though she was curled up on her bed underneath a pile of blankets, there was no point to Brenda pretending to be asleep. She was still sniffling too much. Her mother sat on the edge of her bed, turned towards her, and held out her arms. All at once, Brenda was hugging her as though her life depended upon it. Ruby held her daughter for what felt like hours. There were no words.

Brenda had expected a barrage of questions, but she did not get them that first night. Instead, her mother urged her to try to get a good night's rest. Monica brought her a glass of water. She did not expect to sleep, but shortly after her mom and aunt left her room, she drifted off. She woke in the morning to discover that it was just past ten in the morning. No one had called her for school, even though it was the last full day before the high school broke for the Christmas holidays. Everyone must have been very quiet getting ready that morning for her not to have heard a thing.

Her mother seemed happy to see her when she went downstairs. Her father was gone and so was Auntie Monica. After the previous evening, it was a relief to be in a quiet kitchen. Ruby started cooking her breakfast. While the eggs were frying, she asked about setting up a doctor's appointment. The questions after that were not many and they were asked gently, one at a time. Was she going to keep going to school? When she vehemently said no, her mother did not argue. Brenda did not need to bring up the way the white kids—and some of the teachers—would snicker at her behind her back. Her mother knew that. When did she get pregnant? Brenda answered that it had to have been in late August because she remembered having her period around the middle of that month. Her mother did not pursue things further.

Brenda figured that her parents had talked between themselves. Maybe they had not discussed things the night before when her dad was still too angry, but they had definitely talked in the morning. Early, she figured. Her mother and father would have gotten up extra early although they had probably not slept much the night before. They would have sat at the kitchen table, sipping coffee. Not even Monica would have been present. Between them they had decided things. Brenda was not sure what all those decisions were, but her parents had definitely come to conclusions of their own. By now, they knew that there was nothing they could do except be supportive and kind. They had talked and then her father had gone down to his boat. She suspected that he would spend a lot of extra time working on the *Queen* in the coming weeks.

SEVEN

While Monica and Ruby had been reluctant to talk much about anything that morning, Rebecca, Millie, and even Thomas had been full of excited chatter. It was the day of the annual Kitsum Elementary School Christmas Concert. Listening to her youngest nephew and nieces, Monica learned about the incredible amount of work yet to be done to set up for the evening's festivities. They needed parents, Becky and Millie said pointedly, to come to the school and help.

As her nieces had directed her, Monica showed up at the school's main entrance shortly before the first bell rang. She easily spotted the principal, as he was the tallest person around. She had heard about Gary Ashton from Ruby and the kids over the past few years, and she felt like she knew him already. Extending her hand and introducing herself, Monica told him that she had been enlisted by her nieces and nephew. Gary laughed and told her that she could start immediately.

Monica spent the first part of the morning making the concert programmes on the office computer. Gary had handed her a scribbled draft, which she had typed up with fancy fonts and colours before adding some holiday clip art. Then she printed the five hundred sheets he had requested. She knew that nearly everyone in Kitsum attended the annual concert and that every adult got a programme. It felt good to be preparing something that was actually going to be used. And, she could not help thinking, it was a good day to be out of the house too.

When the programmes were finished, Monica went to the gym where boxes overflowing with Christmas decorations sat on the lower bleachers. A freshly cut bushy pine tree lay on the floor. She was thinking that she was never going to be able to do all the required decorating by herself when the recess bell rang. First a few, and then a lot of kids, noisily entered the gym. Monica began asking questions. Within minutes, she found out that many of the students had very clear notions of what needed to be done. Older girls began hanging bells and angels along the walls. A young girl who looked barely old enough to be attending school told her that the stars always went on the far walls. An older boy informed Monica that the Christmas tree went in the front corner. He and the group of kids beside him appeared to know exactly how to put it up. She did not even have to direct; once the tree was standing, the kids began hanging sparkling ornaments and wildly colourful garlands.

Monica strongly suspected that Gary delayed ringing the bell to end recess. The students were so happily involved with decorating that it seemed heartless to stop them. When they finally did have to return to their classrooms, Monica only had to put away the empty boxes and hang a few missed items.

Gary offered her half a sandwich from his own lunch bag and a cup of stale coffee from what looked to be an overused coffee maker. She declined the beverage, but ate the sandwich. She was still chewing when he asked her if she was able to help in the afternoon as well. Monica nodded. She was genuinely happy to stick around, even if she was the only "parent" volunteer in sight. She would be sure to ask Becky and Millie about that later at home.

Against one wall of the small staff room stood stacks of oranges in boxes. Covering the entire span of countertop were piles and piles of nuts and candies and packages of brown paper bags. Into each lunch bag, one of the teachers explained to Monica, went two mandarin oranges, two candy canes, a handful of peanuts, another handful of mixed nuts, a couple of chocolate Santa Clauses wrapped in foil, and two handfuls of assorted candies. The task that Monica initially saw as so simple took her all afternoon.

She remembered the sheer thrill of receiving a Christmas treat bag as a child at the old Kitsum hall. The warmth of the memory stayed with her as she filled bag after bag. She had never thought before that any effort went into preparing them. Comparatively, she could not recall a single instance of having done anything at her Vancouver job that seemed as worthwhile as filling those bags with treats for the kids.

Monica returned to the school gym early that evening. Not only did she double-check the decorating job; she also casually watched and listened for other people's reactions. It was during that pre-concert time, before the bulk of the parents and community members had arrived, that Gary first approached her about working at the school after New Year's. One of the teacher aides—he explained quickly while fastening a student's "antlers" to her headband—was leaving. He did not know Monica's plans, but he wondered if there was any chance that she might be interested in the position. To her own amazement, Monica found herself telling Gary that she would seriously think about it, and that it all depended on whether or not she decided to stay in Kitsum. It was the first time she had admitted aloud to anyone that she was even thinking about staying.

"The job's yours if you want it," Gary said. He explained that he would be gone over the holidays, but back in Kitsum on January 2nd. She could let him know between then and the start of school. He would keep his fingers crossed.

Maybe it was the job offer and the confidence in her that Gary so readily expressed; maybe it was having spent most of the day helping set up for the Christmas concert; maybe it was the enthusiastic hugs and proud comments from Millie and Becky and Thomas; whatever the reason, Monica enjoyed the Kitsum Elementary School Christmas Concert very much that year. It had been too long since she had last attended. Saul had always managed to delay their arrival home until after the concert was over. He did not understand why she wanted to watch kids—most of whom she did not really know—performing plays and other presentations that often were somewhat incomprehensible. He did not find any attraction in listening to "silly" Christmas carols. These things bored him, Monica supposed.

Kitsum Elementary School had opened in 1967. She had been nine years old and just beginning the fourth grade. She remembered the day clearly. Even though she was certainly old enough to walk to the school by herself, especially since the first school building was within sight of their old house, her mother had walked there alongside her. Her father, she recalled, had been out fishing. A lot of parents were at the school that morning. It was a big deal, a huge deal. It was the first year for longer than anyone could recall that all of the school kids had not left for the residential school down south. Only in retrospect was Monica able to realize how much effort many of the parents and others in Kitsum had put into getting that first school established. The arguments with the Department of Indian Affairs alone would have deterred — and did deter — many other communities. DIA funded the residential schools, but they were not in the habit of "handing out" funding to communities they did not consider capable of operating their own schools. After years of argument, Indian Affairs had finally given Kitsum a small amount to "try out" the school idea. It was an amount that would have made any other school district in the province laugh, sneer, or cry. The funding was meant, Monica could see today, for one thing only. They wanted to ensure that Kitsum Elementary School did not succeed.

DIA was wrong. Parents and Kitsum community members were not going to give up. The school was a donated two-storey house. Walls were removed and replaced. New washrooms were outfitted. Desks, books, and supplies were shipped in on the freight boat from town. Most of the stuff, Monica remembered, was second-hand. Everything was new though, to people in Kitsum. It was that day, at nine years old, that Monica had decided to do well in school. She had not told anyone, but she had made a silent promise to herself that she would be a good student, good enough that she would never have to go back to the Indian Residential School ever again.

It took a few years for many of the Kitsum kids to begin attending. Some of the parents, she recalled, were skeptical at first, or afraid of the warnings from the priest about what would happen if they did not continue to send their children to the church-run residential school. That old priest, Father John, had thought nothing of threatening hellfire and damnation. He had also told more than a few parents that the RCMP and social workers could take their children. She was lucky; Monica had known that for a long time. Her parents were among those who fought the hardest for the Kitsum school. They had refused to be bullied by Father John, just as they had refused to be shoved aside by Indian Affairs. There was never any doubt that she would be one of the first students enrolled at Kitsum.

It was easy to reminisce here at home. In Vancouver, there always seemed to be something else going on, something more important than merely stopping to think. From her perch on the bleachers, Monica spotted Martin and Junior in the gym doorway. A minute later, Ruby and Brenda followed. She was instantly relieved that her niece had come. They were still early enough to get good seats up front where they would be able to hear almost everything, even from the very shyest children. Monica nearly skipped over to join them. Brenda looked less miserable than she had the evening before. She had taken the time to French-braid her hair. Maybe, Monica thought, she felt better now that the whole stress of telling her parents had lifted. Brenda gave her a tight-lipped smile. That *was* something. However, Monica saw that she also seemed distracted; her attention focused on the doorway. She was waiting for this Michael person, Monica figured out quickly. She followed Brenda's frequent glances. Yes, she would like to see this guy herself.

Shortly after seven o'clock, Gary Ashton stood in front of the packed gymnasium to welcome everyone. Brenda was still twisting in her seat every few seconds, trying to see the door.

Silently, Monica urged her niece to not let the disappointment ruin her evening, to just never mind this guy who was causing her so much worry.

Later at home — once the kids had calmed down a little from the thrill of their performances and all the community's enthusiastic cheers and applause, plus the candy in their Christmas bags — Monica followed Brenda into her bedroom. Twice earlier in the evening, Brenda had started to ask her something, but had then changed her mind. In the privacy of her own room, Monica waited to see if she would make a third attempt.

"He wasn't there," Brenda started.

"Michael?"

"Yeah…I was going to talk to him tonight. Tell him that my parents know now." Brenda tried to sound like she was talking about something of little importance. This attempt at self-assuredness was rather premature.

"It would have been too busy there anyways," Monica consoled.

"Yeah, I guess. Still, I was thinking that he needs to know. Maybe he's already heard. I can't see how though. But he is the father and he should know."

Monica nodded. Her niece was right, although she had already had months to tell the guy.

"I was thinking…maybe you could tell him? I've been putting it off, you know, and I think it's because I just can't do it."

She looked pleadingly at Monica. The older woman watched her niece mimic the little girl pout — her lips pursed, the corners of her mouth down — that had once made her giggle. However, that time had passed. Monica could not make herself laugh now. If she had to admit the truth, she was a little annoyed. Brenda was not acting like an adult at all, not even like a responsible teenager. The manufactured pout made her look like a spoiled brat.

"I can't ask Mom or Dad. You don't have to go to his place or anything. He works at construction, on the new houses. It wouldn't be very hard to find him there when you're out walking around."

Monica was tempted to just say no. In fact, a loud voice inside her head told her to do precisely that. This was something that her niece needed to take care of herself. Brenda continued to stare at her with those moist, round, pleading eyes. Monica remembered her mantra of the previous day. *Support Brenda, support Brenda.* In the end, what really convinced her to agree was the thought of Brenda dissolving back into tears.

"Well, I'll see if I can manage to run into him."

Monica did not even know the guy. What was she supposed to do, have the construction crew point him out to her? She did know that he was the late Cindy Clydesdale's son, and the late Earl and Sally Clydesdale's grandson. Growing up in Kitsum, it was normal to have some idea of how your relatives, your neighbours, and your fellow community members were connected. Monica knew that Michael's uncles were Fred and Murray. She knew that Cindy, Michael's mother, had been around Ruby's age. She remembered Ruby talking about how they were once good friends. Michael would have been one of the younger kids when Monica went to Kitsum Elementary. The more she thought about it, the more certain she became that he had not attended. The Clydesdale kids, she was pretty sure, had all kept going to the residential school.

A few days before Christmas, Monica had finally had enough. Brenda kept imploring her with her eyes. Her silent begging all but bored holes into Monica from across the kitchen table. After she had helped Ruby clear up the lunch dishes and saw that the kids were engrossed in a television show, she grabbed the jacket she had borrowed from her sister — the ones she had brought from town were definitely too thin — and headed out the door. She would go down to Village Beach first. Yes, a walk on the winter beach would give her time to think.

Monica waved at Nona, sitting by her kitchen window as usual. Brenda liked to make frequent jokes about her nosiness. The old lady did not even try to hide her constant vigilance, her daily watching of the comings and goings at their house. Monica had always liked her though. Nona was lonely, that was all; she did not have much to do with her days except to see what her neighbours were doing. She resolved to visit her soon and find out the latest about Charlie: whether he was still in Hartley Bay, how many kids he and Molly had now, when Nona had talked to him last, all that family news Nona would be more than willing to tell her.

The beach was empty except for a few roaming dogs. The sky was grey; a southeasterly wind had picked up and was pushing masses of dark clouds quickly across the sky. It would rain soon. The residents of Kitsum were likely safely inside their houses or out last-minute Christmas shopping in Port Hope or Campbell River. She walked. She paid little attention to the living room windows lined up to face the ocean. Monica watched the swirling flocks of seagulls landing beside the fresh piles of torn kelp and seagrass that the latest tide had swept into the upper beach logs. She watched a pair of ravens who easily forced the gulls to move away from anything too interesting. She examined the clam and crab shells that had washed up with pieces of driftwood and coloured plastic. When she reached the north end of the beach, she made her way around the storm-tossed debris to the path that followed along the mouth of the Kitsum River.

She should have asked Ruby's advice. That would have been the sensible thing for her to do. She suspected that her sister would have been annoyed, feeling that Monica was meddling or interfering. She had already said yes to Brenda; that was the thing. There was no way to go back and change that now. She would go as far as Jimmy's Store and get a few things for the house before walking back along the new loop road. Yes, she would take a look at the new houses that were going up. That was all. If she happened to see this Michael on her walk, then she would talk to him. If she did not, then there was little she could do about it. She would tell Brenda that she had searched for him, but could not find him, and it would be better for Brenda to find another way to communicate with the man.

"Road" was a pretty generous term for what she walked upon; that was her first impression of the new loop. Not that the other roads in Kitsum were in such good shape either. It was more that the new one was especially narrow and rough, being made entirely of sharp blast rock. The first section where Monica walked above the Old Top Road was incredibly steep. She would hate to ever see a kid riding a bike down that. Still, beyond the visible harshness caused by blasting out the new road and building lots, Monica was pleasantly surprised. The promised eight two-storey family homes looked fairly close to completion. That alone was a big event for Kitsum. What impressed her even more was the view. The road was high enough up the mountain that even in the winter greyness you could still see for a long ways. It was quite spectacular, really, standing on the hillside looking out at the expanse of Kitsum territory. Every new house and lot seemed to have some view of the village and harbour below. She would come up again soon, on a sunny day, and bring a camera.

Monica was passing the last new house. The loop road was already beginning to slope back down towards the village at the place where she saw him coming towards her. He had his head down and he was wearing a dark green raincoat. She should not have been able to tell who he was, but something told her that this was Michael Clydesdale. There was a slight sway and lightness to his step, as though his feet barely touched the ground. That was how Cindy had once walked. She remembered. When he saw her, he looked up and nodded noncommittally. He neither slowed nor quickened his pace. He had already passed her before Monica turned and managed a tentative "Michael?" His feet stopped and he turned back towards her.

"Yes."

"Michael Clydesdale?"

"Yes."

Summoning up her courage, Monica extended her hand in greeting. "I'm Monica Smith…Brenda's aunt."

Michael shook her offered hand and appeared unsurprised. Just as she had figured out who he was, Michael would have been able to guess her identity as well. He said nothing though; he merely waited for Monica to continue. She had expected embarrassment or anxiousness from him, but what he presented to her was calm patience.

She cleared her throat. "I didn't mean to stop you on the road like this," she began. It was a lie, and she regretted it as soon as the words had left her mouth. From the unchanged look on Michael's face, she guessed that he knew it too. "Brenda asked me to speak to you. I didn't know if I'd get the chance. Look…she's pregnant. She wanted you to know…as the father. Brenda did not know if you had heard."

Michael nodded. That was all. There was neither shock nor protest. He displayed not a trace of emotion. He just nodded as though Monica had told him that it was going to rain. "Yes," he said. "I've heard."

Monica waited for him to say more. Instead, he moved as though to resume walking.

"What do you intend to do?" Even though her voice had risen only slightly, Monica felt like she was yelling.

"There's nothing I can do," he said plainly.

Monica stared at him, stunned by the answer he had just given. Michael stared back. In the end, it was Monica who looked away first. The prominent cheekbones, the jet-black eyes, the tightened lips; he looked so much like Cindy. Instead of the lecture she had half-prepared on behalf of her niece, she mumbled something about just wanting to make sure that he knew and needing to get going.

All the way home, Monica reviewed the encounter in disbelief. She had become agitated and even somewhat angry. This Michael had turned out to be absolutely nothing like she had expected. He had completely refused to be drawn into her anticipated discussion. She had known that he was older than Brenda, but Monica had still imagined him as a kid. A kid, this guy was not.

Monica repeated the short conversation for Brenda. It certainly was not difficult to recall; he had said so little. Her niece clawed and grasped at every word, trying to garner from them even the smallest hint of additional meaning.

"Like I said, he didn't talk much. He nodded when I told him. He said yes, he had heard. Then he didn't say anything so I asked him what he intended to do. He looked sad, I think. Maybe not. He looks a lot like his late mom, Cindy. I guess that's what made me think he looked sad. When Cindy had that expression, she was definitely sad. But Bren, I can't say for sure that it's the same with him. Maybe he's just quiet. Maybe I surprised him. His answer to me was 'there's nothing I can do.' I'm sure that's exactly what he said: 'there's nothing I can do.'"

Monica knew that she was denying Brenda the solace that she desperately craved, but she could not make up something that had not been said. She knew enough to be cautious of creating false hopes. Monica sat down beside her niece and squeezed her shoulder.

"I know this is hard, Bren, but you need to just forget this guy. You hear me? That's all you can do. Try to put him out of your mind and look out for yourself. Take care of yourself and your baby."

Brenda sniffled and then defiantly tilted her head. Suddenly it looked like she wanted to argue. She pushed Monica's arm away.

"Yeah," she muttered. "I can take care of myself. I'm okay."

After a few minutes of silence, Monica did the only thing she could think to do. She left the room. She supposed that her words must have sounded pompous and superior, but what else was there to say? She could not shake the feeling that she had likely made things worse rather than better.

Monica confided in her sister early the next morning when the two women were alone in the kitchen. Martin had already left for the *Queen*, and there was time to sit at the kitchen table and enjoy another cup of coffee. Monica repeated to Ruby the same snippets of conversation that she had shared with Brenda. Monica even admitted how foolish she had felt when Michael had refused to say more.

Ruby shook her head sadly. She understood. That was what Monica missed most when she was away from her older sister, that security in knowing that someone else understood her so completely.

"Martin already talked to him."

"You're kidding?" Monica could only sputter. There had been no sign. No one had breathed a word. Brenda certainly did not know that her father had talked to Michael at all. No wonder this guy had been able to remain so calm in front of her. She was just giving him old news.

"*Do not* tell Brenda." Ruby interrupted her thoughts with the firm order.

"No…no, I won't, Ruby. But what did Martin say to him?"

"I don't know."

Monica felt the old impatience bubble within her. How could Ruby not have asked Martin exactly what happened? She stared at her older sister, silently begging for something more.

"Martin said he told that guy to leave Brenda alone," Ruby said.

She looked out her window. Monica knew that the conversation was over.

EIGHT

Brenda was livid. How could Monica have screwed up a straightforward message? And how could Michael have given her the answer that he did? She had convinced herself that Michael was different—more responsible and respectful than so many of the other Kitsum guys—but he was just the same. She had not led a completely sheltered life; she had heard her share of coarse male laughter, derogatory comments and snickers, and the old "use them and lose them" lines. More than anything, she felt humiliated. Not only was she humiliated in private, as though that would not have been bad enough; now she was humiliated openly and in front of everyone. She could feel the disgrace dripping from her pores; it was out in the open for anyone to witness.

Auntie Monica tried to act extra cheerful and to be overly helpful. Brenda did not want to be cheered up and she did not know what possible help her aunt could now provide. At least her mother knew to stay out of her way. It was a rare sunny day, unusually warm for that time of year, and she could not make herself go outside. She did not even want to leave her room. When Monica invited her to go along for a drive into Port Hope for groceries and last-minute gifts, Brenda quite rudely refused. Maybe that response was what finally got her aunt to lay off for a while. From her bedroom window, Brenda watched Millie and Becky happily climbing into Monica's car in her place. Later on, when her mother came to her room and asked her along to visit her grandparents, she said that she was too tired. "I'll go next time," she mumbled in a half-hearted attempt to ease her mother's disappointment.

Over the Christmas holidays, Brenda tried to convince herself that things would change. Michael would have to see her. At the very least, he would phone. The holiday would provide the perfect setting for him to act. It would all work out, Brenda kept telling herself. She tried very hard to make herself believe it.

By the time it was actually Christmas Day, everyone in the house knew that Brenda was pregnant. When her grandparents and Auntie Kate came over on Christmas Eve, it was obvious that they knew as well. None of them would look straight at her anymore. They saw her from the corners of their eyes or with only the quickest of glances.

Brenda had feared some comment or even harsh words from her grandmother. It was not that her grandmother was cruel or judgmental. If anything, she would have described the older woman as caring and supportive. Still, Brenda was afraid of facing her grandmother's expectations. Ruined expectations, she thought bitterly. Without saying much at all directly, her grandmother had always managed to convey impeccably high standards. There seemed no question in the elder's mind that her grandchildren would behave properly and do the right things. Brenda and her siblings were expected to be as respectful and diligent as their father and his sister, their Auntie Kate. It felt like an enormous weight to have to expose herself, not only to her mother and father's disappointment, but also to her grandmother's.

Only once that evening did Kate follow her into the kitchen, hoping for a talk between the two of them. Brenda nixed that possibility by rerouting to the washroom instead. It turned out that it was Becky and Millie who had the knack for taking her and everyone else by surprise by asking all the questions. When was she going to have the baby? What was she going to name it? Did she want a boy or a girl? Their queries seemed to embarrass the whole family. Reality had not completely sunk in. She had barely accepted being pregnant; she was not ready to consider an actual baby. Hanging in the air were all the gossip sessions of the not-so-very-distant past, all the cluckings and groanings over young

unmarried girls getting "knocked up." Here she was—Brenda
Joe—just another one of them. Already, without a doubt, people
in Kitsum were talking, and this time about her.

NINE

It was the morning after New Year's Day and Monica's last chance to go to Campbell River before the start of school. She had made up her mind to accept Gary's job offer. Ruby had been openly happy at the possibility of her staying in Kitsum. Martin, as quiet as he had been lately, had broken into a large grin and congratulated her. Brenda had actually, for a little while anyway, seemed like her youthful enthusiastic self again.

Before she had time to change her mind, Monica slid her cover letter and her resume into Gary's mailbox. The only big thing left for her to do was to tell Saul. For that, she needed an overnight trip to Campbell River. She would get a hotel room and telephone him from there. He deserved that at least—a proper conversation instead of a rushed call from the wall phone in Ruby's kitchen or the phone booth in Port Hope.

Martin insisted that she take the truck. The weather forecast for the next few days was clear and cold; snow covered the mountains behind Port Hope. The truck was equipped with good winter tires and chains if she needed them. Stowed behind the front seat was an extra blanket, a long-lasting flashlight, and a bag of Ruby's emergency snacks. Martin casually placed a snow shovel at the back of the pickup. Monica almost commented that she half-expected him to throw in the chainsaw that he usually packed in case of trees down along the way, but she held her tongue. She did not want him to interpret a joke as a lack of thankfulness on her part. She set off that morning with more preparations than she had ever made for a trip to Vancouver.

The gas station in Port Hope was just opening when Monica pulled the truck up to the pump. Another older truck was already ahead of her. To her surprise, she recognized Michael Clydesdale. The embarrassment she had felt that day on the new loop road returned in a rush. She wished that she could avoid the guy, but it was too late. He had already seen her. He nodded in her direction and she could have sworn that there was the briefest hint of a smile on his face. Monica managed to nod in return and deliberately looked away.

"Here." She looked up as he passed her the fuel nozzle.

"Thanks." She concentrated on filling Martin's truck. She only glanced up when she heard his footsteps moving away. Before she could completely relax though, he was back. Yes, he was standing beside his truck, watching her.

"Are you heading to Campbell River?" he asked.

"Yes." She supposed that he was only trying to be polite, and making the most of an uncomfortable situation. "Yes, I am. For the night."

"Me too," Michael said, then appeared to pause.

Just get in your truck and take off then. Monica did not say this out loud.

"Hey," he continued. "I wanted to apologize to you. I don't know if I sounded short with you when we met on the road over there. I was taken by surprise, that's all."

It was the most that she had heard him say. She nodded again, not really wanting to answer.

"I'd like to talk," Michael said. "That is, if you're willing? We could maybe have coffee in Campbell?" When she did not reply immediately, he added "How's three o'clock? This afternoon. The café at the Highliner. I can meet you there."

Before Monica could say anything in reply, he climbed into his truck. This Michael had practically given her an order. She wondered if he realized that. Damned if she'd be told what to do by some punk. He could sit in the Highliner and wait all afternoon, she thought. She would not be there.

Monica had intended to use the long drive to carefully plan what she was going to say to Saul. There was too much going on at Ruby's for her to take the time she needed. Most evenings in bed, instead of getting things clear in her head, she fell asleep almost immediately. Now, instead of preparing her speech for Saul, Monica found herself spending the first part of her trip thinking about Michael.

The guy was a puzzle. She was usually pretty good at reading people, but she could not figure Michael Clydesdale out. How Brenda had ended up with him, Monica could not imagine. Brenda flirting and trying to get his attention, she could see. Brenda was not too different from herself as a teenager. And that's what teenagers tended to do: they tried out their new-found abilities to attract the opposite sex. Michael was definitely an attractive young man, so sure, she could see Brenda smiling at him or tossing her hair or giggling hello. She could see her niece hanging around the construction site, too. Was Michael so easily impressed? Or distracted from his work? Was he the type to be drawn into something so foolhardy? Monica just did not know.

Or had he taken advantage of Brenda? Anyone who would do that would surely display some trace of guilt or shame. Wouldn't he be nervous or twitchy or evasive or hostile or something? Maybe he was just a drunk. If there was anywhere a person might drink in Kitsum, it was at his place. The problem with that scenario was there was absolutely no way Brenda would be partying at the Clydesdales. She would have been known there and her parents would have found out quickly. She would have been yarded home and grounded for life. Maybe they drank somewhere else. Monica knew that she was grasping at straws here. But what else could have happened? Michael did not look like a boozer, but appearances could be deceptive. People did stupid things when they were drunk. It was probably as simple as that. Monica was pretty sure that Brenda had exaggerated the extent of her relationship with Michael. She would go have coffee with this guy, she decided suddenly. She would find out more.

Monica had already reached the Kitsum River Canyon. She pulled the truck over onto the widest part of the shoulder. There was only a slight crust of dirty snow. Walking carefully, she retraced her way back to the curve where she had a clear view of the canyon. She could see far below the roadway, where once-bare boulders were now covered by powerfully rushing white water. Months of rain and snow had swollen the river to at least twice its summertime size. Unlike in the ocean, where waves never stopped moving, here in the river, the biggest waves appeared to stand at attention. They retained their form while constantly flushing the running water through them.

She spoke aloud to her mother and father. "I'm staying in Kitsum," she said. "With Ruby and Martin and Brenda and Junior and Thomas and Becky and Millie. I'm going to be fine. We're all going to be fine."

She stood silently for a few minutes and then slowly returned to the truck. Her mind was calmer now. She inched the truck up the mountainside and around the corners. There was no one else on the road.

Poor Saul, she thought. Five years ago, when they had first gotten together, he had worshipped her. He had treated her as though she were some treasured and revered icon that he had the supreme good fortune to hold. Admittedly, the adoration had been intoxicating. Maybe she had needed it at the time. She had been Lady Monica tapping out favours with her royal wand. Of course, it had all been a fairy tale that could not last. Perhaps a year earlier, she had yelled at Saul "I'm not your Indian Princess." He had not understood; he had blabbered on about never having seen her that way. She had remained silent, not because she believed him, but because she knew that it was pointless to get him to admit to his own lie.

Every Sunday morning, Saul would bring her breakfast in bed. He had purchased a gold-trimmed tray with thin metal legs that folded out to balance on the mattress. He would often decorate it with fresh flowers or an ornament he had picked up at one of the garage sales he liked to frequent on Saturdays. Of all the white doves and stately carriages and fairy tale figurines he had chosen, she had preferred the frog that had accompanied her small glass of orange juice one morning. She had saved that one because she liked the bulging eyes, the speckled throat, and the greenish-brown colour.

Saul's timing had been impeccable. He had never brought the tray when she was still asleep or when she had first awakened. He brought it after she had used the washroom and stretched her legs. That had taken a lot of care, Monica conceded. He had to have waited and waited to determine the right moment.

The thing Saul never understood was that Monica had only pretended to be pleased. He had gone to a lot of trouble and the whole scenario had obviously meant a lot to him. She had not wanted to disappoint him by telling him the truth—that eating in bed made her feel lazy and slovenly. It made her think of her Uncle Dan eating supper while reclining on his couch, oblivious to the bits of food that he spilled around him. As a child, when they had visited, she had avoided sitting on that couch even when the only alternative was sitting on the cold uninsulated floor. The idea of sitting on the remains of his messy meals had made her cringe.

Saul was in love with Indians. He considered himself one of the few anthropologists who truly understood Native peoples. He had told her exactly that on a number of occasions. For anyone who might doubt his depth of comprehension, there was the example of his Native girlfriend. Monica had warned him about making her a showcase. Once again, he had not understood, or at least, he had pretended not to understand. In the end, she had found it easier to bow out of most of the conferences and university events.

In another five or six years, Monica calculated, Saul would have a house in Ottawa. No, just outside of Ottawa. In his yard, he would have flowers and plants and trees, definitely trees. They would be oaks or elms or whatever it was that grew back there. He would fret with his new wife over academic papers and dinner parties and the next big research grant. Yes, he would be perfectly content. He would slowly rise to a certain prominence in his field. He was a smart man. It would not take him too long to get on the successful career track he wanted.

As Monica neared the end of the rough logging road, she was already anticipating the last few hours of fast driving on the smoothly paved highway. Then she noticed that Michael's truck had pulled over. Vehicles commonly broke down or had blowouts on the Port Hope road. If he was having trouble, she would have no choice but to stop. She kept her foot on the brake, waiting to either drive onto the highway or pull off the road altogether. Then she saw his old truck start up and merge ahead of her. Michael had been waiting for her to be sure that she had made it through the road safely. Martin had done the exact same thing when she had driven her car back to Vancouver alone a few years ago.

Monica walked into the Highliner Hotel a few minutes after three o'clock. She would leave quickly if Michael was not there. Then she spotted him. He was sitting beside a window in the rear of the café, watching the entrance. Monica saw him motion with his head. If she could have seen his eyebrows, she knew they would have been raised. It was that familiar Kitsum signal for "over here." She crossed the blue patterned carpet and slid into the booth. The table separating her from Michael seemed slender at best. She looked across at the young man and managed a smile. He smiled back.

"I haven't eaten yet," he said, shifting his gaze to the menus. "Have you?"

Shaking her head, Monica looked down. None of the listed items appealed to her. When the waitress arrived, she asked for the daily special—a hot beef sandwich. It was the speediest order that she could make.

"Well," Michael started.

"Well," Monica mimicked. "We're here."

"Yeah."

"I'm worried about my niece."

"Is she okay? Is she going to be okay?" Michael sounded genuinely concerned.

"She'll be all right, I think. She's having a hard time right now though."

Monica saw the grimace tighten his face like a fist.

"Look, I'll say my piece here, okay?" Michael waited for her to nod, to give her assent. "You can tell Brenda what you want out of this. That's all I can do. Look, I couldn't really talk before by the construction site. I was still at work and I was on my way back from phoning in an order for more nails…"

Monica sighed.

"I'm sorry, not that it helps anything. Believe me, I know that I should never have taken up with Brenda. It's not her fault. She's still too young. I know it's my fault. But there's nothing I can do about that now, is there? Not a damned thing." Michael took a long drink of ice water, but Monica sensed that he was not finished. She had come here to listen, and listen she would.

"I was flattered, I guess. When she started talking and flirting with me. Martin Joe's daughter. I mean, she's a nice girl too. She tried to act all grown-up and cool like she went out with lots of guys and stuff, but I could tell she was…*is* a nice young woman."

Michael stopped talking and Monica could not resist asking the question that both of them had to see hanging in the air. "Well, how could you, then?"

Michael grimaced again. His voice took on a bitter quality, and for a second Monica was afraid that he was about to get angry, very angry. "How could I? You don't think I've asked myself that question? Christ. I'm not going to start giving you details, if that's what you're after. Let's just say that I tried to dissuade her. Not hard enough, obviously. But I definitely tried. You know," he let out a hoarse laugh. "Your family thinks I'm an asshole. I guess they have that right. But if I had been more of an asshole before, and told her to get lost or not to come back, none of this would have happened. Man, I was trying to let her down easy. To show her, you know, that whatever she had imagined about the two of us was not going to work. I was trying to not totally wreck her confidence or anything."

It was Monica's turn to take a drink of water before speaking. "Martin talk to you?"

"Yeah."

Michael was not going to elaborate. Kitsum men, Monica thought. Like Martin, Michael was tight-lipped. She was the intruder, even for bringing things up. She decided to change tacks.

"Brenda's in love with you, you know."

"Brenda thinks she's in love with me. It's all some dream world to her. Believe me, it's all in her imagination. I bet by now she's probably realized. Even if she hasn't admitted it to anyone. She must be more embarrassed than anything else. She's stuck with the harsh reality now. You think I ever fooled myself into thinking that she really loved me? Forget it."

Monica could not say anything because Michael was close to revealing the truth. In fact, it surprised her that he had understood things so clearly. That had required some serious, honest reflection on his part.

"Okay," she said.

At that point, she did not want to hear any more about her niece. She lowered her eyes to the tabletop and stared at the hints of stains that had been absorbed into the polish. She felt vaguely dirty discussing Brenda's private life. It hardly mattered how true or untrue any of it might be.

"You're thinking maybe you shouldn't have asked for this?" Michael said quietly. "And I'm thinking maybe I should have kept my mouth shut, eh? Look, I'm sorry. I'll always be sorry. That's what I got."

Monica nodded sadly.

The waitress arrived with their meals. Monica wished that she had not ordered anything. Her stomach did not digest well whenever she was nervous or upset, but she had not eaten more than a piece of toast that morning. She began picking at the food in front of her. Then she realized that she was actually eating. She could hear Michael chewing ravenously.

"You want tea or anything?" he asked her after a while.

"The water's fine," she replied. He was trying to be nice. She would try too. She wished the meal to be over as soon as possible.

Michael persisted in attempting more neutral conversation. "Are you staying here...at the Highliner?"

She tensed at the question, and he noticed.

"I saw the truck in the parking lot, that's all," he laughed. "I'm not psychic or anything."

"Oh," she laughed nervously. "Yeah, I am. Just overnight though. I needed to do some shopping and make some phone calls."

"When are you going back to Vancouver? Everyone in Kitsum knows you live in Vancouver."

For a moment it felt like a friendly conversation. "Everyone, eh?" she said lightly. "I'm not going back. Not right now, anyways. Gary— the school principal Gary Ashton— he offered me a job at the school so I'm going to try that for a little while."

"Hey, that's good. I wasn't going to stay either when I came home in the spring for my mom's funeral, but they offered me the construction work. I didn't have anything else going on, so I thought, what the hell? It would be good to stay home for a while."

Monica found herself relaxing to the sound of his voice. Michael did not talk to her like she was a meddling old aunt. He talked to her like an acquaintance. At the same time, he looked at her the way a man looks at a woman. That was what had unnerved her when she had spoken to him on the road. Monica had spent too long in Vancouver. The men she had associated with there were colleagues at work or friends—mostly fellow academics—of Saul's. Those men were tightly buttoned types who kept their sexuality hidden; some pretended that it did not even exist. Michael, she was pretty sure, would have found them ridiculous.

"I'd better be going," she told Michael as soon as the waitress brought the bill.

He insisted on paying, and she did not argue. Monica climbed the first set of stairs so that she did not have to wait in front of the elevator. She was fairly certain that she had turned the corner halfway to the second floor before Michael had time to leave the café.

Saul had phoned Ruby's the day before New Year's Eve. That was how Monica learned that he was in their Vancouver apartment, packing for "their" move east. He had wanted her to leave Kitsum the next morning to join him. He had sounded surprised, in fact, that she had not already been in the city awaiting his arrival back. That was exactly what Monica had done in the past; she had cut short her visits home to Kitsum so that she could be in Vancouver when Saul got there. After not hearing from him for nearly two weeks, beyond a very quick Merry Christmas call that she took in the midst of all kinds of activity in Ruby's kitchen, Monica was amazed at how arrogant Saul sounded on the telephone. She was deliberately vague in response. Only after she had hung up did she admit to herself that she was confusing Saul on purpose. Maybe, just maybe, he deserved a straight answer from her.

Saul's flight to Ottawa was in two days. Monica could not delay any longer. Trying to plan out her conversation was only making matters worse. She filled the hotel room's coffee maker and watched the small pot gradually fill. Instead of thinking about Saul as she waited, she found herself thinking about Michael and their lunch together. Once they had stopped talking about Brenda, the conversation had turned pleasant. She was not comfortable admitting it, but she had actually started to enjoy herself.

The coffee was ready. She needed to concentrate on Saul. Monica dialed the familiar number. It had been her phone number too, only a few weeks ago. A part of her hoped that Saul would be out or that he had already had the line disconnected.

"Hello," he answered on the second ring.

"Saul. It's me."

"Monica. Thank God. Where are you?"

"I'm in Campbell River, Saul. But I'm not going to Vancouver. I've taken a job in Kitsum. I can explain it all, but Saul, listen. I'm sorry for not phoning sooner. I should have, but you know how crazy Ruby's place can be. There's always someone in the kitchen and I wanted to talk to you alone."

"Monica, what are you talking about? You've taken a job in Kitsum?" He pronounced Kitsum as though it were a disease. "Did I hear that correctly? What about your job here?"

"I've only really decided in the last few days, Saul. I needed the holiday time to think. I quit that job at DIA. You know I've always hated it. And the principal at the school at home asked me if I'd be willing to work. I thought about it a lot, and I think this is a good chance for me to stay home for a while."

"You didn't tell me any of this."

"You've been busy. I didn't want to mess up your planning and preparing and everything." Monica knew that Saul was just big-headed enough to buy at least part of an excuse like that.

"When did you quit your job? I don't understand, Monica. You were going to transfer to their Ottawa offices."

"No," Monica corrected him. "I wasn't going to transfer. You thought it would be a good idea. I hated that job in Vancouver. Why would I want the same job in Ottawa?"

"I wish that you told me all of this sooner. You wouldn't necessarily need to stay in the same job, for heaven's sake."

Saul always acted like he knew everything about the Department of Indian Affairs. If she didn't speak up quickly, Monica knew that he would begin a long round of explaining to her exactly how the bureaucracy worked. "It's too late now," she said. "I've already quit. And I've already committed to something else. I'm starting on Monday at the school. I promised."

"This is coming as a complete shock to me, Monica. I can't believe you're unloading this news on me at this late date when I am frantically organizing my notes and papers. I start at Carleton on Monday, you know." He emphasized every syllable of "Carleton."

"Saul, you're shouting." Monica felt herself growing more and more annoyed. She gulped the coffee. "I said I was sorry. I know I should have told you sooner."

"We'll figure this out," Saul said in a slightly quieter voice. "You need to come over here, at least to pack your stuff. Get the first ferry in the morning. It's only a day, but it will have to do."

"I am not going to Vancouver, Saul. There's no time," Monica said firmly. "I've taken what I wanted already. I don't want the rest of the stuff."

"What am I supposed to do? Clean up your mess?" Saul sounded furious.

Monica knew that she had not left any "mess," as he called it. Everything remaining in that apartment, in another circumstance, Saul might have argued belonged to him.

"Are you insane?" Saul roared into the phone. "I have to fly out in one day. I'm going to be jet-lagged as hell on my first day at my new position. And that, Monica, is thanks to you. This apartment is just going to sit here. I'm supposed to throw my money away paying rent because you couldn't be bothered to pack?"

It was tempting to react to Saul's anger, and indeed, Monica felt herself moving closer to doing so. Bolder than outrage though, out of the wisps of foggy uncertainty that still clouded her mind, an understanding emerged that was quite clear. She simply did not care enough to grapple any longer. She was even able to hear some of their conversation from a distance. Her voice remained flat.

"Listen to me, Saul. I do not want anything from the apartment. I am not coming to Vancouver. I am starting work—just like you—on Monday. In Kitsum. I need to stay home for a while. I do not need to move to Ottawa."

"So you've made all these big decisions on your own, eh?" Saul's voice was now dripping with sarcasm.

"They are my decisions, and I have made them. Yes. Good luck at Carleton."

"We need to discuss this, Monica."

"That's what we're doing."

"Not on the phone, for God's sake. You need to be here where we can talk face to face."

"Well, I'm not, Saul. That's just how it is. I have to go."

"Monica, please, please…come to your senses."

"Saul, I'm hanging up now. This call is costing me a fortune."

Monica hung up the receiver. Saul could blame her all he liked. She just could not listen to him anymore. Saul would convince himself—he was already well on the way to convincing himself—that she had blindsided him. He had ignored every signal that she had sent him over the past few months. He was so wound up in his career and his new move that he could not see anything else. She began to pace up and down in the small hotel room.

She was so tired of explaining. She had spent the last five years beside Saul and every year—every single fall—he had failed to remember why the first major rainstorm made her feel so sad. As though she had never articulated a single thing about it, she had to once again explain to him why she just wanted to stay in at that time of year and talk on the phone to Ruby or Brenda, or why she did not want to go out to dinner or a movie to "cheer up" or "take her mind off things." He never saw that by forcing her to undertake all that explaining, he had altered her feelings for him beyond recognition. She was exhausted. She did not want to explain anymore.

It was not until she was safely back at Martin and Ruby's that the world of Saul and Vancouver fully receded. Apparently, Saul had telephoned shortly before she had gotten back, with instructions for her to return his call as soon as possible. Monica laughed as Ruby mimicked the words and tone. Her older sister had become quite good at imitating Saul over the years. Neither of them displayed the slightest expectation that Monica should actually heed the directive.

While Ruby cooked supper, Monica recited almost the entire phone conversation of the previous evening for her. Ruby nodded, shook her head, and winced at what Monica considered all the appropriate times.

"You know, Rube, I don't even feel like Saul and I have split up. It's like it has been a long path toward ending, and I've only finally reached the exit. I should feel bad—and I do in a way—but mostly I am just glad that the arduous journey is over."

"I guess that's why you and him never got married, eh? Never had any children?" Ruby was not really expecting an answer. She had understood everything that her younger sister had told her and she had understood more besides.

"Yeah." Monica realized that her eyes were welling up. "Yeah, I guess."

Monica waited until Brenda went back upstairs that evening. She tapped lightly on her door and entered the familiar bedroom.

"Bren, I got the job. I'm staying."

It was Brenda's old smile that responded to her news. There was the hint of perfect white teeth, the raised cheeks, and the glistening round eyes that she knew so well.

Then those eyes narrowed slightly. "You fighting with Saul or something?"

"I wouldn't say *fighting*." There was no point in trying to hide the situation from her niece. "We're more or less over. He got this wonderful job in Ottawa."

"More or less?"

Monica smiled. Unknowingly, her niece had just assured her that she had done the right thing. "Okay, we have definitely split up. I'm just not so sure what Saul thinks."

"Do you care?"

"Some. That's the best I can do. I hope things work out for him and everything. He's a good guy in his own way. I just can't be a part of it, that's all."

Brenda appeared deep in thought. "Yeah, I can see that," she finally responded. "Still it must feel kind of funny, kind of lonely without him. You've been together for a while now."

On occasions like this, Brenda reminded Monica of Ruby. She was sensitive; she was smart; she was insightful and compassionate. Brenda might have displayed those characteristics somewhat sporadically in the past, but she was definitely growing into them.

"It feels good though," Monica admitted, "to be Saul-free."

"Saul-free." Brenda tried out the new word. They both laughed.

"Actually, I ran into Michael in Campbell River, Brenda."

The laughter died abruptly. "Did you talk to him? Was he by himself?"

The newfound maturity that Monica had marvelled at in Brenda had vanished. "Yes, he was by himself. And yes, I talked to him."

"What did he say?"

"Nothing new. I can't remember his exact words this time. He feels bad and he said that he was sorry for what happened with you, Bren."

"And?"

"Well, I believed him when he said that he was sorry. He doesn't seem like a liar."

"So what's he going to do?"

"I don't know, Bren. He seems to think that there isn't anything he can do. He's got the idea that leaving you alone is for the best."

"How does he figure that?"

Her niece's face was turning red; her voice was growing louder. "Listen," Monica said. "He's a lot older than you. You're sixteen and he's…twenty-three or twenty-four, I'm guessing. That's a lot."

"I'm not a kid."

"I know. What I'm trying to say is that Michael has been living on his own for who knows how many years. He's in another world. He likes you—he said so—but he's got all these experiences behind him that tell him a long-term relationship for the two of you is just not going to work. I can't help it, Bren. I agree with him."

"Did he say all that?" Brenda was justifiably suspicious.

"No," Monica admitted. "Those are my thoughts."

"But he said that he liked me?"

"Yeah."

Brenda knew as well as Monica that "like" was not such a strong word and that it was not close at all to what Brenda desired.

"He must think that I'm a fool." Brenda was near tears.

"I don't think so. I mean that I didn't get that impression at all. He said that you were a nice girl. He seemed to respect that."

"Oh God!" Brenda was now crying.

Monica wanted to hug her niece and erase every word that she had uttered.

"Brenda," Monica spoke firmly. She could not leave her niece like this, not this time. She had to come up with something. "There's nothing for you to feel badly about. You are a beautiful, smart, and talented young woman. You're still growing up. Believe me, I know. I remember what it was like to be sixteen. I remember what it was like to flirt and fool around with guys, older guys."

"Yeah, but you didn't end up pregnant."

"No…no, I didn't. I was lucky. By sheer chance, I did not get pregnant. But you know, Bren, I have been doing a lot of thinking these days. Thinking about long-term relationships and what makes them work. What goes into a good marriage, you know? Well, I always think of your mom and dad. They are role models for me. In the last year—maybe longer—I have been comparing me and Saul to your mom and dad. What I had with Saul didn't even come close to what Ruby and Martin have together. There's loads of stuff I don't like about Saul, but that's not it. I could have lived with all that if we had cared about each other the way your mom and dad care about each other.

"I'm telling you about all this for a reason, Brenda. It's got me thinking. My own relationship with Saul—why was I getting the short end of things? Didn't I deserve what Ruby had? A good husband who loves her unquestioningly, who wants and prides himself on the family they have together.

"I do deserve that. That's what I decided. And you deserve it too. More than some casual relationship like with Michael. You deserve something that is deep and lasting. And that is what you will get too. Not this time, but that's not never. You've got to give yourself time. Hell, I'm twenty-seven years old, and I haven't found it. Not yet."

Brenda had almost stopped crying and was staring intently at her aunt.

"Bren, I want to tell you something else, too. I *do* understand. I mean it. I see what you found attractive about Michael. I mean, there was a moment when I could definitely see shaking my tail for that."

Brenda looked horrified for a brief second, then fell back onto her bed chuckling. Monica laughed along with her, but largely out of relief. The last thing she needed to do was depress her niece even more, and for a while the conversation had looked like it was heading in that direction alone. They had made it through. Now all Monica had to do was escape the bedroom as quickly as possible. Then she would not have to mention lunch with Michael at all.

TEN

January passed slowly, the way it always did. Everyone you saw, everyone who called, they all seemed a little subdued, a little quieter than usual. People were less enthusiastic, less motivated, less ambitious about things. The spring was still a long ways away, and there was nothing much to feel excited about. It was like that every year. Short days, made even duller by the constant grey clouds and rain, piled atop one another. Sometimes they got a spell of freezing weather at this time of year, when all the puddles and ground froze up, and when afternoon hours of sunshine made everything glisten and sparkle. There was no sign of that this year, at least not yet. The whole world remained grey.

Charlie's annual winter visit was over for another year. Nona kept expecting Monica to leave. The snow that had fallen between Christmas and New Year's had dissolved. Only on television did snow float like feathers to rest gently upon the ground. On the West Coast, snow was mostly so saturated with water that it became a heavier, more cumbersome form of rain. Still, the roads were clear and Monica's car stayed parked outside the Joe house.

Shortly after school started up again, Carolyn phoned with the news that Monica was now working there. Carolyn had the janitor job at Kitsum Elementary. She had been shocked to find Monica helping Gary in one of the classrooms after school hours.

Monica had seemed cheerful enough, Nona thought. She had stopped by only a week before to invite her to a New Year's Day lunch across the way. Nona knew that she should have gone over, but on that first day of 1986, she was feeling especially depressed about Charlie and the kids leaving. They had been home for

Christmas just as she had wished, but then they had left too, only a few days after they had arrived. It was the darned winter ferry schedule that made them leave so early. Nona had given Monica an excuse about not feeling well. Polite as ever, the young woman had offered to check up on her later. Nona had waved her off, and had assured her that it was nothing serious. Monica had not said a thing about staying in Kitsum or about working at the school.

Nona had just seen Martin at the store, too. He had not said much other than to ask about Charlie and his family's travel arrangements. He had offered to drive her home with her bags though, so she had bought extra flour. The general store and post office were situated at the very end of the village, across the Kitsum River. The building was just off the reserve where the present storekeeper's father had built it when Nona was still a young child. Like his father before him, Jimmy Craig sold groceries, hardware, engine parts, and fishing supplies. His customers were the people from Kitsum, and occasionally, fishermen and boaters from elsewhere. Prices were high, and Jimmy was pretty tight about credit, but his store was a lot closer and more convenient than having to wait for a trip into Port Hope to get supplies. He was also the only way to get mail. Jimmy's father had gotten the post office soon after he had set up his store.

Nona remembered tagging along with her mother during her infrequent visits to the store; mostly it was her father who would go there to deliver fish. Old Man Craig used to buy fish and sell fuel for the boats that day-fished out of Kitsum. When he passed away, Jimmy had let that go. He told the fishermen that he just could not keep offering the same fish prices as they did in Port Hope. When Nona's mother would go to the store, she would ask for flour, baking powder, potatoes, tea, biscuits, and sometimes near the holidays—Nona's favourite—Japanese oranges. All the goods were kept behind the long counter. Old Sam Craig would bring them out, one at a time, and place them next to the cash register. Once everything was there, her mother would carefully count out the money from her change purse and place it on the counter. Only when she was finished would Old Sam — he was not so old then — place her groceries in a box that her mother would carry home. Some things, Nona remembered so clearly. More and more these days, as she sat by herself, she fell into reminiscing.

The next morning, Nona watched for Monica. Sure enough, she left the house before Tom, Becky, and Millie. She left at the same time as Martin Junior. From only a short distance, a person would have thought that she was a high schooler heading down to wait for the school bus. She and Brenda looked very much alike. Lots of people got mixed up and thought they were sisters rather than aunt and niece. So Monica was staying in Kitsum and working at the elementary school; that was something. Nona made up her mind to tell Charlie when she phoned him. If Monica could move back to Kitsum, well, maybe that would get her son thinking too.

Nona was up early a few mornings later, making bread; her cinnamon buns were out of the oven well before lunch hour. She was known for her baking, and even took occasional orders from the community. It was a small amount of extra income, but the activity kept her busy. Through her window, she could see Ruby moving about in her kitchen. She put a lid atop the box of warm buns and carried them across the street to her neighbour. Ruby was thankful, complimented Nona on her baking, and invited her to stay for a cup of tea.

Sitting in Ruby's kitchen, Nona saw that everything looked in order. Ruby was a decent housekeeper; her kitchen was clean and tidy. She was not like some of the younger people. Even Charlie's house was rarely to be found without a sink overflowing with dirty dishes. Nona asked again about the family and Ruby assured her that they were all well. Nona could hear water running in the bathroom. She had watched Martin leave the house hours earlier; she had seen Monica leave in the early morning. She knew the kids had gone to school. That left only Brenda. As though hearing her question aloud, Ruby brought up the subject herself. "Brenda's not feeling so good these days."

"Oh." Nona tried to look concerned.

"Nothing serious," Ruby quickly added. As though to prove her statement, she called out to her daughter. "Brenda! Nona's brought cinnamon buns."

A minute later, Brenda appeared in the doorway. She was wearing old sweatpants and what looked like an ancient sweater of Ruby's. Her face seemed somehow puffier or rounder than Nona recalled. She sat beside her mother and helped herself to a cup of tea and a fresh bun. Like her mother, she praised Nona's baking. As the girl ate and sipped tea, Nona glanced at her sideways. She was used to seeing Brenda carefully dressed for school; she had lost count of how many new jackets the girl wore. She actually could not remember ever seeing the girl in the sloppy type of clothing she had on now.

There was no mistaking it. The normally trim girl displayed a most definite bulging belly. Not too large yet, but a noticeable rounding. On a chubbier girl, one might not even have seen it. Brenda obviously believed that the bulky sweater hid it, but sitting as she did on the kitchen chair, the sweater's bulk gathered behind her and caused the front of the sweater to stretch tight across her belly. Sensing Nona's eyes upon her, Brenda tugged the sweater material forward. My God, Nona thought, so this is their big secret. Their sixteen-year-old daughter is pregnant.

Nervous that she would blurt out something inappropriate, Nona quickly asked about Monica. She only listened in part as Ruby described how her sister was asked to help out at the school, how she and Gary had hit it off right away, and how he had all but begged her to stay on and work with the kids. Ruby was justifiably proud of Monica. The whole family was proud of her. Even Brenda seemed to perk up a little when talking about her aunt. She told Nona that some of the kids even came by the house to see her in the evenings.

Nona went two days without even a whisper to anyone about Brenda. Then on the weekend, Carolyn came by to pick up the bread she had ordered. Nona's relative was in no hurry. She leaned into the kitchen counter and chattered away. Her favourite topic these days was her daughter, along with the fact that Charmayne and her husband were finally expecting a baby. Carolyn could offer infinite detail about what sounded to Nona like a very ordinary pregnancy.

Nona hesitated. If she told Carolyn her news about Brenda and Carolyn spread it around Kitsum, as she was sure to do, then Martin and Ruby would know that she was the one who had blabbed. But, Nona countered, the girl had certainly been to see the doctor or the nurse. Likely both. Her mother would have taken care of that, even if Brenda herself was too shy or embarrassed to make appointments. Nona had seen her going somewhere in the truck. People would have seen her at those appointments. And what of Monica and the kids? Maybe Monica could keep her mouth shut, but Martin Junior, he had friends. Brenda herself had friends. Thomas, Becky, and Millie had to have overheard something in that house. News about Brenda Joe could come from a lot of sources.

She made up her mind to tell Carolyn. Inevitably, that was the way gossip worked. In order to get news from others, one had to—at least occasionally—also contribute news. Nona left out her suspicions about who Brenda had been seeing. They were based upon a single remark that an old friend had made. At the time, that comment had not even made sense. Carolyn was actually quiet for a moment. Nona could not help feeling satisfied with herself. Usually it was her cousin with all the juiciest gossip. For a change, it was the other way around.

"Holy smokes," Carolyn finally exclaimed. It was one of her favourite expressions. "Ruby must be horrified. Mad as hell too, I'll bet."

"She seemed okay to me." Nona felt like she needed to stand up for her neighbour. "I was there not long ago."

As Nona had expected, the news kept Carolyn occupied for some time. First she was mystified, and then she was trying to guess the identity of the father. Nona professed to not having a clue, even as Carolyn was shaking her head in disapproval. "What's been going on over there?" she demanded of Nona.

"Nothing," Nona replied. "It's been quiet."

Carolyn launched into a long tirade about unwed mothers. She actually had the nerve to use Charmayne as a good example of a woman getting properly married before having children. It was enough to almost make Nona sick to her stomach. By the time her cousin was ready to leave, Nona was sorry that she had shared the news at all.

ELEVEN

I t was the big basketball dinner in early February that finally jolted Brenda out of her numbness. Since the holidays, she had stayed almost entirely inside the house. She had gone to a doctor's appointment, and then two appointments with the health nurse, only because of her mother's prodding. The sole person outside her family who she really wanted to talk to was Marcie, but her friend had no telephone and Brenda could not bring herself to walk the distance to her house. When Junior's friends came over, she stayed upstairs in her bedroom. When someone came to visit her mother or father, she hid. Though her mother often suggested it, she did not visit her grandparents. When her family went there for family dinners — her grandmother was big on family dinners — Brenda said that she was not feeling well and stayed home.

However, the excitement surrounding basketball finally proved irresistible. Junior had talked for weeks about the team's upcoming trip to Prince Rupert for the All-Native Tournament. He and their father had spoken about little else. Listening to the two of them, every day there was something to be done. Organization and planning just did not stop. There were practices, ongoing considerations of which players were playing well and which players were not, rumours about other teams, fundraising lunches or bake sales or bottle drives, and travel logistics to work out. The house was all activity, and Brenda was no longer the focus of everyone's muted attention. It felt good to think of something other than herself for a while.

Every year, Kitsum hosted a dinner for the teams going to Prince Rupert. The whole community attended. People brought their best foods: smoked fish, salmon, codfish and halibut, crabs, clams, pies and cakes galore. By the time the day of the dinner arrived Brenda was as excited as everyone else. She spent the morning and afternoon baking raisin and lemon pies while her mother made a huge pot of clam chowder and stacked a platter full of fried clam patties. The sudden burst of activity invigorated her. By early evening, when they were all getting ready to go to the hall, Brenda was even helping to carry things out to the truck.

They arrived early and the community hall was already nearly half full. Everyone in Kitsum had a brother or a cousin or a close relative who was going to Rupert. Every young child was dreaming of someday being on one of the teams themselves. During every free break at the elementary school, the gym was filled with boys and girls practising free throws and layups. Ten-year-olds took turns trying their hand at three-pointers. Then in the evening, teenagers and adults would take the floor.

The Joes settled along the end of one of the long tables. In a row sat Brenda, her mother, Junior, her father, Thomas, Becky, Millie, and Monica. Across from Monica was her Uncle Dan, his wife Linda, and three grandchildren. Brenda had never thought much of Linda, not when the woman had first started staying with Daniel, and not now. Rather than sit beside Monica and have to answer Linda's questions — the woman was just plain nosy — Brenda tucked herself safely beside her mother. When her aunt called old Nona over to sit beside her, Brenda was doubly glad about her seating choice.

She watched Junior. This was a huge event for him. His head bobbed constantly towards the doors and towards his teammates. Quickly and repeatedly, his eyes scanned the hall. His legs and feet shuffled rhythmically beneath the table. It was impossible to sit anywhere near her brother and not continue to feel excited. Brenda was glad that she had come.

Dinner was served first. After everyone had eaten and the tables had been cleared, the teams and their coaches were called up front. Junior and the crew of guys he had played ball with since elementary school made up the Kitsum Intermediate team. They called themselves Kitsum Storm. Martin had coached that team in the past, and this year, he was an assistant coach. He stood up and addressed the boys. He talked about how well they had played last year, and how they had won the trophy for being the most sportsmanlike team, and how he hoped that this year would go just as well. Martin talked about how he had brought the boys out clam digging at Lone Point on the *Pacific Queen* a few nights before. They had dug hard and helped one another, and together, they had made a good chunk of the money needed for the team's travel costs. The hall was absolutely quiet. The boys stood completely still. After he had finished speaking, Martin presented the coach with an additional cash donation. Everyone cheered.

Other community members followed. Each of them stood up with words of advice and donations. When it looked like everyone was done, the Kitsum Band Chief and Council Members went up to the front of the hall and presented a cheque. It must have been a big one, because the already happy head coaches and team members smiled even wider. All the basketball players started clapping and stamping their feet. That got the people clapping all over again. Clapping and stomping. It was a wonder the hall could contain that overflow of encouragement, enthusiasm, and support.

Full of good food and in the midst of family and community, Brenda forgot that her slim, well-dressed figure had been replaced by this strange, swollen version of herself that she no longer recognized. For a while, it no longer mattered that she was obliged to wear the baggiest, most nondescript clothing possible. It did not matter that even her hair—which so recently had been long and thick and a rich deep brown that so readily caught the light—was now stringy and dull like so many worn strands of old rope. The health nurse had calculated that Brenda had gained over five kilograms since her first visit in late December. She had also offered suggestions for exercises and eating healthy meals. Brenda had ignored her.

Marcie came over to see her after the speeches had wrapped up. Brenda saw across the tables that Gabriel stayed on his grandmother's lap. "I'm really glad that you came," her friend said. Brenda smiled.

"I missed you. You and Gabes."

"Me too. Come over tomorrow? Please. Just me and Gabes will be home. Mom and Dad are heading for Campbell River."

All of Kitsum was in the hall that evening. Everyone had seen her and nothing horrible had happened. The idea of Brenda remaining hidden in the house all day suddenly seemed foolish. Yes, she would go out to Marcie's and feel the sunlight again. Things would not be so bad. There was no sign of Michael. His aunt and uncle sat in the bleachers. Maybe he had left town. He was gone, invisible; he did not even exist. It was better that way.

TWELVE

Monica threw her energies into working at the elementary school. She left the house in the morning darkness and arrived back home in the evening darkness. She knew that there would be more time to do other things in the spring when the days were longer. For now, work and home were enough.

Tom, Becky, and Millie were especially helpful. They were obviously proud to have her at their school and they wanted her to stay. They explained routines and common practices more effectively than some of the teachers. They told her what past aides had done, and informed her clearly of what they had definitely liked and what they had definitely not liked. Millie told her that the teacher aide who used to work in her class stunk. No one wanted to sit too close to her because she smelled so strongly of perfume. That was why the little kids did not want to read with her. Tom told her that he did not want anyone trying to help him with his math unless he specifically asked. Teachers and aides who pushed their noses into his work only annoyed him. "They think I am too dumb to figure things out by myself," he said.

She enjoyed helping at the school in a way that she had never enjoyed working in Vancouver. Not a day went by without her receiving hugs from children and even the occasional parent. Gary made time to answer her questions and offered her a steady stream of educational resource materials. The man had been teaching for over two decades; there was little that he had not thought about, at least concerning elementary school and its students. It had taken Gary only a few days to decide that Monica should become a teacher herself. It quickly became a sort of running joke between them, but like the hugs from the children, his belief in her abilities gave Monica daily confirmation that she had done the right thing in staying home and taking the new job.

There were seven teachers at Kitsum Elementary, including Gary, and five teacher aides, including herself. All the teachers were from outside Kitsum. Gary and three other teachers stayed in the village in the teacherages across the playing field from the school. The other teachers drove in each day from Port Hope. The aides were all women from Kitsum, and one of them served as the school's receptionist. Doreen Brown, who was a well-respected elder in the community, had been brought into the school specifically to teach Kitsum language, and to lead the kids in learning Kitsum songs and dances. Monica tried to help out with that as much as possible. She wished that Doreen had been teaching language and songs when she was in school. The elderly woman never made fun of her for learning along with the young students. In fact, she smiled and nodded encouragement at her often. Within only a few days, Monica had divided her time between helping Doreen and helping out with the Grades 4-7 classes.

Gary's Grade 7 class ran the most smoothly. It was obvious that he genuinely appreciated and respected his students. The students mirrored his attitudes right back at him. They rarely spoke badly to him, and even when they grimaced or groaned about assignments, that seemed to be with a positive spirit. Of course, Gary, being such a good teacher, needed the least help in his classroom.

Monica spent a lot of her time helping Helen, the Grades 4-5 teacher, and Marge, the Grade 6 teacher. It did not take long for Monica to also come to respect Marge. The fact that the provincially funded elementary school in Port Hope had more resources and funding than the federally funded on-reserve school in Kitsum was a topic of frequent discussion. Marge rarely took part in these conversations. Monica initially thought that she — as so many people outside the community tended to do — somehow took offence at their criticisms of the provincial schools. Then one Monday morning, the woman showed up at the school with a complete set of individualized reading plans for each of her students. She had worked the plans out during her evenings at home with the unofficial help of the Special Education teacher in Port Hope. After that, Monica made sure to sit in the "library" at the back of the classroom each afternoon, and spend at least ten minutes listening to each student read to her individually.

Compared to Marge, Helen was extremely outgoing. She was a veritable bubble of enthusiasm and excess energy. Almost every day, she invited Monica over to her place for tea and a visit. Monica's string of excuses did not appear to deter her in the slightest. As for Becky, she raved about Helen. According to her second-youngest niece, Helen was the best teacher ever! Monica thought that Helen's classroom was barely controlled chaos. What little order there was seemed to hang by the thinnest of threads. Helen believed fervently—and she was happy to tell anyone who would listen to her rant—in letting students work at their own pace. That was fine for students like Becky who actually sat down and did their work. As far as Monica saw, it did not seem to go so well for the kids who chose not to do much in the way of work at all.

Monica's role as the "disciplinarian" in Helen's classroom evolved quickly. At first, she only spoke up when Doreen was trying to teach. Someone had to settle the kids down so that the older woman could actually be heard. For Monica, it was a matter of basic respect. At home, Becky was quick to point out that she was too crabby at school. Across the kitchen, Ruby arched her eyebrows and stifled her laughter. "I'll try to be less of a crab, okay, Becks?" Monica grinned at her sister.

"Sounds like you're doing okay at the school," Ruby remarked after Becky had left the room. "No big problems, then?"

"No, not really. Nothing I can fix anyways. It's easy to see that the school is short-staffed. I don't get into classes of the younger kids at all. So the school definitely needs more aides. Gary goes on and on about needing Special Ed teachers, which is totally true. I mean, there are kids with special needs in every class. Like a couple of kids in the first grade who are obviously hard of hearing. And there's definitely some kids with other issues. It's too much, and the teachers can't get it all done by themselves."

"Gary's been trying to get funds for more support staff for years. Since he got here." Ruby kept up with education issues in Kitsum. She had been on the PTA since Brenda started school. "They do have Special Ed in Port Hope. But it's a provincial school. We get to fight and wait for Indian Affairs to keep underfunding us. It's been like that since the school started."

"Yeah, Gary's giving me stuff to read on fetal alcohol syndrome and some of the problems it can cause. I've only started to understand some of it. There's a lot to consider, but there are also a lot of strategies and methods that can be used to help those kids more."

"You've got the time, Monica. These problems aren't new. They've been around for a long time now. And they're certainly not going to be solved overnight."

"Yeah, I know." Monica chuckled.

"What is it that Gary is always telling you? Take your time."

"Yes, it *is* good advice."

When the letter arrived, Monica realized that she had been expecting it for a while. Saul did not give up easily. He professed to understand the reasons why she had not wanted to move to Ottawa. He claimed to understand that she missed her family and wanted to be closer to her sister. He was not completely wrong. Saul believed that the problems between them could be worked out. He declared his ongoing love for her. The letter closed with his "deepest hopes" that she had not given up on their relationship.

Monica was touched. Perhaps she had more feelings for Saul than she cared to admit. Then as she read Saul's words a second time, Monica began to feel guilty. She had not told Saul that he was moving to Ottawa by himself until two days before his flight.

That was just plain mean. She could have at least informed him earlier that she was considering staying in Kitsum. What kind of a person was she?

After reading the letter a third time, it occurred to her that Saul very much intended for her to feel guilty. She knew how to read the subtext of Saul's written words, and what was worse, he knew that she knew. Did he—a man of his intelligence—really think that making her feel badly about not moving to Ottawa with him was going to help restore their relationship? Did he not realize that the very guilt he was trying to create would quickly morph into anger? Saul's same old arrogance was glaringly apparent. Monica could not believe that she had ever been blind to it in the past. The time she had spent apart from him had helped her to see him more clearly.

She did not procrastinate this time. She sat down and wrote a letter of her own. Another man would not have stooped to such trickery. Did he really want to manipulate her into recommitting to their relationship? A relationship that would not even be based upon truth and honesty? The more Monica thought about it, the more she was convinced that Saul had ignored everything that she had said to him on the phone in Campbell River, and before that in Vancouver. She was through explaining to Saul. If she had any doubts in her mind earlier, they were now gone. The letter she wrote was concise and to the point. Millie could have understood it.

She carefully copied Saul's new address onto the envelope she got from Ruby. Instead of waiting for someone to go to the post office, she made the drive into Port Hope herself and paid for express delivery. This thing with Saul had gone on long enough. The sooner he admitted that it was all over, the better off they both would be. Monica did not expect to hear from him again.

Monica was searching through the school's supply room but she could not find the projector she was looking for. Frustrated and dusty from moving old boxes and bins—some of which looked as though they had not been moved in years—she began to shove things out of her way. Then she heard the door creak. Feeling like she had been caught doing something that she should not have been doing, she turned around. Linda's daughter was staring at her and casually holding the door open with an experienced extended foot.

"What you looking for?" Carolyn demanded.

"Marge wants the projector for tomorrow. I can't find it anywhere." Monica tried to be polite; it was all she could do.

"Try the old teacherage."

Only when Monica looked confused did the woman explain. Carolyn led her outside and around the back of the school building. She stopped at a door that Monica had assumed was an emergency exit no longer in use.

"Check in here," Carolyn directed as she selected one of her many keys.

Monica had never gotten to know Carolyn well. Linda had married their Uncle Daniel after his first wife had died and their children had grown up. Carolyn and her daughter—that was Charmayne, the one who had caused all that trouble with Martin—had been living on their own then. She and Ruby saw her occasionally at big family birthday parties or dinners, but she could not remember ever exchanging more than a few words with her.

During her short time at Kitsum Elementary, Monica had already noticed that the woman worked hard. There were two janitors for the school. Carolyn was supposed to concentrate on cleaning while the other janitor worked on maintenance and repairs. However, it was clear that she did most of the work. The railing outside the main school door had been broken since the Christmas holiday, yet the inside of the school was freshly cleaned, mopped, and tidied every day.

Monica expected Carolyn to disappear after opening the door, but she followed her into the rooms. "It's supposed to be a teacherage but none of the teachers wanted to stay in here. Too small, I guess. There's just the one room here, plus a tiny bedroom and bathroom. Still, the lights and heat and water work fine. I just started putting extra stuff in here because nobody was using it for anything else. No point wasting space."

In the hard electric light, Monica looked around at the combination kitchen and living room. The only window was boarded shut. Cobwebs hung from the ceiling; the air was stale. No one had been in here for quite a while. She surveyed the school materials; there were a lot of old textbooks that could just as well be thrown away. The projector was easy to spot, sitting on what was intended to be a kitchen counter.

When they were outside again and on their way back to the classrooms, Carolyn offered to carry the projector box. "How's Brenda?" she asked as she took the heavy box from Monica.

"Fine."

"She's not in school anymore?"

"No, she's not."

"How come?"

Monica remained silent.

Once she was back in the classrooms and free of Carolyn's questions, an idea began to percolate in Monica's head. Ruby and Martin's house was crowded. With Brenda home all day now, the place had seemed to shrink even further. For over a month, she had been sleeping in Tom's room, forcing Tom to move into Junior's bedroom. Surely the boys wanted some space of their own. What if Gary let her have those small storerooms? Carolyn did say that they had been intended as a teacherage. Monica could clean it all up, get the window replaced, and then she would pay rent if they wanted. She would still spend a lot of time at Ruby's, but the privacy would be good for her. A place of her own — she had not had that for a while.

The next day she broached the subject at lunch hour. She had been working for over a month by then; she was doing a good job and she was not going anywhere. Gary thought about her query only briefly before tentatively agreeing. He would run her proposal by the Band Office, and if they approved, he would do up a written agreement.

THIRTEEN

Monica left for Campbell River before the sun was up on Saturday morning. She had convinced herself that if she left for home early enough on Sunday morning, she would be able to beat the bulk of the forecasted snow. Over the preceding week, she had scrubbed and scoured, and then made a list of the things that her new place needed. She had vowed to not take too long to accumulate her own furniture and household goods and return all the items that Ruby had so generously lent her.

Once she had checked back into the Highliner, Monica drove straight to the shopping mall. It was the exact same mall that she and Brenda used to make fun of for being so tiny compared to the malls in Vancouver. She loaded her car with a random assortment of goods: everything from thick, cream-coloured bath towels to a small stereo to a full-sized coffee pot to a yellow soap dish shaped like a duck.

Next, she paid for a bed, and arranged for it to be delivered to Port Hope. They did not deliver to Kitsum, the salesman told her. Monica already knew that — Ruby had told her exactly how the furniture store operated — but she asked why anyway. She wanted to hear for herself the argument for a store "policy" that made no sense. Only when she knew that the flustered salesman was worried about losing the entire sale did she agree to pick up the bed in Port Hope. She would have to ask Martin for yet another favour, or borrow his truck again. Ruby claimed that the bed she had lent her was an extra one, but Monica knew that it was Tom's. Her nephew had been sleeping on camping foam since before Christmas. She needed her own bed, and whatever she thought of the salesman and his shop, this was her best option.

More than a little satisfied with herself and how the day had gone, Monica returned to the Highliner. She intended to eat in the café, and then watch television and read in her room. She was scanning the menu—with her newly purchased weekend newspapers waiting for her in the plastic bag at her elbow—when she heard his voice.

"You're here again." Before she could reply, Michael Clydesdale slid onto the seat across from her. "Are you eating alone?"

She nodded and realized that, despite her trepidation, she was not unhappy to see him. A familiar face from Kitsum was always welcome amid the strangeness of town.

"You hang out at the Highliner?" Michael made a sort of grimace to let her know that it was not a serious question, and then laughed at his own joke.

"Do you?" Monica laughed back.

By the time their meals arrived, they were speaking easily to one another. Monica spoke of buying things for her new place and told him how much she was enjoying working at the school. Michael talked about his work up at the new subdivision. It was almost as if the two of them were friends.

"Kitsum can be pretty nuts on the weekends. Well, maybe not where you are, but at my Uncle Fred's. I come to Campbell quite a bit. I usually stay with my old foster parents—Mitch and Allison. They're pretty great people. Allison is Métis from Saskatchewan and Mitch is a carpenter. He's always giving me tips on how to do things with the houses we're working on right now."

When he saw that she was listening to him, he continued. "They've been to Kitsum, you know. They drove me out before my mom's funeral, and stayed to pay their respects to my uncles and Auntie Ethel too. They took me in when I was a haywire punk," he laughed. "Anyways, I forgot that they were going to be gone this weekend. I felt funny about staying in their place alone. I mean I know where they keep the hidden key for emergencies and all

that, and they wouldn't have minded me using it, but still, I never
mentioned ahead of time that I'd be around, so it's just easier if I
stay here at the good old Highliner, too.

"Yeah, the Highliner—I mean, all the *best* people stay here,"
he added.

Monica laughed and shook her head. Michael could be funny.
This time, she had no difficulty eating her dinner. In fact, she
felt famished. Between bites, she managed "I haven't seen you
around Kitsum."

"I work all day. I go home, eat, then go to sleep. That's about it."

"Yeah, short days this time of year, too. After work, there's no
time to go anywhere."

"Not like the city, eh?"

They talked about living in Vancouver. She was surprised to
learn that Michael had lived there during some of the same years
that she lived there. They finished their meals, drank more tea, and
it seemed like their conversation had only begun.

"You feel like going for a walk?" Michael asked her. "Help
digest the food."

"Sure." Monica answered quickly before she had time to think
too hard.

She could not have said how long their walk lasted. She only
knew that it was twilight when they started out, and dark when they
returned. Bundled up against the winter wind blowing down the
channel, they walked along the sidewalk that bordered the water's
edge, and headed down to the docks. Unlike in Kitsum, the Campbell
River fishermen's floats were well lit. Michael pointed out the boats
he recognized: *Pacific Provider*, *Haida Warrior*, and *North Wind*. She
was keenly aware of the touch of his hand on her elbow and upper
arm as he guided her across the few frosty sections where patches of
ice might have formed. She dared not look at him then, afraid that
he would see on her face what she could not admit to herself.

Whenever Michael moved slightly ahead of her, Monica found
herself staring. His black hair lay partially over his jacket collar.
His shoulders were broad, his waist narrow. He moved smoothly,

at home in his own body. *What was she doing?* she wondered more than once, and more than once she refused to contemplate an answer. It began to rain. It was not a heavy downpour, but the large, slow drops were steady. The wind had not let up either. Monica had to brace herself to keep from shivering. They turned back toward the hotel.

"You probably have plans?" Michael asked her.

"Plans?" She did not understand.

"Plans, you know, plans," he said slowly with a smile. "Like what you were going to do tonight? You know, bingo, bars, plans."

"Me?" Monica laughed. In the last year or so, Saul had begun to give her strange looks when she laughed too loudly or too often in public. Here, it seemed that her laughter could flow freely. "I'm going to watch TV and read the paper," she said firmly.

The closer they got to the Highliner, the less they spoke. Words that had come so easily earlier in the evening now seemed to carry enormous weight. Monica could hear every step they took. She looked down at the sidewalk and watched their legs move, their strides equally spaced. Simultaneously, she dreaded and anticipated the bright lights of the lobby. The closer they got, the more she knew that she would invite Michael back to her room. From his lengthening silence, she sensed that he knew it too.

Monica woke up smiling. She could see a dim line of light entering the room where the heavy drapes did not quite join together. Michael lay sleeping beside her, his bare chest gently rising and falling. She moved closer to him and he turned to meet her. When she awoke again, the crack of light was brighter. Michael's eyes were open. He was watching her.

"How long have you been awake?"

"Not long," he answered, and for no apparent reason, they both laughed. Monica felt like she could laugh all day.

Once they had dressed, she opened the room curtains and saw all the snow. Her car was buried beneath a sea of white in the parking lot below. Every vehicle was now nothing but a mound of snow. The worry of getting home did not even hit her immediately; at first she just stared without comprehension.

From behind her, she heard Michael. "We'll take the truck. I've got good tires and chains. There's plenty of room for your stuff. I'm sure they'll let you leave your car here...considering."

They waited to leave Campbell River. They had to wait until they got news that the highway had been ploughed and the grater from Port Hope had gone over the length of road between the turnoff and Kitsum. It was now a matter of driving slowly and carefully. The long drive back to Kitsum—that even at the best of times would have made Monica nervous—did not worry her too much this time. Michael would be driving; she would be safe.

Perhaps it was his having to pay extra attention to the driving that caused the uneasiness that entered their conversation. On the previous day, they had talked about their jobs and families, and about living in Vancouver and Kitsum. Today the conversation did not flow nearly as smoothly. Mostly they spoke in short snippets, commenting on the radio programs or the music. Three or four times, Michael told her jokes that made her groan and roll her eyes. Both of them, it turned out, liked to sing along with songs on the radio. Monica heard Michael doing it shortly into the drive. Then about an hour later, she caught herself doing the same thing. Just as she was about to stop, she heard Michael join in. Neither of them was very musical, Monica thought wryly, but then as the song went on, she gradually let her voice grow louder and louder.

"Hey," Michael said when the song ended. "We sound good together."

That made her blush. She could not remember the last time that she had felt her cheeks grow so hot so quickly. She did not dare say anything or look at him. Nervousness filled the truck cab. By the time Michael was helping her unload her groceries and purchases in Kitsum, they were being almost formally polite to one another.

There was no sign of Michael—not for three days after he dropped her off. On the second day, Gary asked her if she was all right. On the morning of the third day, he asked her if she might be coming down with something.

"Maybe I've got a cold," Monica told him and actually believed it. As soon as the final school bell rang, she went straight to her place with the aim of taking Helen's advice to drink lots of hot herbal tea and get more rest. She had barely slept the night before.

She was awakened by a knocking at her door. Fully dressed, Monica sat upright quickly. It was already completely dark outside. She had no idea how long she had been asleep. She had sipped half a cup of tea and then she had gone to lie down; that was the last thing she remembered. Squinting at the stove top, she saw that it was nearly six o'clock.

"Coming," she called in a still cloudy voice.

Monica opened the door to Michael. Without thinking, still dazed by sleep, she stretched out her arms and nearly fell towards him. She hugged him hard, not wanting to let him go.

"Hey," he finally spoke. "I'm glad to see you too. You going to let me in?"

"Sure, sure." Monica spoke between chuckles. Somehow, this man made her want to laugh.

"I brought you another lock," he explained. "I'll put it on for you. I noticed when we dropped off your stuff that you didn't have a decent lock on the door." From his jacket pocket he pulled out a new bolt and chain and a screwdriver. "You can't trust the drunks around here, you know. Better to be careful."

Monica was waking up fast now. She was suddenly conscious of her rumpled appearance and the messy bed that was clearly visible through the open bedroom door. "I must have fallen asleep."

"Must have," he mimicked, and she was laughing again.

Michael stayed with her that night. Within a few days, they had established a new routine. They would wake and eat early, and then Michael would stop by his place to change and gather what he needed for work that day. Then in the evenings, he would drop off his tools at home and return to Monica's for supper.

Monica refused to think too much about what was happening. She only wanted to know how good it felt to be with Michael; she only remembered how horribly empty those three days had felt away from him. Things had never been this intense with Saul. In the beginning when she and Saul had seen each other once or twice a week, Monica had carried on with her classes and assignments, her readings and research, much as she had before they had met. It came as a complete shock to her now that whenever Michael was gone — even though she understood that he was at work or at home — she felt like she could not function properly. She definitely could not concentrate. She had to go through the motions of what she needed to do without being capable of really thinking about it. When Michael was with her, Monica was in a state of utter happiness. She could not recall ever having been so happy. She could not keep from smiling, laughing, and beaming.

That first weekend together in Kitsum, neither of them had any desire to leave the small apartment. It was late February; the skies were completely grey; rain poured down endlessly. The apartment was a warm cave in a storm. It was a cocoon. She did not think beyond its walls. She managed to emerge from its embrace only long enough to phone Ruby and tell her that she was exhausted from the week and that she was going to spend the entire weekend sleeping. Ruby did not sound like she completely believed her, but she did not question her further. It was enough of an excuse to keep her sister and nieces and nephews from coming to look for her. At the time, that was all Monica wanted.

On Monday morning, first Becky, then Millie, asked her where she had been all weekend. She even caught Tom watching her suspiciously as he hung up his wet jacket. Their mother had expected her for supper on Sunday; the girls were clear about that. Monica got the message. She may have been tired on Saturday, but surely by Sunday afternoon, she should have been rested enough to see her family. After school, Monica went to Ruby's. She had to at least tell her sister. It would not do to have Ruby hear about Monica and Michael from someone else. She and Michael had already driven in from Campbell River together. Who had seen that? Who had seen Michael coming and going from her place? This would have all been just gossip to Monica except, of course, for her niece Brenda. The slightest thought of Brenda and her reaction caused Monica's stomach to clench tight. She was not ready for that; she would do her best to hold that one off for as long as possible, but she had to let Ruby know what was going on.

At her sister's house, Monica practically pushed Ruby into her bedroom. Monica was not prepared to stay at the house all evening to wait for a chance to speak to her sister alone. Using the bedroom for a private talk was the only quick option. Brenda and the kids were in the living room watching television. Ruby was obviously annoyed at being interrupted from cooking dinner, but at least she did not complain out loud. She just looked quizzically at her "baby" sister.

Monica had been in Ruby and Martin's bedroom only a few times over the years. She realized that she had not done more than knock on the door or drop off laundry there since she was a teenager. It was not that the room was formally off limits or anything; it was more that everyone treated it as a sort of private space. Monica suddenly felt shy. She kept her eyes on the tiled floor.

"Sorry," Monica started. She knew that she was going to be apologizing for this for a very long while. "I know this isn't a good time, but I'm sorry I didn't come over on the weekend."

"Were you sick?"

"No," she reassured Ruby. "I'm fine. I'm great. School's good. The place is good. Everything's good." Monica had the feeling that she had to get her words out rapidly or she would not be able to utter them altogether. Still, she hesitated. "The heat in that apartment is set too high. It gets really stuffy if you don't open the window a little."

Ruby stared at her. They both knew that Monica had not dragged her into the bedroom so that she could tell her about the heat at Kitsum Elementary School.

"I have to tell you, Ruby. I have to. It's not something I ever thought would happen. I never would have planned or imagined this happening. It's too strange."

Ruby waited wordlessly for her to continue. Monica looked away from her sister and back at the floor. Even with the regular scrubbing and mopping that she knew the floor got, the tiles had yellowed over the years.

"You know I went to see Michael Clydesdale...to speak with him about Brenda." She waited for Ruby to make a noise in response. "Well, I ran into him again right after New Year's when I went to Campbell River. We had lunch and talked, mostly about Bren. Then, when I went to Campbell last time to get stuff for the new place, well, there he was again. Anyways, Rube, it's not like I expected to be attracted to him or anything. Farthest thing from my mind. Hell, Ruby, I didn't expect to like the guy. I really didn't. After everything that happened, I thought he was a real asshole. But I did. I did like him. I do, I mean. I like him a lot."

She dared a brief glance up at Ruby. Her sister's eyes had narrowed and her head was ever so slightly bent forward; Ruby was watching and listening to her very seriously indeed.

Monica was almost too frightened to speak. It was too important; it all meant too much to her. How could she explain to Ruby how Michael's hair shone in the winter sunlight, how his body moved sleekly and easily as if he flowed rather than walked, how his arms made her feel safer and more loved than she had ever felt? Ever imagined possible? How could she say?

"I'm in love with him," Monica told her sister in her smallest voice.

"What?" The sound emerged from Ruby not so much as a word being spoken but as an angry guttural response to pain.

"I'm sorry."

Ruby stared at her—her eyes were wide open now—for what felt like a long time. Suddenly, Monica was a little girl again waiting to be reprimanded for losing her jacket or for being out past curfew on a school night. In the end though, Ruby merely shook her head sadly. "I have to get supper ready."

"Yeah, I have to go too," Monica managed.

She knew it was a futile wish, but she wished it anyway. If only her sister could hug or touch her now and assure her that all would be well again. That was not going to happen. She no longer had any right to expect it to happen. Ruby brushed hurriedly by her on her way back to the kitchen. Monica did not attempt to look at her again. She fled the house before her nieces or nephews could notice.

FOURTEEN

Brenda hurried out of Marcie's house in a daze. What her best friend had just told her! That her favourite of favourites—Auntie Monica—was seeing Michael Clydesdale! There was no way. Someone had started a rumour from bits of old gossip. That had to be it. That sort of thing happened all the time in Kitsum.

It simply could not be. Marcie herself had admitted that it might not be true. She was getting her gossip muddled with her own distress about being forced to move with her parents to Campbell River. Yes, that had to be the case. She was upset about the move herself. Her friend did not want to leave Kitsum. It was not even her idea. It was not fair. Nothing was fair!

So much confused energy propelled Brenda that she arrived home in what felt like mere seconds. Once there, she could not sit or calm herself down. She left the house quickly and headed for the lake trail, the first place she could think of where she would be completely alone at that time of year. It was not until she had actually reached the lake and was staring across at the stunted bog forest that her mind began to slow enough for her to think somewhat coherently again.

She would need to calm down until she knew what was going on for sure. Marcie's gossip had likely originated with Carolyn. Everyone knew that woman was one of the meanest gossips around and that she did not like their family. Troublemaking, that is what she would have been doing. Brenda came up with a plan. Not a great plan, but at least one with some chance of working. She would ask Thomas and Becky when they got home from school. They would probably know more than anyone. Millie was too young yet; she would only get mixed up and say that Auntie Monica's boyfriend was the principal or someone else who had only spoken to her.

The hard part was waiting for Tom and Becky to get home from school. She actually had to stop herself from racing down to Kitsum Elementary to meet them as they exited the school building. She only had under an hour to wait, for heaven's sake. She needed to control herself. Her mind was spinning. Monica had not visited them lately. Was her aunt avoiding her? What did her mother know?

Her best friend was leaving Kitsum. What about that? She had just got Marcie back, and now she was going to lose her again. Her throat felt like it was closing up. Brenda had to force herself to swallow, to breathe. Please, please, please, she chanted. Let it all be a mistake.

When Becky got home, Brenda followed her into the bedroom that she shared with Millie. Her sister had a puzzled look on her face; she could see that Brenda was mad about something. She just could not figure out what it could be.

"Auntie Monica works in your classroom?" The words came out like an accusation.

Becky nodded.

"Have you been to her new place?"

Again her sister nodded.

"Who stays there?"

"Auntie Monica stays there," Becky said.

"Who besides your aunt? I heard someone else lives there too."

Becky looked confused. "I think she stays by herself."

"But you're not sure?"

"I think I'm sure."

"But you're not, eh? Because I heard that Auntie Monica has a new boyfriend." Brenda tried to soften her tone a little. She knew that she was scaring Becky unnecessarily. "I'm trying to find out who he is, that's all."

"Not Saul?"

"No, not Saul," Brenda almost screamed.

She saw the tears well up in her little sister's eyes and knew that she should ease up on the questioning.

"I said *new*. A new boyfriend. Monica has another boyfriend now."

"I don't know, Brenda…I don't know."

Becky was openly crying now. Brenda walked out of the room. She went to Tom's room next. He was still young enough to be afraid of his older sister. She would find out what was going on from him.

"Marcie was telling me that Auntie Monica has a new boyfriend." Tom did not speak very loudly, and Brenda had to lean in to hear him. "Yeah, I think so," he answered.

"Who, Tom?"

"I forget his name."

"Think, Thomas." Brenda stood over her brother, waiting.

"I dunno, Bren. I'm sorry…"

"Christ, Tom. *Think*."

"I really don't know."

Brenda took a deep breath. She tried to hide her anger from her brother. He had always had trouble remembering names. Badgering him would get her nowhere. She turned instead and went back to her own room.

She had left Marcie's too quickly. She should have pressed Marcie to go over every detail of what she had heard, and then to reveal where she had heard her news. Maybe there was something her friend had missed telling her. She would have to wait for the next day and she would have to start the conversation all over again. Brenda paced to and fro.

She would have to wait for the kids to go to bed. Her whole life, she thought bitterly, was now nothing but waiting. Junior went out to the hall for basketball as usual. The winter hours had been extended until ten o'clock so that the teams could get ready for Prince Rupert. No one had wanted to change them back once that tournament was over.

"You want tea, Mom?" She knew that with her father out herring fishing, her mother would enjoy her company at this time of night. Some evenings, she felt bad about going upstairs and leaving her alone on the couch to stare at the television.

Her mother nodded appreciatively. Brenda did not find it hard to talk to her, especially with her dad away. Ruby had really been nothing but kind since Brenda had told her about being pregnant. There was no reason not to bring up the subject of Monica and her new boyfriend. "Marcie told me something today…" She brought the tea and took a seat on the opposite end of the couch from her mother. "About Auntie Monica."

A look of shock flashed across her mother's face. Brenda watched that initial look turn quickly into one of weariness and resignation. Suddenly Brenda knew that her mother had anticipated the very conversation they were about to have, and that scared her. "Wait…what did Monica tell you?" she managed.

It took her mother a long time to answer.

"She didn't mean to hurt you."

That simple statement was all Brenda needed to confirm her worst fears. Marcie's news had been true after all. Her own aunt—her aunt who was like a big sister—was doing this to her. She had been doing this to her for who knows how long, behind her back. Not only had Michael Clydesdale not become Brenda's boyfriend; he had somehow become Monica's boyfriend. It was too horrible to fully imagine.

"Tell me," she ordered her mother.

Once again, her mother took ages to begin. "I guess Monica first talked to this Michael because you asked her to. Anyway, that's what she told me." She looked at Brenda with sad eyes.

"Then, Monica said she wasn't satisfied with whatever this guy had said to her, so she went to talk to him again. She didn't tell me, Bren, that she was doing any of this. I would have told her not to bother. I mean, she was talking to him for nothing."

Not nothing, Brenda thought with alarm, but talking to him because she had asked her to talk to him.

"Brenda." Her mother was serious. "You are not to tell your father that I told you this. He never wanted you to know...look, he went to see Michael himself. Not long after you told us about being pregnant. So it was stupid of Monica to go, after Martin had already spoken to him."

"Dad?" Brenda could not believe it.

"He didn't ask me, Bren. He just told me after he'd seen him."

"And?"

"Well, I guess your father told him not to bother you anymore."

Brenda shook her head. She had waited for months to hear from Michael. Then to find out that her own father had prevented it! Her chest felt like it was about to explode.

"How could he? How could Dad tell him that?"

"But Monica didn't know that. I guess she thought that she could help you out by talking to him. So she met up with him in Campbell River. She didn't tell me much, Bren. Just that they started to see each other after that. I can't imagine what she was possibly thinking. I really can't. The only reason Monica told me was that she was afraid of me—and you—hearing it from someone else. I guess Monica expected me to tell you but...I just couldn't, Bren."

Brenda wanted to call her aunt every nasty name that she had ever heard. At the same time, reverberations of what her father had done pounded inside her head. Her mind was a boiling cauldron of chaos, swirling and churning. All of it—her being pregnant, her father making mysterious arrangements with Michael, Monica luring Michael back to the teacherage—it was all completely incomprehensible. None of it made sense. The world she had always known and trusted had disappeared, only to be replaced by this distorted horror story version. She sat on the couch, her tea now cold beside her, and stared into a darkening storm.

FIFTEEN

Winter days passed so slowly in Kitsum that it always came as a surprise to realize that spring had nearly arrived. Suddenly a person realized that the days so abruptly abbreviated were growing longer again. Temperatures rose. Rain fell more often as drizzle or heavy mist than as torrential downpours. The community was coming alive again after its long hibernation. Even Brenda, Nona noticed, was once again taking daily walks.

Nona had begun to take her tea at a small table beside her living room armchair. From there, she could gaze out her front window at the expanse of Kitsum Harbour. Herrings were schooling in the bay. Eagles perched on the shoreline trees and rocks. Flocks of seagulls flew spirals in the sky and landed to float upon the water alongside masses of ducks. Sea lions barked day and night, diving and resurfacing while eating their fill of the small fish.

The marine radio was busy with herring fishery news and weather predictions. After the Barkley Sound opening, Nona knew that Martin would be heading back up the coast to their area to fish. Then the *Pacific Queen* would tow his herring punt and gillnets up to the Central Coast for more activity up there. He and the other herring fishermen followed the same routine every year. Harry had fished herrings, too. Some years, when they had to wait especially long for various openings, he had been gone from home for over a month.

Like everyone else in Kitsum, Nona eagerly awaited the herring spawning. Then the whole of Kitsum Harbour would be white with the milt of the male herrings as they let go over the eggs the females had laid. Everyone would have a tree out, hoping for thick coatings of *kwukmis* on the branches. She could no longer do that herself anymore, but Martin Junior had assured her that he would be out with his grandfather and that they would put a tree down for her. She used to love taking part in all that exciting work with Harry and Charlie. They would cut down small hemlock trees along the shoreline, and pick up stones the size of bowling balls to use as anchors. Harry would tie a rock anchor to one end of the tree and secure a buoy to the other end. Then they would drop it from the skiff into the waters wherever the herrings were spawning the most. Across from Frank's old cabin used to be a good spot. Inside Corner Beach, too. Harry said that the herrings liked to spawn on all the eelgrass that grew under the water there. Nona would go along in the boat to check the trees, sometimes once, sometimes a few times, every day. Then she would watch as Harry and Charlie hauled them up to see how many layers of eggs had accumulated. It only took a day or two for their trees to be thick with spawn. Then they would pull them into the boat and Nona would spend all day on the floats cutting up the branches. Before long, there would be large pails full of *kwukmis* and layers of coarse salt. Then they would have enough *kwukmis* to last them through spring, summer, and fall.

She saved less now that she was alone. Charlie got his own from wherever the Hartley Bay people got their herring eggs. Still though, by herself she could easily go through forty or fifty bags. And fresh *kwukmis*; there was no better food on Earth. Nona had watched the herrings moving in and out of the bay for over a week before they started to spawn. Then Junior stopped by to tell her that they had put trees out. A day later, he offered her a ride to the floats with her bags and containers.

Nona plucked the thickest pieces of *kwukmis* from the branches and shoved them into her freezer bags. She could not resist eating some. The fresh stuff was just too delicious. Whenever she happened across a particularly thick branch, she put it into her smaller bucket to cook fresh after she got home. She listened as a few feet away from her, Susan Joe began telling her granddaughter about how they used to dry branches of *kwukmis* on long racks in the sun and breeze. Nona nodded along in agreement. She recalled her own mother setting up such racks and hanging the boughs that were full of eggs. She remembered how her mother had soaked the dried *kwukmis* before they were allowed to eat it, so that the eggs puffed back up. Susan carried on with her story, telling Brenda about all the places near Kitsum where herrings spawned.

Seeing Nona's containers full, Junior offered to pack them up in the truck and drive her home. It seemed like the afternoon had passed too quickly. Others, she knew, would be back on the floats the next day to store away more *kwukmis*. She would be at her house then, with enough for a single person already put away in her freezer and fridge. Yes, she would be eating pots full of *kwukmis* for days.

She was eager to tell Charlie about the spawn and her *kwukmis* too. It was with that thought in mind that she said goodbye to Brenda, Ruby, and Susan. She would phone her son as soon as she had her bags safely stowed away.

He was home too! As she knew he would be, Charlie was excited and happy for her. The herring spawn near Hartley Bay was still weeks away, or so he figured. She had no idea where herrings spawned on the North Coast. Her son told her the names of places, but they were all meaningless to her. She had no connection to any of them. Not like around Kitsum, where she could name every point and every beach for miles in both directions. Here she could remember where a particular family came from, where coho salmon went up the creek to spawn, or where to dig clams or pick salal berries. She could recall whole streams of information, of history and knowing, tied to so many places. Here, she knew what places meant to people.

Maybe it was eating all that *kwukmis* that put Nona in such a happy, youthful mood. She decided the very next evening to accept her son's invitation to visit. That day, she felt daring and bold. Why not go to Hartley Bay for a few weeks? She could spend some time with her grandchildren. What did she have to lose? Before she could change her mind or find some reason not to go, she phoned Charlie. She could tell he was surprised to hear from her again so quickly. "I'll come up then," she told him. "That is, if you still want me to. Just let me know when to be ready."

He sounded really happy; Nona was glad of that. He laughed a little and told her that the kids would be excited to see their grandmother again. Nona expected that would have been the end of their conversation, but her son seemed to want to stay on the line. This was uncharacteristic of him, but maybe he really did miss her. He asked more about the herring. Were they still spawning? In which areas had they spawned? Did everyone get lots of *kwukmis*?

Nona told him as much as she knew and teased him about having fresh *kwukmis* for lunch and dinner. Charlie groaned enviously. Once the herring talk had subsided, Nona again expected Charlie to say good night. Instead, he blurted out, "So how is Brenda?"

It was Nona's turn to be surprised. Her son looking for gossip; that was completely unlike him. He had never been particularly close to Brenda. He had gone fishing with Martin a few times over the years but mostly he had fished with his own father. Other than that, he had not had too much to do with Martin and Ruby's children. They were all quite a bit younger than him.

"She seems all right," Nona answered carefully. "She was down at the floats doing *kwukmis* with everyone."

Charlie seemed to wait for more. Nona could not think of much else to tell him. Brenda had seemed cheerful, at least until she saw Monica. Or that was how things had looked to her. "I guess that's to be expected," her son pronounced.

Nona had no idea what he meant. "You mean the moodiness that goes with pregnancy?"

"Well, that too, I guess."

This was the strangest conversation with Charlie that Nona could remember. What was her son getting at? Maybe she was just drowsy from all the recent fresh air.

Charlie talked about Brenda being young and capable of getting over things. Then he said that Brenda and Monica would be close again, that there was no taking away the fact that the two of them had grown up together and were part of the same family. Her son — usually so straightforward — was speaking to her in riddles. Nona raised her voice in frustration.

"Hang on…what has Monica got to do with all of this?"

Charlie's voice grew quieter. "You mean you didn't know?"

"Know what?" Nona did not often get peeved with Charlie, but she was well on her way.

"I just assumed you knew. That's the only reason I brought it up."

"Charlie, you'd better tell me what is going on."

She heard her son take a deep breath. He'd been talking to Michael Clydesdale recently on the phone. He liked to talk to a few of the guys from back home, and he had stayed in touch with Michael over the years.

"Anyways," her son said cheerily, "I can't help but be happy for Mike now. He's finally found someone he can trust and rely on."

Incredulous, Nona nearly shouted, "Brenda?"

Her son spoke to her as he would to one of his children. "Not Brenda, Mom. *Monica*."

Nona could tell he was sorry to have ever initiated this conversation with her. She chided herself for all her stupid questions, but it was too late to take any of them back. She changed the subject.

"You know, you could make a quick trip down and find out how everyone is doing yourself. I'll be sure to save you lots of *kwukmis*."

SIXTEEN

The excitement of *kwukmis* had lured Brenda out of the house. Like everyone in her family, and everyone in Kitsum, she absolutely loved *kwukmis*. On the floats, she worked alongside her mother, grandmother, grandfather, Auntie Kate, and Nona. She peeled chunk after chunk of the thick layers of herring eggs from the hemlock branches and stuffed them into her waiting mouth. The sun was shining; the sky was clear blue with mere wisps of cloud. Most of Kitsum seemed to be out and in a good mood. Even the seagulls drifting alongside the floats—who were scooping up leftovers and squawking their apparent good fortune—seemed to be in a state of casual celebration. Indeed, Brenda relished the crunch of the popcorn-like eggs between her teeth as she cut the branches full of *kwukmis* into smaller pieces and eagerly filled their totes. She found herself smiling and laughing easily.

There were five long "fingers" to the village floats. Tied up to those fingers were an assortment of fishing boats, small motor boats, rowboats, and canoes. Even with most of the trollers and herring punts gone for the fishing openings, the floats still looked fairly full. At first glance, the gillnet drums, buckets, ropes, chains, and tools appeared to merely litter the floats. Upon closer examination, the fishing gear proved to be sorted into easily distinguishable areas, according to which skipper it belonged to, and where that skipper generally tied up his boat.

When Brenda was not looking at the *kwukmis* or her mother or grandparents, her eyes were drawn to the *Queen's* gillnet drum at the end of the finger. Even after what her father had done, she still missed him.

She was staring at the drum when she heard the commotion coming from the other direction. She turned her head and saw the schoolchildren coming down the ramp. Gary was at least a head taller than everyone else, so he was easy to see. No sooner had she recognized them than she heard Thomas shout in their direction. Brenda and her mother returned the greeting. Then, before Brenda had even finished lowering her arm, she saw her aunt. Only slightly taller than the students, there was Monica, waving and smiling. Brenda stared. She watched as her aunt helped some of the girls with a branch that was heavily loaded with *kwukmis*. Suddenly it felt like everyone else on the floats vanished. All she could feel was her aunt's presence; all she could hear was Monica's clear voice and the telltale sound of her laughter. Brenda would have recognized that laughter anywhere. She had grown up with it. How could Monica be so happy? What right did she have to all the joy in the world? The *kwukmis* in Brenda's mouth turned to rubber. It was no longer a perfect day.

When her mother asked her to go down to the floats with them the next day, she almost refused. However, the thought of more fresh *kwukmis* was overpowering. On a Saturday, Monica would likely be off in town shopping. Besides, her aunt would know full well that Ruby and her family would be down at the floats doing *kwukmis*. She would not dare show her face. Why shouldn't Brenda be out enjoying her favourite season with her mother and the kids?

The day went well until later in the afternoon. The sun—already low in the sky—was not too high above the western mountains. Her grandfather and brothers had brought in the last of their trees hours ago. Her grandmother and Auntie Kate had already gone up, as had most people. The last of their bins was wedged in between herself and her mother, and it was nearly full. Another few branches, and it would overflow. One tree full of *kwukmis* lay on the far side of her mother.

Brenda wondered if her grandfather had already promised that last tree to someone. They no longer had the room, since Junior had brought most of their full totes to the truck. He was getting tougher, she noted. All that working with their father and grandfather, and all the basketball training, was paying off. Parked near the top of the ramp, she noticed her brother stopping to speak with two people on their way down. Brenda resumed cutting up branches. Her hands were getting numb now, even from a light breeze. At that time of year, so early into spring, any wind was enough to bring back the chill of winter.

When Brenda looked up again, Junior and the two people following him were standing in front of her and her mother. Monica and Michael! It was the first time she had laid eyes on Michael in nearly six months. It was too late to pretend that she had not seen him or Monica. They were right there and she was staring right at them.

"Hey," Monica said, as though everything was perfectly normal, as though the world was not threatening to blow apart.

Brenda wanted more than anything to flee, but there was no escape. The thought of having to raise her bloated body from its spot on the railing of the float kept her glued in place. She managed a nod and nudged closer to her mother.

"Peter said that you should take that tree there," her mother said, tilting her head in the direction of the full tree.

Brenda realized that her mother was speaking to Monica. How could she? How could her grandfather? Give Monica *kwukmis* after all she had done. How could they?

Monica prattled on. Brenda recognized the excitement over *kwukmis* in her voice, but there was something else there as well. Her aunt was actually nervous. Three times, she heard her repeat herself about thanking Peter. Michael remained silent. *Just take the tree and go*, Brenda felt like shouting.

Then, of course, her aunt could not just leave things alone. "How you doing, Bren?" she asked quietly.

Raw anger gave Brenda the strength to glare up at her. "How the hell do you think I am?" was on the tip of her tongue, but out of the corner of her eye, she saw the lines around her mother's eyes tighten. "Fine," she answered grimly and looked away.

Maybe Monica wanted to avoid a confrontation too. Her aunt held her tongue after that. She stepped past Brenda and picked up the loaded branches. Michael was watching Monica and the *kwukmis* as though they were the only things that existed in the world. Leaning on her mother, Brenda heaved herself up and headed for the truck. She doubted that anyone was paying the least bit of attention.

SEVENTEEN

Not long after all the *kwukmis* had been collected—Monica remembered specifically that it had been during the third week of March when the herrings had spawned near Kitsum—she received a visitor. She was getting ready to leave the sixth-grade classroom when she heard a series of small knocks on the nearby main door. Thinking it was only students looking for something to do, she ignored them. She would just tell the kids that everyone had left on her way out. However, the tapping did not stop. It only grew louder. Irritated now, Monica gathered her papers to take home and flung the metal door open. There, standing under the brief overhang, was Saul. She would have been no more shocked to see the pope himself at her doorstep.

"Saul," she managed. "How did you know I was here?"

"I went to Ruby's first. She gave me directions." Saul smiled. "It's good to see you."

"I'm just locking up. Everyone's left for the day." Monica fumbled in her pocket for the key to the deadbolt. Carolyn never failed to complain if one of the staff forgot to lock a door. It did not occur to her to invite Saul into the school. Monica stepped outside, turned the key, and stood looking at this man with whom she had once lived.

"Ruby mentioned that you had your own place. I was a little surprised at that news. I just assumed that you'd be with your sister as usual."

There was nothing wrong with Ruby telling Saul where she lived, she told herself. It was not a secret. What else was her sister supposed to do but tell Saul where to find her? "Come on," she said, and began walking around the building. Even half a step behind, Saul seemed to tower above her.

"I needed my own spot," she explained. "I was taking Thomas's room and that didn't seem fair, not for such a long time, anyways." She held the door open and told Saul to have a seat on the small blanketed sofa. "I'll make tea," she said. "You still drink tea?"

"It hasn't been that long." Saul tried to laugh. "Yes. I still drink tea."

Before the tea was even ready, Saul began talking. She figured that he had to have prepared his speech well in advance. "I kept thinking of phoning, Monica. Then I realized there was too much to explain on the telephone. I don't know how many letters to you I started and tore up in frustration. Finally, I realized that the only thing that would do was for me to come here and talk to you in person."

Monica pretended to busy herself with selecting cups. Did he expect her to congratulate him on his decision or his showing up out of the blue? "Do you still take honey?"

"Yes, of course. Thank you."

Monica looked hard at Saul. He was wearing a light green golf shirt with its top two buttons undone, and new blue jeans. She saw that he had dressed to appear casual. It was one of a few "looks" he used. The faint beginnings — or endings — of a tan showed on his neck. The muscles of his arms flexed ever so slightly as he reached for the teacup. He still worked out, she thought. Three times a week, and once every other weekend. He would not have changed his routine. She thought that she should be polite and ask him something. "How's Ottawa?" she ventured.

"It's..." For a second, she expected a sincere revelation, but then he seemed to revert to a prepared speech. "It's different. I'm enjoying the university. They seem to appreciate me; there's lots of support and interest in my research. And then, there's nothing like being in Ottawa close to the archives. The sheer amount of material there is absolutely astounding. Ottawa really is the centre of things, in a big way. But Monica...it's lonely too. I miss you."

She did not answer. Instead she concentrated on the small table. She sat on one of the two kitchen chairs. That was the only place to sit, other than on the couch beside Saul. Out of the corner of her eye, she watched him taking in the room. She tried to see it all as he would see it. The books stacked on the floor, the armchair full of laundry, the dirty dishes on the counter beside the tall scented candles she had picked up at the market in Port Hope. The dried flowers in a pink-tinged vase on the windowsill, and the photos of her nieces and nephews stuck with magnets onto the refrigerator. The cream-coloured curtains that offset the arrangement of beach stones and shells on the new bookcase. How did it all appear to him? Monica had taken immense pride in every item she had added to this room. It irked her now, to see Saul so casually looking everything over. She glanced at her wristwatch and saw that Michael would be home soon. That was Saul's own fault, she told herself. He should not have come.

"Can I use your washroom? I had a long drive."

Monica nodded and waited. Now that he was here, she wished that she had thought to invite him into the school instead.

It was not the same affable Saul who exited the bathroom. She recognized the furrowed forehead as a sure sign of anger. Just what had he seen, exactly? Nervously, she looked to the window and door.

"Expecting someone, Monica?" Even his voice had changed.

"Michael." She cleared her throat. "Michael Clydesdale."

"That didn't take you long."

Monica felt like telling him that it was none of his business, but she held back her words. "He's from Kitsum. Like me," she said instead, and then wondered where that had come from. "He lives here. With me."

"So I travelled all this way...for...*this*. I know you didn't like the idea of moving to Ottawa, even though it was important for my career. I understood that, or so I thought. But Monica, I never dreamed there was someone else. You didn't even have the guts to tell me. I should have known. Your refusing to come back after Christmas. Your treating me like a fool."

"Now wait a minute, Saul. It's not like that. Michael had nothing to do with my not wanting to move to Ottawa or not going back to Vancouver. I already explained that to you on the phone and in my letter. I was as honest as I could be."

"Yes, honest Monica." Saul practically spat the words. His voice was louder now. "Did you think I was too stupid to notice how interested in Kitsum you became? After years of barely wanting to come here, you suddenly had this need to be home all the time."

Saul was getting uglier. Monica cursed herself again for inviting him inside the apartment. She should have had it out with him in the schoolyard, the way the kids did. Then she could have walked away, and slammed her own door in his face. "Look, Saul, I am not going to listen to baseless accusations, especially not in my own home…"

They both heard the doorknob turning. They both watched as Michael entered the room and took a cup from the shelf. He poured himself some tea and settled onto the second kitchen chair before venturing an introduction. "Michael Clydesdale," he said, extending his hand to Saul.

Saul ignored it. "I've heard," he muttered.

It took him but a moment to recover. Monica knew that Saul would have been horrified to see himself as intentionally rude. Then he leaned over and shook Michael's hand. "Saul Arbess," he said clearly.

Michael did not betray a thing. Saul could as easily have been a parent of one of the schoolchildren, a teacher, or one of Monica's relatives. He sipped his tea and prepared himself to listen.

"You see…Michael…I've travelled here to Kitsum, to ask Monica to come back to Ottawa with me."

Only Michael's presence saved Monica from complete outrage. How dare Saul? She clenched and unclenched her fists beneath the small table. Michael reached for the candy dish that Monica had set out the night before. Tilting it slightly forward, he offered it toward Saul. "Candy?"

"No…no thank you." Saul looked confused, maybe even afraid. He had studied Aboriginal peoples and cultures and languages for so many years, and yet he still stiffened whenever he passed a Native man on the street. He would have never thought that Monica noticed, but she noticed every single time. Reality for Saul never quite matched his research.

Not taking his eyes from Saul, Michael removed his hand from the dish and rested it atop Monica's. He stretched his legs beneath the table and stifled a yawn. Monica inched sideways on her chair and leaned against him.

"I'm not going anywhere," she said quietly.

Without another word, Saul rose and left the apartment. Monica and Michael sat in the stillness, finishing their tea. Once she felt certain that Saul was not coming back, Monica got up and started supper.

Monica watched as the blinker at the entrance to the harbour cast its light over the trees at First Point. From the beach fronting Kitsum, she and Michael watched the moon rise in the eastern sky. Neither of them had much to say. Monica believed that something of consequence had been settled that day. She had also made a profound commitment to the man standing beside her. Michael suggested that they stop by his uncle's house on their way home. Monica recalled having been there only twice before, years ago when she had gone there with other teenagers to party. She nodded and followed Michael. It was not far.

Ethel and Fred were obviously surprised to see them. They invited them to stay for tea, and nodded courteously when Michael introduced Monica. They already knew who she was, but they followed Michael's lead. Ethel poured tea and sliced fresh bread for the table. Then she explained to Monica how they were related, something Monica had never clearly understood and would have been too embarrassed to ask about directly. According to Ethel, her mother and Monica's mother, Joan, had been first cousins. Ethel's mother's father and Monica's mother's mother were siblings. Ethel explained the relationship with care. It was closer than Monica had realized. Maybe it was because of all the deaths that she did not remember the connection so well. That older generation was all gone by the time she was a child, including Ethel's parents and her own mother's parents. Joan had been the oldest one in her family still alive when she and Ruby were growing up.

The four of them, along with Michael's Uncle Murray, sat in the kitchen having tea and bread with peanut butter and jam. There was not too much conversation after Ethel's explanation; there were definitely plenty of awkward gaps in their talk, but Monica could not say that it was wholly uncomfortable. Ethel and Fred clearly made an effort to smile and appear friendly. There was no way that Michael or Monica could feel that they were not welcome. Occasionally, Fred or Murray said something to Michael about work or the fishing coming up. They talked some about the herring run that year. The stretches of quiet did not seem to bother Michael. Monica watched him calmly sip his tea. She noticed that he held his cup — not by the handle but opposite the handle with his whole hand — exactly like his Uncle Murray. When Michael said that it was time for them to leave, Ethel told Monica to give Ruby her best.

On the walk home, Michael kept his arm around her. "They're pretty quiet when they're not drinking," he observed, partly to himself. Then he began to hum. By the time they reached the school, he was singing.

One day, there was one of those bursts of hot sunny weather that appear unexpectedly in the midst of the usual chilly wetness of mid-April. Monica and Michael decided to pack a lunch and leave early in the morning to walk out to Lone Point.

"My mom used to like to party here," Michael told Monica as they took their first rest break at Corner Beach. "I remember being out here lots when I was a little kid. They'd build a fire, and sit around it. It was lots of fun in the daytime. Me and some of the other kids, we'd run all over, all the way to Sandy Beach sometimes. The part I never liked was heading back home in the dark. I'd have to watch out for my mom all the time. She'd be pretty loaded by then and it wasn't easy in the dark. We never brought flashlights. I don't know how many times I thought that I had lost her..."

Michael had not talked much about his mother or about growing up. Monica, in contrast, seemed to constantly be remembering aloud. Living back in Kitsum brought all her old memories to the forefront. Seasonal events, people, sounds, even smells; they were always triggering recollections. She was about to tell her own story about Corner Beach—the one about the day that she and Ruby, along with preschoolers Junior and Brenda, had been within touching distance of a mother deer and her three white-spotted fawns—but Michael continued.

"The caves there." He pointed up the beach toward the hollows in the rock face that had been worn deeper and deeper by centuries of waves pounding the shore. "That's where they'd take her."

The look on his face kept Monica from interjecting.

"My mom," he answered softly as though she had spoken. "Even as a little kid, I knew what for. I guess it just seemed normal then. Christ, I was just a dumb kid. I thought about it later, as a teenager, and it pissed me off so much. Still does, actually. Those men—and I still see some of them around Kitsum—they abused the hell out of my mom."

Monica did not say anything. She stepped closer to Michael. His childhood had been quite different from hers. He had often told her how lucky she had been, and she did not doubt the truth of that. They had walked a fair ways past the caves before Michael spoke again.

"You know what still gets me? They were there too...my uncles, Fred and Murray. Plenty of times, they were there and they just let those guys take advantage of my mom. Their own sister!"

"It was the booze, Michael," Monica said softly. "You know it was the booze."

"Yeah, I do know that. They would do anything for a bottle or another drink once they'd started. The nuns at school—at Christie—they made it sound like they were just depraved somehow. Savages, without morals. Heathens. That Sister Margaret, she was the worst. I was maybe seven years old and she'd tell me that my uncles were drunks…that my mother was a whore…that they were all going to hell.

"Back then, I believed her. Part of me, for sure, believed. I'd get back home at Christmas or in the summertime, and I'd hate my uncles for a while. I'd try to stay away from them, but I didn't have anywhere else to go. Uncle Fred and Uncle Murray, they'd see how I was, but they'd just keep taking care of me anyways. Feeding me, showing me stuff on the boat, taking me fishing until gradually…I'd forget about what those damned nuns had said."

Sandy Beach was visible in the distance. At its far end was Lone Point. Monica squeezed Michael's hand. Though this was all bad stuff that he talked about—horrible stuff—learning about his past made her feel closer to him. He was speaking these things aloud and acknowledging them, and also in that acknowledgement putting them further away where their rawness could scratch less at the heart. They sat together on a partially dry log that had been pushed above the high tide line. The sun was hot now, so hot that Monica had to remove the sweater she had been wearing. A pair of bald eagles glared down at them from a single treetop branch. The forest was predominantly spruce here, dark and seemingly impenetrable. However, they both knew of a multitude of ways inside the woods; there were bear and other animal trails, natural openings created by fallen trees or bushes bent by the wind. Once you were past the initial thicket of growth spurred on by direct sunlight, the forest opened into far more accessible spaces beneath the upper canopy of branches.

"Allison talked it all out of me. Made me face some of that anger that built up as a kid. That anger I didn't or wouldn't admit that I carried around, and for sure had no idea how to control. I was lucky. Just lucky to end up with her and Mitch. They understood.

Not in the way counsellors and those types 'understand,' but she knew what I was going through. She didn't say too much but I guess her own growing up was pretty tough. She's a real caring person. She was the first one who ever told me straight out that everything wasn't my fault. It may not have been the fault of my mother or my uncles, but it certainly was not mine. That was the start, you know. The start of me learning how to let go of blaming them all the time. To look at them instead and see all the good, how hard they tried, how much—despite impossible situations—they had tried to do for me."

Michael had promised to bring her to meet Allison and Mitch when they next went to Campbell River. She already knew the bare bones of how he had ended up in their home. Michael had told her that when he finished Grade 7 at the residential school, his uncles had wanted him to stay in Kitsum even though his mother had moved to Vancouver. The high school in Port Hope was opening and some Kitsum kids were attending. It was in response to Monica telling him about her staying home for Grade 12 that Michael had told her about that. They had joked about it then, about how Monica could have started "dating" him when he was in Grade 8. Before he got the chance to stay home and go to school in Hope, however, Social Services had stepped in. They deemed Fred and Ethel unsuitable as guardians and placed him in a foster home in Campbell River. After two of those foster homes—and getting into a whole lot of trouble—Michael had been placed with Mitch and Allison.

The section of shoreline covered with boulders took the longest to cross. For close to a kilometre, they passed a field of wet rocks made slippery by strewn kelp, seagrasses, and the slime left by tide after tide. They knew enough to take the long route, largely above the high tide line, where the biggest rocks appeared only sporadically and where it was possible to sometimes weave their way through the boulder field across gravel and pebbles. The last long section of beach was a leisurely stroll. They stopped to examine particularly strange looking pieces of driftwood, battered plastic bottles imprinted with Chinese or Japanese characters, floats that had broken from fishing nets, and a hodgepodge of remnants tossed by the sea onto the shore. They remembered other occasions when they had walked the beach, and they agreed that for both of them, it had been a long time — too long.

They reached Lone Point by early afternoon. The walk had taken them nearly four hours. Michael made a fire. They unpacked and began to eat their sandwiches, watching the driftwood burn and staring out at the open Pacific. Waves, even on such a calm day, pounded the gravel beach. Each wave carried a hundred, a thousand, tiny little pebbles back and forth, back and forth. Monica and Michael made plans to come back some other weekend. They would come in the summer, and bring blankets, and sleep under the stars. The possibilities were as vast as the ocean in front of them.

EIGHTEEN

It was not until her father got back from herring fishing—not all the way back to Kitsum, but back to Port Hardy at the top end of the Island—that Brenda's mood finally altered a little. She only had two months left in her pregnancy, and the days had brightened. Her brothers and sisters no longer returned from school in semi-darkness; they actually had time to play outside before being called in for supper. Monica had not been over to the house, not even once. Brenda told herself that she would be satisfied if she never saw her aunt again.

It was early afternoon when the phone rang. Ruby—anxious and cranky since Martin had been away for well over two weeks—answered on the second ring. From across the living room Brenda could tell that it was her dad. Her mother's voice went from dull to thrilled immediately. After she had hung up, her mother beamed with replenished energy.

"He's in Port Hardy," she told Brenda. She sounded as excited as one of the kids. When her mother was happy like that, Brenda thought she even looked like one of them. The beginnings of wrinkles, the ever so slight stoop, the weighted shoulders—they all seemed to vanish.

Her mother's happiness was contagious. Just as the arrival of herrings and *kwukmis* was an anticipated annual celebration, so was their father's annual return from herring fishing. The whole family already knew that they had done well on the *Pacific Queen*. Her father had phoned home every time he had gone in somewhere for fuel or food. There would be new clothes for all of them and lots of groceries. Ruby still felt ashamed for having ruined the couch and television, and she had never mentioned new furniture, but Brenda guessed that was on the list as well. Thomas, Becky, and Millie took it to be a second Christmas.

"You going to see him?" Brenda asked. She had already assumed that her mother would go to Port Hardy to meet her father. She did that almost every year.

"The kids are all in school," her mom started. "If I take them out now, they'll miss the whole week. I don't know."

All of them had taken a week off school the previous year. That had been lots of fun too, staying in the hotel and eating out and buying stuff. Mostly it was fun to fool around on the *Pacific Queen*, and to listen to their father's stories about fishing that year. What was her mother's issue with this year?

"I'd like to go," her mother ventured.

"You should," Brenda agreed.

Ruby remained quiet. Perhaps she had guessed correctly that Brenda did not want to go to Port Hardy. It was bad enough seeing people from Kitsum. She did not even go into Port Hope for fear of running into anyone, but the prospect of seeing her father's fishermen friends was too much. Was her mother afraid to leave her home alone? Was that preventing her from going to meet Martin?

"I can stay home and take care of the kids. We'll all be fine."

Her mother hesitated, but Brenda became excited by her own idea. "I'll get them up for school, and make sure they don't stay up late. If we run out of anything, Junior can charge it at Jimmy's."

She half-expected a refusal from her mother, or at least an argument. Instead, her mother seemed to catch her enthusiasm. "Are you sure?" she asked.

All her life, Brenda had seen her parents as her parents. It had only dawned on her in the past few months that they were also a couple. She had begun to recognize that her mother yelling at Tom for spilling the juice or Millie for soaking her last pair of dry shoes was perhaps not about Tom or Millie. Brenda felt foolish for taking so long to see that her mother's irritability had more to do with missing her husband, especially when he had been gone for such a long time. This year, she was pretty sure, had been worse than others. With all the worry Brenda had brought into the household, plus the crap about her father and Charmayne, her mother was having a tough time. "Mom," Brenda said firmly. "You should go. Me and the kids—we'll be okay."

Her mother did not need any more convincing after that. Packing for the trip would take only a matter of minutes. Brenda told her mother that she could leave right away, but she insisted on telling the children her plans first. She would leave before Martin called back though.

"He said he'd phone again this evening. You can tell him I'm already on my way up."

Brenda smiled at that one. Together they sat waiting for Junior, Thomas, Becky, and Millie to get home from school. Brenda was impressed; despite her mother's childlike excitement filling the air, she still had the patience to wait.

Junior did not argue. In fact, he barely commented. Brenda knew that he was old enough to make his own arrangements if he wanted to go to Port Hardy badly enough. It was the younger kids who seemed unexpectedly understanding. Her mother's promise to take them all to Campbell River when she and their father got back seemed to satisfy them. Just like that, their mother was heading out to the truck to drive up to Port Hardy.

Brenda could not say that anything bad or even unpleasant happened over the next few days. However, the sunny days full of their bright promise were replaced by rain-full gusts and dark greyness that rolled in from the southeast. Once again, spring had been subdued by the still formidable power of winter. For the most part, the kids stayed on their best behaviour. Junior kept to his routine, leaving for the hall after supper and arriving back at the house just after ten. Thomas, without being asked, helped Junior with splitting, packing, and piling firewood. Thanks to the two of them, there was always a full pile beside their stove and plenty of small dry pieces to stoke the fire back up each morning. Becky and Millie willingly helped with the dishes after supper and even made extra efforts to keep their bedroom and the living room tidy.

The storm that was hanging onto Kitsum meant that their father could not bring the *Queen* down on Wednesday as he had planned. "It's no problem," Brenda told her mother over the phone. "We're all fine here. See you on the weekend."

She had spent more time than she could remember with her mother during the past few months. Brenda had believed that the break would do her and her mother some good. Now that she was alone, she began to realize just how tiresome her mother's routine could become. Dishes had to be done after every meal; laundry needed to be separated into darks and lights, along with heavy clothes and light clothes; floors had to be swept and mopped; garbage had to be taken out; bread had to be punched first thing in the morning. She had never really noticed just how gruelling her mother's housekeeping schedule could be. By herself, Brenda did everything just as her mother would have wanted it done. The house itself knew the rules.

By the third day, Brenda felt like she was sleepwalking. She was exhausted. How did her mother come up with fresh energy every day? Where did that supply of patience and enthusiasm come from? To braid Millie's hair just because she wanted it in that style. To bake cookies in the evenings instead of just letting the kids run off to the store. To truly care that meals were properly prepared, and that laundry was neatly folded. Only the year before, the thought of keeping house like her mother had not even registered with her as a real possibility. She had been looking forward to going to university. She may not have talked about it openly, but she had prepared the whole scenario in her mind. Her grades were high; she would get scholarships. Then she would move to Vancouver and stay with her Aunt Monica. What a cruel joke that was! Now here she was, doing the same daily house chores over and over again, worrying about dirty dishes and soiled clothing and mopping floors. A baby was going to make it permanent. The future she had once envisioned had disappeared.

The kids were all at school when her grandmother came to visit. She brought a casserole that they could heat up for supper. Brenda was grateful for that. She was also sure that her gran was there to check up on her. Her mother had probably asked her to do so. If the old woman saw her granddaughter's nervousness, she kept that to herself.

Brenda felt self-conscious for actively avoiding her. Even so, her grandmother sat calmly at the table, drinking her tea and nibbling at one of the biscuits Brenda had put out. She seemed to have all the time in the world. Brenda jumped up to check the wood stove and then to finish the lunch dishes. Her pretended busyness did not drive her grandmother away though. The old lady merely waited until she had run out of excuses to leave the table.

"I've missed you," her grandmother told her, once she had sat still long enough to hear.

She had never said a single thing about the pregnancy. Her silence had only confirmed in Brenda's mind that the old lady was disappointed in her, even ashamed or embarrassed by her situation. "I understand how it is," her gran told her now. "I really do. I wasn't always old, you know. I was young like you once."

Brenda tried to steel herself against the lecture that she had long expected to be coming. There was nothing she could do to avoid it now.

"I don't know if your father has ever told you...I had a baby too, when I was sixteen."

Her father had most definitely not told her any such thing. She stared at her grandmother in utter shock. She had expected advice or carefully veiled criticism, but not a revelation like this. Her grandmother was sixty-seven years old. Not too long ago, there had been all kinds of joking about her receiving her old age pension.

"I told your father when he was a teenager. I'm sure he remembers."

Brenda was confused. She waited for her grandmother to explain.

"It was long ago, before I married Peter. The baby…he was a little boy…he died. He was born alive, but barely. He only lived for one day. He had trouble breathing right from the start. We were at home, my mother and I, here in Kitsum. There were not many people here then. People lived all over at that time, some at Lone Point, some at Sandy Beach, some even where Port Hope is now. In fact, there was no road, and Port Hope didn't even exist yet. Not by the same name, anyways. *Yakshilth*, we called that place. The name describes how the beach runs along beside the river there.

"Back then, there was no hospital, doctor, or nurses. My mother and I were home alone when I went into labour. She heated the house as hot as she could make it. We had a drum stove that my father had made. I wondered why she was making the house so hot. I was sweating something awful, but she told me that it was better for the baby to be nice and warm once he was born. He came out all right because my mother helped me. She knew all about helping women have babies. She knew how to clean him and wrap him when he was born. I watched her make sure all the mucus was out of his nose and mouth. Even so, he was stuffy sounding right away. She kept checking and rechecking him. We named him Tooch-aa after my father's brother who had passed away a few years before that.

"I think my mother knew right away that he wasn't going to make it. She had that worried look on her face like she had whenever she knew something bad was going to happen. I was only sixteen, I didn't know anything. I thought she was just worried about me because I felt so weak. She told me to just stay on the bed and rest. I must have drifted in and out of sleep all that day, and then I remember waking up, and my mother was crying and praying."

Her grandmother paused to take a sip of tea. "But that is not why I am telling you, not to scare you. There are hospitals and doctors now. Your baby will be fine.

"I'm telling you because I understand how you feel. Me, I went to the Indian Residential School. When I was home that summer, I would have done anything not to go back. I begged and begged my mother not to send me back, but she was stubborn. She wanted me to finish school. So I thought, no, I'll just get married and then she won't be able to send me. Only..." Her grandmother laughed dryly.

"I had no one to marry me. They were strict back then. Parents and families arranged marriages. You couldn't just go around with anyone you wanted. But I started sneaking out with...I won't tell you his name now. When you're older, I can tell you if you still want to know. When summer was over and my mother was getting ready to send me back, I told her 'No, I'm getting married.' Oh, what my mother had to put up with from me!"

Brenda sat absolutely still. She would not have washed another dish now for anything.

"Anyway, my mother didn't really believe me. She thought it was just a trick so I wouldn't have to go back to school. I had to tell her who it was, this man I was going to marry. Only this man, he had not said anything about getting married. We'd fooled around all right, but he'd never mentioned marrying me."

The glint in her grandmother's eyes was suddenly a mischievous one. Brenda could not contain herself. "Grandma!"

"What?" Her father's mother laughed. "You think you invented it? I haven't always been an old woman."

Brenda was now eager to hear the rest of the story. "What happened? What did you do?"

"I had to tell this man what I'd told my mother. I didn't even like him that much, but I told him that we should get married. He said that was fine with him. Only I guess he didn't really mean it, because a few weeks later, he left Kitsum. You might say it was lucky for me the freight boat that brought the kids to the residential school had already come and gone. Then in the spring, we heard he was living down south with another woman. I don't think he ever knew that I was pregnant.

"I guess Martin never told anyone. Maybe your mother, I don't know. The old people around here, they'd remember. Peter, he wanted to marry me anyways. He said it was over and done with, and he was glad that I never married that man.

"Brenda." Her grandmother looked straight at her. Her gaze did not waver. "For a long time I felt guilty. Guilty and afraid my feelings had affected my baby. I don't know. My mother said I was just too young. But I was angry. Very angry all the time. I was always sorry for myself and not thinking about the baby at all. I am not saying that you are as foolish as me. I just want you to be careful, you know."

Her grandmother finished her tea. She seemed to know that Brenda needed time to think about what she had told her before she could really make sense of it all. She rose to leave. "You come see me whenever you want," her grandmother said. Then she walked out the door.

Brenda was left alone at the kitchen table. She was still stunned. First her father goes out to a drinking party and fools around on her mother, and now she finds out that her grandmother had a baby before she married Grandpa Peter. Had she ever really known her family at all?

The unasked-for advice! Did her grandmother think she was being negligent, or not caring for herself properly? No, that was not it. She knew that her grandmother still cared about her. She cared about her so much that she had shared a story that might have been embarrassing and even shameful for her. Tears ran down Brenda's cheeks.

She was still sitting at the table when Tom, Becky, and Millie got home. "Told you I'd beat you," Tom yelled to his sisters as he attempted to push the kitchen door shut before they could enter.

"Hey…hey!" Brenda jumped up to prevent the door from being wrecked. There was no longer any time to think.

Ruby kept her word. The weekend after she and Martin arrived back in Kitsum on the *Queen*, the whole family was off to

Campbell River in the truck. The doctor who saw Brenda at the Kitsum Health Clinic, a Port Hope doctor who drove out to Kitsum once a week, had referred her to a doctor in Campbell River. She was instructed to make an appointment with this new doctor and arrange for him to deliver her baby. It worked out that the kids could have their weekend in Campbell River and Brenda could see this Dr. West on the Friday afternoon when they got into town. If she did not factor in her doctor's appointment and the constant burden her own body had become, she could say that the family trip to Campbell River was just like old times.

The appointment went well. Instead of a dozen or more people ahead of her like at the Kitsum Clinic, there was only one conspicuously pregnant woman waiting at the new doctor's office. The chairs were stylish and comfortable. They were actually spread far enough apart so that no one needed to crowd the person sitting next to them. When she entered the examination room, Dr. West looked up at her and smiled. He appeared relaxed and calm rather than rushed and anxious the way Dr. MacLean invariably did when he was in Kitsum.

Dr. West checked everything. He explained each test and each new prodding, telling her what they revealed. He said that her blood pressure and weight were slightly high, but well within healthy levels. Also, the baby's heart rate was strong. The length of the baby—determined by a cloth tape measure like the one her mother used when working on sewing projects—was exactly what it should be at this point in her pregnancy.

"I want to see you by the end of May, and no later, for another appointment here in Campbell River," he told her pleasantly and firmly. "After that, you'll need to stay in town for the delivery. We have June 15th as your due date, but really it could be any time around the beginning of June or later."

Brenda nodded obediently. She had expected such instructions because they were given to all new mothers from Kitsum: move to Campbell River or another city at least two weeks prior to your due date. Medical Services would put you

up in a motel and give you a meal allowance, and then you would
wait. Her own mother had done the same thing. It was strange
how Dr. West's statement of the facts made the experience seem
more real. She tended to ignore most of what she heard from
Dr. MacLean. She mainly saw him just to keep her mother from
nagging and worrying. Dr. West seemed different, like someone
she could trust. The end of May was only a month plus a week
or two away.

Dr. West asked her to think about who she wanted with her
at the delivery, and if she wanted natural childbirth, and if she
was going to be breastfeeding. He made her feel like she had
choices. He did not pressure her for immediate answers either. He
simply told her to think about his questions and make decisions
before the next appointment. Perhaps, she thought, she had not
completely lost control over her own life after all. She left the
appointment feeling uplifted.

Brenda's good mood lasted throughout the following day
while shopping with her mother and her sisters. In fact, she was
happy all the way back to Kitsum. She awoke at home in her own
bed, and felt better than she remembered feeling in a very long
time. Her mother could barely hide her surprise when Brenda
announced that she was off to visit her grandmother.

Brenda thought about the choices presented to her by the doctor.
Ruby, of course, would be with her when she had the baby. Beyond
that, she could not really imagine. Every time she made up her
mind to ask her mother about natural childbirth, she wondered
what the alternative would be. Un-natural childbirth? And what
about breastfeeding? She felt hugely pregnant now; her belly
protruded like some overblown basketball. Her baby kicked and
squirmed inside her. When she stood in front of the full-length
mirror on her bedroom door and lifted her shirt up, she could
actually see its movements. Still, she put off any further discussion.
She was too embarrassed to bring up the topic of actually having
the baby, even with her mother.

She often wished that Marcie was still living in Kitsum. Brenda knew that her friend had stayed in Campbell River too; Marcie had quite a few funny stories about living in the motel, taking taxis, and waiting in the doctor's office. She had ended up having a C-section because her labour was not progressing properly. She had even shown Brenda the scar that ran along her belly, and then she had made a joke about that too. In retrospect, Brenda realized that she had simply not known enough to ask Marcie for more details.

It was obvious that her mother was getting more and more excited at the prospect of becoming a grandmother. After making an entire set of blankets, she had begun to crochet baby booties and sweaters. Brenda had watched her pick out more wool in Campbell River and ponder over various colours. "White or yellow," she had wondered aloud, and Brenda had only shrugged. She had no preferences. Her mother's anticipation was contagious too. Even her father had started making jokes about being a grandfather and taking his grandchild fishing. Brenda smiled each time he told one, but in truth, she did not find any of them particularly funny. A couple of times, Brenda overheard him calling her mother "Grandma."

Just as their earlier dismay had depressed her, their blooming enthusiasm now made her feel vaguely ill at ease. Things were just simpler for them. For Brenda, nothing was completely clear. One day she felt like she was still a happy child; the next she felt near ready to be a mother; and another day she felt like a teenager with a bad attitude. It was like being out on the *Queen* in a stormy sea with the wind and waves pushing at her from all directions. She could still steer all right, but it took a whole lot of effort.

NINETEEN

By the middle of May, Brenda had her arrangements in place. The process was not very difficult at all. She had gone in to see the Community Health Representative at the Kitsum Clinic. She relayed to her the doctor's information and passed on the form that Dr. West had completed. The CHR — everyone referred to her by the abbreviation — took care of everything after that. Brenda had not even needed to ask her mother about accompanying her to Campbell River.

She found that slightly disappointing. She had imagined sitting nervously alone with her mother one day in the kitchen at home. Brenda would quietly but earnestly acknowledge that she knew her mother did not like to be away from the kids for long, but this was a special circumstance. She needed her very much at this time. It was going to be an official reconciliation of sorts, a kind of fresh start to their relationship as mother and daughter. Before she could even bring the matter up though, a whole scenario had already been put into place. Her mother would drive her out to Campbell River and stay with her until the end of the following week, when her father would bring everyone else on the *Queen*. It was as though the CHR and her parents — and who knew who else — had created the perfect plan without even consulting Brenda about her wishes. So much for having choices! Immediately, she felt guilty at the thought. How could she even dream of complaining in the face of everyone's thoughtfulness?

During the long drive out, Brenda finally broached the subject of natural childbirth with her mother. There really was no one else she could possibly ask, and she would have to tell Dr. West something that very day. Her mother explained that natural childbirth just meant that a woman did not take any medication during her labour. Some women were given pain medication in the hospital, and others chose not to take any drugs because they were worried that they might distress their baby. Brenda wanted to ask her mother what she had done, but she waited instead. If her mother wanted her to know, she would tell her. Brenda did not even bother with the breastfeeding question. She could remember her youngest brother and sisters being breastfed. She also remembered them crying after her mother no matter how Brenda or Monica or her father tried to soothe them. She had already made up her mind back in Kitsum that breastfeeding was not going to work for her. For most of the trip, the two women travelled in silence.

Brenda had been looking forward to the stay in Campbell River. She had been inside the house in Kitsum for too long, and she was also just plain tired of being pregnant. At least in town, she figured that the waiting would be easier. She could go out whenever she wanted and not worry too much about what people thought of her. They were only strangers. In town, there was always the promise—or at least the possibility—of something close to adventure or excitement.

Staying at the motel with her mother was not what Brenda had expected. Without needing to cook for everyone and clean up after the kids, her mother was more relaxed than Brenda had seen her in months. The transition was so obvious, Brenda could not help but notice it right away. In a carefree manner, Ruby suggested movies and restaurants. She even suggested having a picnic lunch out at Seymour Narrows at the spot where they sometimes stopped for a short break on the long drive home to Kitsum. During these excursions, her mother reminded her very much of Monica. Back at home, Brenda did not notice the similarity of the two sisters too often. That was because, she now recognized, her mother was always so busy being her mother. She acted "old." Noticing the resemblance did not annoy or trouble Brenda. Instead, it was a source of comfort. It was like having Monica — the Monica of the days before all of this happened — there with them.

Except during evening telephone calls home, Brenda had her mother's full attention. It was not the smothering attention of home either, where it felt like her mother was treating her like a child, overloading her with maternal ministrations and advice while dealing with Junior or packing snacks for Becky and Millie's field trips. It was a different kind of attention; more as though mother and daughter were simply two women taking care of one another. The comments her mother made, those that Brenda would ignore in Kitsum, seemed to make sense to her in Campbell River.

By the morning of her third doctor's appointment, her mother noticed that Brenda had "dropped." She explained that the baby had moved down, and that the added weight would probably make her feel like she needed to pee every few minutes. Then in Dr. West's office an hour later, what did the doctor say to her? That the baby had moved down into position to be born, and that she might feel increased pressure on her bladder as a result. Brenda could not believe that she had so casually disregarded the knowledge offered by her mother, a woman who had five children. She had loved and raised all of them without fanfare or even much in the way of acknowledgement.

Brenda had advised her mother that she should wait in the truck instead of accompanying her into the doctor's office. Returning there after her appointment, Brenda reached over and laid her hand on her mother's shoulder. It was the first time in a long while that she had initiated such a gesture of good feeling.

"I'm sorry," she sniffled. "I've been so horrible to you. To everyone."

Ruby clasped her daughter's hand. "It's okay, Brenda. We're your family and we love you. All of us, we know it's been a hard time for you."

"Oh, Mom…" That was all Brenda could manage before she burst into tears.

The day after that doctor's appointment, Brenda ran into Marcie. Her mother had suggested shopping at the supermarket in the harbourfront plaza for lunch materials and Brenda had readily agreed. Sitting in restaurants got tiresome pretty quickly. Having strangers watch her while she was eating turned out to be more disagreeable than knowing the people who looked at her. She and her mother were carefully choosing fruit when Brenda spotted her best friend.

Without thinking about any attention that she might attract, Brenda called out as she would have in Kitsum. Marcie spun around instantly. She was already chuckling by the time she stood in front of Brenda and her mother. After the hugs and a few jokes about Brenda's by-now huge belly, Marcie was all questions. When did they get into town? When was Brenda due? Who was her doctor? Where were they staying? It scarcely mattered that they were in the middle of a crowded grocery store. Seeing one another again and sharing their news, that was more important than what any of those onlookers might have thought. Brenda glanced at her mother and, seeing her smile, she began to answer Marcie's questions.

After she had finished with her explanations, Brenda began to ask questions of her own. Where was Marsh living? Did she have a phone? Brenda had no number for her, and had been unable to contact her earlier. And where was Gabes?

Marcie hesitated. She suddenly looked nervous, gazing down at her feet instead of at her friend. Brenda was impressed with her mother. She noticed Marcie's reaction and excused herself to carry on with her shopping. Quickly, she began pushing her cart toward the opposite end of the store. Just like that, the two girls had their privacy.

"Social Services took him," Marcie said softly.

"What?" Brenda sputtered. She was too shocked to remember to speak quietly.

Marcie sighed. When she spoke again, Brenda had the feeling that it was only to avoid another outburst, or another barrage of queries. "You know how my mom and dad are. Well...they've been partying a lot since they moved here. But one day, they weren't drinking at all, but it was pretty edgy in the apartment, with everyone cranky and all. So I went out to the mall, just to look around. I just wanted to be gone for a little while, that's all. Mom told me to leave Gabes. She promised she'd look after him. She wasn't drinking, so I left him. Anyways, while I was gone, this social worker showed up and I guess my mom had started sipping. I don't even know where she got her stuff because I swear there was nothing in our place. Dad was gone somewhere. I don't know what the hell happened. It sounds like Mom and the social worker got into some kind of argument. All I know is I got home and Mom was pretty drunk by then, and Gabes was gone."

"So what did you do?" Brenda could not believe what she was hearing.

"Mom was blubbering about the welfare, so I kind of figured it out, but by then it was after five. Plus, we don't have a phone. I went to their office the next morning. They made me wait all day there. Kept sending me to see different people, but mostly just made me wait. I didn't know what else to do. I just wanted to find out where he was."

Marcie stopped herself for a moment. She looked at Brenda as though uncertain whether or not she should continue. Brenda tried to look encouraging. Marcie seemed to square her shoulders a little, and when she spoke again, her voice had a hard edge to it.

"I'm getting him back though," Marcie said. "They...Social Services...want me to get my own place. When I get that all set up, I can get Gabes back. I will too. I've already been looking around. Me and Dale. He's a guy I've been seeing. He's helping me."

Brenda did not know what to say. Too many questions that she sensed did not have the answers she wanted to hear flashed through her mind. She looked toward her mother for support, forgetting that she had already disappeared down one of the shopping aisles.

"I've got to go," Marcie said woodenly. "I'm supposed to meet Dale, but I'll come see you soon."

Brenda repeated the name of the motel and the room number. Then she watched her childhood friend rush away. She could tell that Marcie was embarrassed and ashamed, just as she used to be when she was a little kid and her parents would miss the school's open house or bake sale. Just like back then, there was nothing that Brenda could do to make the situation any better. Brenda hurried out of the store, hoping to catch Marcie on the sidewalk or in the parking lot. At least she could hug her friend. Her body, however, refused to move quickly enough. By the time she had managed to exit, it was her mother and only her mother waiting for her beside rows of discarded shopping carts. Marcie was nowhere in sight.

Once inside the truck, she told her mother everything, or as much as she had gotten out of Marcie, anyway. "That's too bad," her mother replied. Brenda wanted her to burst out in anger or sorrow, or at the very least to offer some sort of advice, but her mother did not add anything to her bland response. Ruby had always liked Marcie, but she was certainly not sticking up for the girl now. How could her mother be so caring and loving yet also act so coldly?

Brenda could not understand how Marcie could be so matter-of-fact about it either, or how she could talk about losing Gabriel with that distant voice. In a weird way, that was what bothered her the most. This was the friend she had shared tears and laughter and outrage and every possible emotion with since they were both small children. How could Marsh talk to her like she was a stranger? Marcie was not the sort of person who could describe what had happened to her own son with so little feeling. That was not who Marcie was, and Brenda knew that.

"Mom," Brenda said as they were taking the bags into the motel room. "Where would they have taken Gabes?"

"I don't know, Bren. A foster home, I guess."

"Does Marcie even get to see him?"

Brenda had heard of plenty of kids in foster care. You could not grow up in Kitsum without hearing about people's kids being apprehended, or horror stories from those kids who had been in foster care. Michael, she could not help but think, had spent time growing up in foster care. But face it, his mom had been a drunk. It was not like she could look after him. What was Social Services supposed to do with him?

"Marcie spent all her time watching Gabes, you know," she said to her mother. "She loves him. She never neglected him or took off on him or anything. So how could they take him away?"

"We don't know the circumstances, Brenda," her mother answered quietly.

Brenda resented her reasonableness. She glared at her mother. Didn't she care?

Seeing that her daughter was not about to let the matter drop, her mother relented. "It's her parents, I'm guessing. More than Marcie. Marcie's young. The welfare, they look out for that. I know she's a good mother, but where is her support? Half the time in Kitsum, her mother and father were gone, leaving her alone with her son. And she did a good job, sure, as good as she could. But, think about it, Bren. Auntie Kate said that she had to get some of the guys over to her place to cut wood for their stove. Her parents left her at home in the middle of winter without even enough wood for Marcie to keep the stove going to warm the house. Kate had to give Marcie a food voucher for Jimmy's just so that she could get diapers and some food in the place. I'm guessing that the welfare workers here in Campbell River are not as understanding as Kate. They don't know Marcie from a hole in the ground. All they see is a young mother with alcoholic parents and they automatically think she's irresponsible or negligent."

"I'm scared for her, Mom."

Her mother nodded. "Yeah. Me too."

"You know, Marcie was miserable in Kitsum sometimes. All alone at home, not being able to go to school anymore or do much of anything outside her house. But you know, she was happy too.

I don't know if she can take care of herself here in town. I mean, does she even know how to rent a place by herself? Where is she going to get the money? And who is this Dale anyways?"

"I don't know, hon." Her mom shrugged and turned the television set on.

Brenda ignored the loud blare of an ad for dish detergent. "I knew she was getting pretty frustrated watching Gabes all the time by herself. I guess I'm worried that maybe now she's got her freedom back, she won't try all that hard to get her son back. But she loves him. I know she loves him. And Marcie sounded so weird. Not like herself at all. She sounded so different. God, I hope she comes over. Maybe, you can talk to her, Mom? Would you?"

"Okay, Brenda." Her mother sighed. "Sure."

What she did not say was that Marcie was not coming over. Not today and not the next day. They both knew that.

TWENTY

By the time the rest of Brenda's family arrived on the *Pacific Queen,* it seemed like she and her mother had already been staying in town for much longer than the ten days that had actually passed. Brenda knew that the journey around the northern end of the Island took one day and one night, and she imagined the trip as though she had travelled with them. Becky and Millie would have slept for a lot of the way. Junior, for sure, would have alternated shifts steering with Martin. Thomas would have taken shorter shifts when the others were making coffee or cooking something to eat. Brenda had been on the *Queen* since she was a baby—and perhaps since before she was even born. She knew the routine on board as well as she knew the routine of their house in Kitsum. She could easily picture her family running up the West Coast, around the Brooks Peninsula, past Winter Harbour, and then around Cape Scott. They would have cruised by Port Hardy and then down the inside passage between the eastern side of Vancouver Island and the Mainland.

When they were not sleeping, Becky and Millie, and probably Thomas too, would have sat on the hatch cover, watching the expanse of ocean and the distant shoreline and the silhouettes of mountains. In the cabin, Dad or Junior would have been in the skipper's seat, one of them steering while the other sat in the deckhand's seat, watching out the front windows. The days had been almost summery; the cabin windows would have been open to the cooling ocean breeze. The water would have been a deep blue-green, glimmering in the sunlight. Maybe, in this late stage of pregnancy, she was becoming overly emotional. The thought of being out on the *Queen*—instead of cooped up in a motel room that appeared increasingly dingy and less exciting with each passing day—nearly made her cry.

Her father had used the excuse of needing to paint the bottom of the *Pacific Queen*. That was why, he had explained weeks ago, he was bringing the boat to Campbell River. He needed to get the boat out of the water and hoisted up on the marine ways there. Then he and Junior could scrape the barnacles and grass that grew on the wooden bottom and repaint it with fresh copper paint. While he was at it, he could put the new propeller on. "Have to get the *Queen* ready for fishing," her father had said. It was exactly what he said every year. Brenda smiled at the familiar voice inside her head.

Brenda knew, just as her mother knew, that her father did not have to bring the *Queen* all the way to Campbell River just to paint. He had planned to travel all those extra hours just to be with her and her mother, and so that everyone in their family could be there. When he arrived at the motel room, with Junior, Tom, Becky, and Millie bunched behind him, Brenda hugged him hard. It was the first time she had hugged her father in a very long time.

The quiet motel room was filled with the hustle and bustle of the entire family. Suddenly there was a surplus of not only noise, but also movement. There was constant talking and laughter. In the small room, or for that matter in the cabin of the *Queen*, Brenda found herself as excited as her younger sisters. During the short time she and her mother had been away from Kitsum, she had missed everyone terribly. How could she have ever wished them away?

It happened on the second day. They had all been down to the marine ways to see the *Pacific Queen* being hauled out of the water. She and her mother had watched as even Millie took her turn at scrubbing a year's worth of growth off the bottom of the boat. They had eaten buns from a nearby bakery that were stuffed full of cheese, sandwich meat, lettuce, and tomatoes. They had washed them down with cartons of apple and orange juice. Brenda had felt cramping since early that morning. She shifted and changed position as she had grown used to doing. Her hips were sore. Her back hurt. She tried to ignore the pains that had become a part of her daily life.

It was not until they were all sitting at the Chinese restaurant where her father had brought them for supper, that Brenda started to wonder if her "cramps" were in reality the "contractions" that her doctor and all the books talked about. She had no way of really knowing. Formerly, she had held a low opinion of all those young women who had claimed they were in labour, only to be sent back home by the doctors and nurses to wait additional weeks and months before they could actually have their babies. Now she knew the question that they all had wrestled with. How are you supposed to know the real thing when it happens? There were so many pains and cramps—which was the particular pain to watch out for? She made up her mind that she would ask her mother if the pains continued into the evening.

The kids dove into their meals. Her mother and father exchanged more news from the past week. They talked on the phone every evening. Brenda wondered how there could possibly be anything left to discuss. She fidgeted where she sat. As soon as she was semi-comfortable on the cushioned chair, her hip would begin to ache or another pain would make her want to stand. She assumed that her mother was not paying attention to her; those eyes and ears that had been hers alone were now diverted by her husband and her other children. However, it was Ruby who paused over her plate to ask if she was all right.

"I'm okay," Brenda said as she felt her belly cramp again. "Lots of cramps today."

That, of course, caused everyone to stare at her. Even Millie quit eating. She immediately wished that she had omitted the last bit about the cramps, but now it was too late.

"Let's go to the washroom," her mother suggested. Brenda rose from the table without delay and followed her mother to the rear of the restaurant, silently thanking her. Even the short walk felt better than sitting. Once they were inside the restroom, her mother began to time the "cramps." Brenda realized that it was for exactly this reason that her mother had insisted on buying herself the wristwatch with the second hand when they had first gone shopping in Campbell River.

"Tell me as soon as another one starts," her mother instructed.

Four minutes apart, her mother determined. Almost exactly four minutes. Were the pains getting stronger?

"Just since we got to the restaurant," Brenda admitted.

Her mother smiled broadly. There was no trace of the panic Brenda had seen on television shows. Her mother was excited, but she remained calm. "I think baby is coming," she told her daughter.

When Brenda and her mother returned to the table, her father and brothers and sisters all stared up at them. They waited for Brenda or Ruby to say something. Martin and Junior looked especially ready to jump. Still with a grin on her face, her mother announced to her father, "I think it might be time to bring Brenda to the hospital."

Millie began to chatter nervously, but her father shushed her with a stern look. "I'll drive," he said, rising from the table.

It only took seconds for her parents to arrange for Junior to pay the restaurant bill and then to take the kids back to the motel room to watch TV for the evening. In the truck, Brenda wondered if her father had eaten even half of his meal before she had disrupted everyone. He had worked on the *Queen* all day; she had seen him stop for only a single bun and a few swallows of coffee. She pictured Junior and the kids walking back to the motel. How far was it? Eight, maybe nine blocks. She distracted herself by watching the traffic. Was this really it? There were no alarms or explosions of celebratory light, no moments of sudden awareness or epiphany; there was just another ride in the truck, this time to the hospital.

The hospital check-in was all business. They had her information; they had to find her a room; she had to change into a hospital gown. The nurses checked her blood pressure, her heart rate, her temperature, and asked her questions about her contractions. When had they started? How many minutes between them? One nurse asked her mother if she was going to be staying. Her father appeared ill at ease. He stood a step behind her mother. No one asked him anything.

If Brenda doubted that her cramps — or contractions, as they were being called — were enough to merit a trip to the hospital, her doubts subsided by the time all the hospital processes had been completed and she was finally admitted to her "own" room. The pain that gripped the entire middle section of her body was definitely real, definitely more than the discomfort she had been feeling earlier in the day when standing around by the *Queen*, or even sitting at the restaurant.

After the nurses had left the room, Ruby hugged her and Martin smiled nervously. "You're going to have a baby," her mother whispered over and over again.

Brenda's memories of that evening were jumbled. A scene here, a scene there, the faces of her mother and father, the words and directions from the nurses, and the footsteps of the doctor when he arrived. Time made no sense. The evening seemed to go on for days, but it was gone in an instant. Her father left the room only once to phone the motel and check in with Junior. Brenda was suddenly afraid that he had abandoned her. She was hugely relieved when he returned. She had never imagined birth to be like this. She had no time to think, no choice but to follow her body.

Brenda's baby girl was born just before midnight on June 7th. After all the pain, she was utterly amazed by its sudden absence. A profound and immense feeling of relief overcame her at the sight and sound of the tiny infant girl who had come out of her own body. She felt such a rush of love for this child that all of her anxieties went away at once. Here was her baby, her own daughter, healthy and beautiful in her own arms. And above them were her beaming parents. All of them were encircled in an almost tangible aura of love.

That glow remained throughout the morning as her mother and father returned to the hospital room with her brothers and sisters in tow. One by one, they held the baby. Each of her siblings inspected and marvelled at the tiny fingers, the chubby cheeks, the thick dark hair, and the hint of a dimple on her chin.

"I'm naming her Jasmine," Brenda pronounced when Millie asked for what had to be the hundredth time. "Jasmine Ruby Joe."

"Well, Jasmine Ruby Joe," Junior said, looking down at the infant he was holding. "Want to come copper painting with Uncle and Grandpa?"

That got everyone laughing, of course. Junior could be pretty hilarious sometimes. Brenda was relieved. No one would have questioned her choice of name, but they might have fallen silent or shown some sign that they disapproved. Instead, they had all laughed and the moment had passed.

Brenda was still feeling so good that she could not even get upset when the nurse—the one she did not like—came into the room to tell them that they were making too much noise. Furthermore, there were too many people in the room outside of visiting hours.

"Got to get the *Queen* back in the water," her father said lightly. "It's high water at noon."

The plan for the day had to have been agreed upon or at least understood by everyone earlier. Once the stern nurse had left the room, everyone except for her mother began heading out. "We'll be back for visiting hours," Junior announced with a raised eyebrow. Millie and Becky giggled even as they pulled the door shut behind them. Brenda and her mother stifled their laughter. It was impossible to ruin the family's good mood.

Brenda reclined on the raised bed. Her mother sat in the green armchair beside her. Just in front of her mother was the clear plastic baby bed on which newly named Jasmine slept. For the rest of the morning, neither Brenda nor her mother said much. They merely stared at the sleeping child, transfixed.

Only the nurses disturbed the stillness. Two of them bustled in—a nice older woman and the younger one Brenda thought of as "evil." They came to check Brenda's temperature and blood pressure, to change her "pads," to direct her to take a shower "if she wished," and to scrutinize Jasmine. Brenda was thankful that, when the time came, it was the kind nurse who took the baby's blood from her tiny red heel. She passed the screaming infant directly to Brenda and apologized profusely. She really did look sorry to have disturbed them all.

It was the evil nurse who insisted that Brenda breastfeed right in front of her to ensure that she was "doing it properly." When Jasmine did not immediately latch onto her breast, the nurse leaned over Brenda and began pushing at her breast, trying to force the nipple into the wailing baby's mouth. Confined by the bed, Brenda could not shrink far enough away from her rough fingers.

"Is that really necessary?"

That earned Ruby an icy glare from the big nurse and a curt comment about needing to teach new mothers so that they got started on the right path. As soon as she took a breath, her mother interrupted.

"I think some privacy would go a long ways," she countered firmly.

Brenda felt like bursting with pride over Jasmine, her mother, and her whole family. The nurse could not leave them alone quickly enough after that. Mother and daughter smiled at one another like co-conspirators. Jasmine was now breastfeeding as though she had already been doing so for months.

"Your grandparents phoned this morning," Ruby told her. "They said to say congratulations and they send their love…and I phoned Monica?" Her mother made the statement into a question. Brenda felt the familiar sting of the name, but she was surprised to find that it was lighter by far than even a few weeks before. "Good," she assented. "Yeah, that's good. She can tell What's-his-name." She meant it as a joke, but neither of them laughed.

TWENTY-ONE

Michael did not mention Brenda or the baby. *Ever*. In fact, after their conversation in Campbell River, neither he nor Monica brought the subject up again. Monica mostly thought of the baby as being Brenda's. Then she had to remind herself that it was also Michael's. She was deliberately ignoring the real situation, having no wish to disturb the warmth of the cocoon she had wrapped around herself.

Then after Ruby and Brenda had gone to Campbell River to await the child's arrival, Monica began to grow more anxious. At first, she waited for Michael to say something, but he maintained his silence. Then Martin left on the *Pacific Queen* with her nephews and nieces. Monica felt like she was going out of her mind with worry on one side and excited anticipation on the other. During these spells, she would bombard Michael with questions about Brenda. When would she have her baby? Maybe today? Boy or girl? Michael listened to her monologues. The biggest response she got from him was a rare shrug of the shoulders.

One night, the phone rang. Monica sat up immediately and stumbled through the dark toward the receiver that she had set to ring as loudly as possible. She had felt Michael shift beside her, his body tense, so she knew that he was awake and alert. "She had a girl," Ruby announced into Monica's ear. "A beautiful, healthy, baby girl."

"Oh my, oh my," was all Monica could respond. She wanted to jump up and down or dance or shout. She grinned so hard, the corners of her mouth hurt.

"They're fine, Mon. Just fine." Ruby knew her so well that she could hear her smiling. "She was born a few minutes before midnight. Eight pounds, four ounces. You should see her head full of hair. And her cry. She's a loud one, that's for sure."

"Oh, Rube! I'm so happy for all of you," Monica gushed. "Tell everyone congratulations. Brenda especially. And congratulations to you, Ruby. Congratulations to *you*."

"A baby girl," Monica said to Michael.

"Healthy?"

"Yeah, everything sounds great. Ruby sounds so happy."

"A girl?"

"Yup, a girl." Monica was still smiling into the darkness. "Congratulations," she whispered. "You're a father and I'm what? Grand-aunt or something. Kitsum way is better. That means I'm a grandma."

There was a split second of silence and then Michael laughed. It started out hoarsely, but the sound rose in his throat to become a full chuckle. Monica could barely see the outline of his face so she could not read anything into his expression. All she could do was listen to his laughter as it echoed off the bedroom walls.

TWENTY-TWO

Brenda enjoyed all the attention in Campbell River. Her father had brought her a vase filled with a dozen pink roses surrounded by wisps of greenery, with a card announcing "It's a girl." Her mother and her younger sisters had seemingly bought every baby dress and bonnet in town. Marcie had even come to the hospital to visit. She had not said too much, but she had held Jasmine for at least ten minutes before a nurse Brenda had never seen before peeked into the room to announce that visiting hours were over.

Just as the hospital room quickly became too small and confining for everyone's excitement, so did the motel room when she and Jasmine were released. The whole city began to make her feel claustrophobic. By the day of Jasmine's final checkup with Dr. West, Brenda could barely contain her desire to get back to the peace and familiarity of home.

As things turned out, the peaceful part of being back in Kitsum took a little longer to come about than she had expected. They had scarcely returned home when her grandparents and Aunt Kate arrived at the house. Not only were they laden with gifts, but they brought with them an entire "welcome home" dinner consisting of trays wrapped in aluminum foil. They had brought so much, in fact, that they had to make multiple trips between the house and her grandfather's truck to get it all into Ruby's kitchen. The phone rang constantly. Though her mother or one of her sisters would answer it, the receiver would invariably be passed to Brenda. Everyone, it seemed, wanted to offer their congratulations, and to ask the same questions.

What was the baby's name? How much did she weigh? How was Brenda?

Her grandmother had knit Jasmine not one but three pink-and-white sweaters, and both a thinner and a thicker blanket. Auntie Kate had an armful of baby clothes. Never one to be impractical, she was the one to give Brenda the much-needed undershirts and bath towels, along with the newest and softest diapers. It was not the gifts alone though; it was the way everyone cooed and marvelled over Jasmine that touched Brenda's heart. Jasmine seemed to feel the safety and love that the family provided; she slept on as she was passed from one set of arms to another.

While everyone was in a celebratory mood, Brenda found the chance to ask her aunt if there might be a way to help her best friend. Kate was a social worker, after all, and Marcie had not been too far from her thoughts, even during the recent week. Brenda could see the effort on Kate's face, and the careful way she moved her lips and jaw to answer. "I'll try," was the best she could do. The provincial workers, in her opinion, were "kinda hard-ass." Brenda knew that if her aunt said that she would try, she would do what she could. Maybe, things could still work out.

Once everyone had left, and the phone had stopped ringing, Jasmine began to cry. Not wanting her mother to take the responsibility—she was already drooping with exhaustion—Brenda took Jasmine to her room. Martin and Tom had assembled the new crib beside her bed. Other than that and a small dresser that had belonged to her grandparents, the room looked just as she had left it. Brenda recalled the many long hours that she had been in this room alone over the preceding months. Now she sat on the edge of her bed trying to convince a screaming infant to eat, to please suckle at her breast, and to please, please, stop crying. Even as she hung onto the wonder of Jasmine's birth and the days that had followed, she could already sense that they were beginning to drift away.

Her father had plenty of work ahead of him to get the *Queen* ready for fishing. Junior rushed back to school to finish the year and write his exams. Tom, Becky, and Millie were eager to catch up with all the end-of-year activities at Kitsum Elementary. Her mother was again busy with cooking meals, washing, cleaning, and taking care of the kids and her father. No one asked anything of Brenda. Now her full-time occupation would be taking care of Jasmine.

Yes, that was true. Jasmine had Brenda's full attention. She woke up and went to sleep seeing, thinking, and breathing her new daughter. As Brenda knew that she would, her mother helped. She walked Jasmine when she was fussy; she changed her diapers; she washed her laundry with the special baby soap. Life in the Joe house continued along, seemingly as it always had. Why that should upset Brenda rather than comfort her, remained a mystery. Her whole life had changed. There had been this monumental arrival of an entirely new human being. Nothing looked the same. How could everyone else go on the way they had before? After all her mom and dad had done for her, she knew that this was not something to talk about with either of them. No matter how she broached the subject, she would appear ungrateful. Also, she feared that she actually might be ungrateful. Marcie would have understood. But where was her friend now?

After they had been home for three days, Monica came to the house. A part of Brenda was truly glad to see her aunt again. A part of her desperately wanted their good relationship back. She sat and watched Monica admire Jasmine. Holding the infant, her aunt was easily as amazed as Becky and Millie and Tom and Junior had been, and then some. Perhaps because of her age, Monica seemed so instantly attached to the baby. Brenda watched as her aunt studied every feature of Jasmine's face: the thick black hair, the long curled eyelashes, the tiny dimple on her chin, the roundness of her short nose.

"Oh Bren," Monica said. "She's beautiful. She is as perfect as Ruby said she is."

Brenda accepted the complimentary words even while a small inner voice told her that precisely what Monica found attractive about Jasmine were the features that made her look so much like Michael. She even expected that Monica would say something about the obvious resemblance. After all, her aunt had always been the blunt one in the family. Even though she was staring at Michael's dark eyes, Michael's dimpled chin, and Michael's broad forehead, her aunt remained silent on the subject.

Instead, Monica motioned to the wrapped gifts she had put down near Brenda's spot on the new couch. Inside the first package she found more baby clothes and blankets for Jasmine. However, the second package surprised her. A pair of jeans — an expensive brand — and a light blue blouse.

"They won't fit," she protested.

"Not today, Bren…but soon."

Monica had an answer for everything. Even so, Brenda had missed that smile so much over the past months, the smile that made everything all right with the world, the smile that made you believe that you could do anything. Brenda had to force herself to not cry. She rose and hugged her aunt, or hugged her as much as she could manage while Jasmine lay sleeping between them.

No sooner had the renewed warmth between niece and aunt surfaced than it abruptly sank again. Monica uttered the words that Brenda would have done a great deal to avoid hearing, the words that she knew were coming despite all her inner pleadings. "Her father would like to see her," Monica said quietly.

Just like that, Monica had suddenly reminded her of the wedge — the canyon — that was between them. Monica was still blunt all right. Blunt and nervy. Even Auntie Kate was not that nervy. From the corner of her eye, Brenda could see Ruby standing still, waiting. She had heard, for sure. If not for her mother as a witness, Brenda might have yelled or sworn or, more likely, given a spiteful answer. She managed to restrain herself. Perhaps she had gained some maturity after all.

"I'm not ready."

When she saw the disappointment on her aunt's face, she had the urge to grind it in, to punish her in the biggest way that she could. She suddenly realized that she had the power here. As quickly as that realization came, alongside it came a gentler knowledge that told her cruelty would be good for no one.

"Not right now," she added, "but sometime…" That was the best she could do.

Her aunt did not stay long after that. They sipped their tea in a silence broken only by her mother's remarks about Jasmine. Monica listened attentively and nodded. Brenda was not the only one who had missed her.

"What am I supposed to do?" Brenda asked her mother as soon as Monica had left.

"Just give yourself time, Bren. You said it fine. You're not ready. You've got the right. This will work out if we all wait for a better time."

Brenda knew that her mother meant the words to reassure her. Which they did, but not as much as she would have liked, particularly when her mother added, "She's got to get to know her father sometime."

How could that not upset Brenda? At first her mother had sounded supportive, and then she had to go and revert to telling her what to do. To make things worse, Ruby provided no clear or specific direction. If she was going to be giving orders, Brenda thought, why didn't she just make them plain so that Brenda could merely follow them instead of having to think things all out? She had mostly said the bit about not being ready because she could not think of anything better to say. It was the most polite thing she could think of at that moment. She was trying to be nice, or as nice as she could be under the circumstances. Why should she have even bothered? After what Monica and Michael had done to her, she did not owe them a damned thing.

When she was taking care of Jasmine day and night, Brenda found it easy to forget that the child even had a father. Jasmine was her baby; that was clear. She belonged to her and her family. Time passed quickly without her having to think of anything more complicated than running low on clean diapers. Before Brenda even noticed, school was out. Her father was mostly fishing. Junior was back out with him as a deckhand on the *Queen*. Thomas, Becky, and Millie were home in the daytime. The girls were especially eager to hold and watch Jasmine, and to tag along beside Brenda whenever she went for long walks. As fussy as Jasmine could be in the house, she always settled down when taken outside.

When Tom and her sisters started attending the summer recreation program organized by the village summer students—Sarah, her old bus partner, was the Youth Recreation Supervisor—Brenda and her mother took Jasmine for walks. Those were Brenda's favourite times. Some days they walked up to the lake or out to Jimmy's Store and along the river there; other days they strolled down to Village Beach and across the expanse of sand and stones towards Kitsum Point. Jasmine slept the entire time, held firmly against Brenda or her mother's chest by the heavy cloth baby carrier. Invariably, the moment they re-entered the house, they would see that the infant was suddenly awake. Awake and starving. Ruby said that she had not done so much walking since she was a teenager; she joked that becoming a grandmother was getting her back into shape.

On mornings when her mother let her sleep in, Brenda knew that was how she quieted Jasmine. Ruby would walk her granddaughter around the outside of the house and down the road to the hill and back. Some days, she walked her all the way to the fishermen's floats. Early in the morning—the sun was just beginning to light up the spruce trees outside her bedroom window—her mother would tiptoe into her room and retrieve the baby as soon as Brenda had finished feeding her. If her father had been home the night before, he would have already left for fishing. If he had not been home—if he had anchored the *Queen* near the fishing grounds and stayed there for the night—her mom would be up anyway. It made sense for Ruby to take Jasmine while Brenda got a little more sleep. It did not take too many mornings before Brenda began waiting expectantly for her mother to come into the bedroom.

"She's hungry again by 7:30 or 8:00," her mother said to her over lunch one day.

"Just bring her back up," Brenda retorted quickly. What was the problem?

"I did that today and you were snoring. You didn't even hear us." Her mother tried to laugh, but Brenda got the message.

"Just wake me up, for heaven's sake," she snapped. Why did her mother tell her to get her sleep, when she didn't really think that she should sleep?

Then there was the morning that Jasmine would not stop crying. Brenda, after a nighttime feeding, had decided to put her daughter into the unused crib. Jasmine awoke screaming. Brenda was still wrapped in her dreams. Maybe Jasmine would stop on her own, she thought blurrily, if she just left her alone. Brenda dozed; Jasmine cried.

There was no tiptoeing that morning. Her mother all but ran into her bedroom. She said not a word to Brenda, but scooped Jasmine from the crib and began to soothe her. Brenda ignored the pair of them and went back to sleep. When she awoke again, the sun was already above the top of her windowsill, which in the summertime meant that it was already after nine o'clock. The house was silent. Suddenly she was afraid. She raced downstairs to the kitchen. There at the table, Ruby was holding Jasmine and feeding her a bottle of formula. The public health nurse and her mother had both talked about "expressing" breast milk for those times when she was away from her baby, but she had barely tried. The whole idea of milking herself like some cow was just too strange, and somehow just plain unnatural.

Brenda felt ashamed. She knew that she should have gotten up, but almost as soon as she had thought that, she had reasoned that her mother was there. It was not as though she had left Jasmine on her own. Hell, if she had been the only one home, she would have been up no matter how exhausted she had been. Everything was all right. Her mother and her baby both looked content. Standing in the kitchen doorway, she had to admit that she felt pretty good herself. It was the most sleep she had gotten in months.

"She likes the bottle?" she asked tentatively.

"Seems to." Her mother did not attempt to pass the baby to her.

From a distance, Brenda could see her mother assuming more and more responsibility for Jasmine. Though right up close, she felt powerless to stop it. The little bit of freedom her mother's responsibility afforded Brenda was too dear, too tempting to give up. Besides, with her father out fishing and the kids at the summer program, her mother had the time. After all, she *was* the expert. She was used to giving constant care. Things would change again in the fall.

One day in mid-July, Brenda stayed home with Jasmine while the rest of her family went to Campbell River. Her father and Junior had delivered a load of fish. They wanted to drive over to Campbell River to pick up more gear and supplies for the *Queen*. Would they all like to go along and do some grocery shopping, her dad had asked her mother. Even before her mother answered, Millie started jumping up and down. How she had heard her father's quiet question from across the room, Brenda could not imagine. That little girl had ears like no one else. Ruby hesitated. There was no longer room in the truck for everyone, not with the car seat taking up an extra space.

"I'll stay home." Brenda tried to sound as though she actually liked the idea. "I'll stay," she repeated. "Me and Jazz."

She could almost hear her mother's gratitude.

Brenda forced herself to fully wake up when Jasmine first cried early that morning. She fed her, changed her diaper and clothes, and only then heard her mother moving around in the kitchen below. It would be good to spend a couple of days alone with her daughter. It would be relaxing to not have her mother's intentional and unintentional vigilance. It would be a relief to not have Becky and Millie asking to hold Jasmine, at least for a little while.

Her mother hugged her hard before she left the house. Everyone else was already in the truck. She was thrilled to be going to town, Brenda realized. She was just like Millie or Becky. Brenda realized that her mother must be tired herself, and that looking after Jasmine must be wearing her out. It was just as well that she had some time away.

The first few hours passed smoothly. Jasmine ate again and fell back asleep. Brenda toyed with the idea of going back to bed, but decided to drink a few cups of coffee instead. She did the dishes that she had told her mother to just leave in the sink. She was about to go upstairs to try on the jeans and blouse that Monica had brought when Jazz awoke, screaming in hunger. She still could not believe how much this baby ate. Not every four hours, or every two hours, or every anything. She wanted to eat *all the time*. Brenda changed Jasmine's diaper as quickly as possible and collapsed with her onto the couch. So much for trying on clothes; she was going to be stuck here for a while. She flicked the television set on and frowned at a game show—there was nothing worth watching at that time of morning—before putting Jazz to her breast. In between sniffles, the baby ate ravenously.

One show ended and another replaced it. Brenda tried to remove Jasmine, but instantly the child resumed her sucking motions. What the hell, Brenda thought, I have all day. She settled into watching a pair of families compete over answers to silly questions. Each time she attempted to put Jasmine down, the baby hung on. She could have sworn that Jasmine knew that the two of them were by themselves in the house.

By lunchtime, Brenda was growing desperate. She left the infant, protected by pillows, alone on the couch for only a few minutes in order to use the bathroom, and the little girl howled the entire time that she was gone. Brenda knew that she could bundle her daughter up or put her in the carrier and take her for a walk. That would certainly calm her down. Except that was

what Brenda always did. This was supposed to be a "special" day
for them together, a day not like every other day. Instead of going
outside, Brenda walked Jasmine through the kitchen and living
room, down the short hallway to Ruby and Martin's bedroom, and
even onto the covered back porch. All the while, she explained to
her daughter "this is where Grandma sleeps, this is where we have
a bath, this is where we wash our clothes." Brenda actually enjoyed
the game for a while, especially as Jazz kept quiet. Was she really
listening to her? Up the stairs she took her, into all of the rooms,
explaining everything.

The whole house tour — even repeated twice — took under
half an hour. As soon as it was complete, Jasmine resumed her
fussiness. Brenda was already tired and the afternoon had only
just begun. It was nearly suppertime when she thought of giving
Jasmine a bottle. They had counselled her at the hospital about
using supplemental bottles of formula; they had told her how
it was not advised in the first few weeks because it interfered
with her own breast milk coming in. Jasmine was already over
a month old, and there was nothing wrong with Brenda's
breast milk supply. Besides, the hospital had included bottles of
formula in both of the gift kits that they had given her when she
was leaving.

She did not remember Millie having a bottle, but then, she
could not recall Millie eating all the time like Jasmine did either.
She had babysat for people and given bottles to their babies, and
she recalled that Marcie had fed Gabriel from the bottle right
from the start. Heck, anytime Brenda was at the hall for a dinner
or event, mothers (and grandmothers and cousins and other
relations) were feeding babies with bottles.

She went to the cupboard and found the formula on the top
shelf alongside packages of dry beans. Some of the ready-made
bottles were missing. They must have disappeared during those
long morning sleeps. If her mother could give Jasmine a bottle,
Brenda could give her one too.

Brenda warmed the formula slightly and then watched her daughter gulp it down. Jazz definitely had experience. She had no trouble at all. The formula disappeared quickly and just as quickly, Jasmine was asleep. Soundly asleep too. For the first time that day, Brenda was able to put her down with some confidence that she would remain sleeping.

She no longer felt like trying on clothes. She no longer had energy enough for a bath or even a shower. She rummaged through the cupboards looking for something to eat. She felt like having chips or a chocolate bar, and of course there were no such treats to be found. Jimmy's store was too far away, and besides, she could not be bothered. She opened a package of biscuits, made tea, then sat at the table, sipping and chewing, sipping and chewing.

The ringing phone woke up Jasmine. Holding her again in one arm, Brenda stood and answered. It was Ruby, phoning to check up on her and her granddaughter. Before she had even finished asking, Jasmine had started to scream again. "The phone woke her, Mom." Brenda had to raise her voice to be heard.

Her mother apologized profusely. Then she asked Brenda if she wanted anything from town.

"Formula." Brenda spoke loudly. "Get Jazz some formula. She won't stop eating."

Within a week and a half, Jasmine was almost completely bottle-fed. Brenda noted with pride that she continued to grow and thrive. Her daughter also began to sleep for extended stretches of time and was content for longer periods between feedings. For the night, all Brenda had to remember was to bring an extra bottle upstairs and leave it beside her bed. Then when Jazz woke up hungry, she would just reach over and feed it to her. Jasmine even seemed to sleep a little later in the mornings. At least that is what Brenda told herself whenever she heard her mother come into her room to bring the baby downstairs.

TWENTY-THREE

It was after school let out and she had all day to herself that Monica's waiting became truly painful. Michael continued working at construction. She took to visiting Ruby early in the mornings. Martin would invariably be out fishing, Brenda would still be sleeping, and Ruby would be in the kitchen, usually with Jasmine. Monica would hold the sleeping child, or rock her when she was awake. Some days, she took turns with her sister, walking her around the small kitchen.

From Ruby, she got daily reports on how much Jasmine was eating and sleeping, and even how many diapers she was dirtying. Every day Monica hoped that Ruby would tell her that Brenda had decided that she and Michael could visit and every day Ruby said nothing. It always seemed that before Monica was quite ready to part with Jasmine she would hear stirrings from upstairs — the sounds of taps being turned on and the toilet flushing. Whenever she heard those sounds, Monica would feel like some criminal sneaking around and would leave the house before Brenda came downstairs.

"When is she going to let you see Jasmine?" she lamented.

"Give her time, for Chrissakes," Michael snapped at her late one Saturday morning. Monica had woken up with the notion that it would be the perfect day for the two of them to visit Ruby's.

"She's had lots of time, Michael. Jasmine is getting bigger every day and you're missing that."

Monica did not often misread Michael, but she did that morning. When he shook his head, she interpreted it not as disapproval of her statement, but as a sign that he was giving up on seeing the baby. He had not wanted to be a father in the first place, she thought bitterly. Now the split with her family was going to become permanent. "She has no right to keep Jasmine from you!"

"She has every right in the world."

"Maybe if you gave a shit…" Monica knew it was the wrong thing to say as soon as the words left her mouth, but she could not take them back. Michael's eyes narrowed. For a fraction of a second, Monica wondered if he would strike her. He stared at her for an excruciatingly long moment.

"Look, I didn't mean that." Her attempted apology sounded feeble even to her own ears.

"I'm going to Port Hope," Michael announced, turning away from her. "Can I take your car?" Before she could reply, he scooped the keys off the counter.

"You know your problem, Monica?" He did not look back toward her. "You're used to getting every goddamned thing you want." Before she could answer, he walked out the door.

Monica was furious. How dare he? She was doing her utmost to make a reconciliation, some sort of an arrangement that they all could live happily with, and what had he done? He had scarcely helped or supported her. His arguments for patience and waiting for the right time were merely excuses for not doing anything. He had stormed off to Port Hope when it would have been the perfect day for him to finally see Jasmine, his own daughter. She paced frantically around the room; it felt even tinier than normal. Suddenly, she stopped, and all of the angry energy that was consuming her vanished. She slumped onto the couch and found herself fighting off the tears. What if Michael was right? What if she was pushing too hard? What if Brenda and Michael ended up hating her for it?

When she looked at the clock, she saw that Michael had been gone for all of twenty minutes. She wanted him back. She would explain; he would understand that this waiting was driving her crazy. She wanted to phone Ruby and tell her everything that had happened and everything that had been said, but she knew that would not do at all. Monica knew, without a doubt, that Ruby would tell her that her situation was of her own making. Basically, that things were her own fault. Her sister would not be wrong.

Monica tried to go back to sleep. Unlike the pacing, the thinking had exhausted her. She would fall asleep and when she woke up, Michael would be home and this would all be over. After a lot of effort, she finally dozed off for what felt like a few minutes; the clock told her that she had slept for over an hour. She was alone and scared. She could not remember waking up that frightened since the days following the death of her parents. She was afraid that like her parents, Michael would not come back. This did not make sense, and yet she could not shed the sense of impending doom.

She forced herself to get up and make tea. This wanting to cry, this sinking into self-pity and expecting the sky to fall was ridiculous. It was a waste of time and it was beneath her. She had never fallen apart like this when she had argued with Saul. And they had argued a lot. Plus, she could scarcely even call what had occurred between her and Michael an argument. She had unintentionally offended him; that was all that had happened. Even when she had tried, she had never been able to hurt Saul like that.

She sat, drinking cup after cup of tea. When Michael had been gone for almost three hours — more than enough time to drive to Port Hope and back — she began to panic. What if something had really happened? What if in his anger he had driven off the road or run into another vehicle on one of the single-lane corners? What if it had been a logging truck? Thoughts of her parents continued to blend with her thoughts of Michael.

"Calm down," she said out loud. Like a mantra, she repeated "calm, calm, calm." She took long, deep breaths, and drank more tea.

When Michael had been gone for four hours, Monica made up her mind to borrow Martin's truck and go out looking for him.

She would wash up and then she would phone Ruby and explain things. Her sister would give her the keys.

Monica heard the car back up into the single parking space. The curtain was not open, but she heard the distinct sounds of Michael opening her car door and trunk. After a brief feeling of intense relief, she was afraid again. She was scared of what Michael would say and what he would do. She froze and watched the door open. Michael entered with grocery bags.

"I could use a hand," he said.

Monica rose quickly and took the Port Hope Market bags. Michael stepped back outside to get more bags from the open trunk.

"You got a lot of stuff."

"Yeah."

"Did you have lunch?"

"Yeah. At the hotel."

She saw that he was not going to return to where they had been before he left. She would not go back there again either. They were wary of one another. Their words were wooden and short. Cautiously, they stood side by side, putting away the groceries. Then Monica noticed that he had bought strawberries. She had to wipe her eyes. Michael did not eat them, but he knew they were her favourites. They must have cost him a small fortune in Port Hope.

On Monday morning, after Michael had gone to work, Monica went to Ruby's. There was still some tension between her and her sister, but Monica believed that the heaviness between them was lightening. There she sat at the old familiar kitchen table, feeding Jasmine a bottle of formula and gently rocking her back to sleep while Ruby mixed dough for bread. Monica could feel herself nestling back into the comfortable safety of family.

"Can I ask you something, Rube?" She waited for her sister to look at her. "Am I being unreasonable…wanting Jasmine to know her father?"

"Of course not. Jasmine has to know her father. He is her father, and there's no two ways about it."

Ruby's declaration convinced Monica of the sincerity and the importance she attached to what she was saying.

"It just doesn't seem to be happening."

"You've got to have patience, Mon. *Patience*. It's not going to happen overnight. There are lots of hurt feelings here. You need to let them get better first. That takes time."

"Sometimes I think they're never going to heal. Period. Just stay the way they are. Forever. That's what scares me."

Ruby shook her head slowly. "You always were in a hurry, even when you were a little kid. You can't rush some things."

Monica took a deep breath. She supposed that she needed to hear this again, this time from her older sister. Ruby had always had the answers. She always seemed to know the right thing to do. How was Monica ever going to learn how to wait?

That day, instead of leaving when she heard Brenda getting ready to come downstairs, Monica stayed. Her niece appeared surprised at seeing her, but she did not seem hostile. There was no glare or look of outrage. There was only a small smile directed down at Jasmine, sound asleep on her lap.

"I think she's getting a tooth already," Brenda said.

Behind her daughter, Monica could see Ruby shaking her head and mouthing a long "no." She could not keep from laughing. Ruby joined in. Brenda, unsure of exactly what they found funny, laughed nervously too. Monica looked into her niece's eyes. They were eyes so much like her own, with faint hints of green and gold shining in the brown. Some of the old Brenda was returning; some of that energy and sheer love of life was coming back. Monica felt good when she left the house that morning. She still wished that everything could be "settled," as she termed it to herself, but she also felt a little more willing to wait.

TWENTY-FOUR

One afternoon, Brenda was out with Jasmine, walking by the school field where Becky and Millie were playing games with about a dozen other kids in the centre grass. Sarah was watching from a short distance away. When introducing her daughter, Brenda realized that it was the first time she had spoken to her old schoolmate since before Christmas.

"Are you going back to school this year?" asked Sarah.

Without really thinking the matter over, Brenda nodded and replied that she hoped so. Until then, she had not—even casually or as a joke—admitted aloud to anyone that she was hoping to go back. Sarah seemed to accept her answer without surprise, and Brenda took that to be a good sign. All the way home she allowed herself to daydream. Her mother would have no problem looking after Jasmine. In fact, she would be glad to spend so much extra time with her only grandchild. Brenda would have to do her Grade 11 again, but that was okay. This time, she would be ignoring all those stupid Port Hope girls anyway. Sarah, and maybe another guy from Kitsum, would be in Grade 12, but that was okay too. She would still ride with them on the bus and spend lunch hours with them. Yes, her mother and father would be proud of her.

Jasmine was still asleep when she quietly re-entered the house. Her mother had gotten Junior and Tom to move the crib downstairs. That way, the baby could sleep and her mother could do all the things she normally did in the kitchen, within easy reach of her granddaughter. "I'm not a spring chicken anymore, Brenda. I can't keep running up those stairs," her mother had said to her the day she had asked Junior and Tom.

Ruby was already working on dinner. Her father and brother, she said over her shoulder, were coming in from fishing. There was a big westerly wind offshore. Brenda immediately started peeling potatoes.

"I've been thinking, Mom," she began. Already her plan did not look quite so perfect because Jazz would wake up any minute, and then her father and brother would be home and then there would be no chance for her to talk to her mother alone. If she had to wait until the next day, she would likely lose her gumption altogether. "I've been thinking that maybe I could go back to school in September. Do my Grade 11 again?"

Brenda could not quite read the expression on her mother's face. She was scared to look too closely. "Oh," her mother managed, and then they both heard Jazz stir. The little girl had not begun to cry yet, or even fuss, but Brenda nearly jumped across the small space between the counter and the crib and picked her up.

That evening, her father said something about Ruby being tired. Could Brenda somehow encourage her to rest a little more? He did not have to say how well that advice would go over. He knew more than anyone how stubborn Ruby could be. At least that was the message Brenda read in his raised eyebrows and slight smile.

"Yeah, I'll try."

"She's going to work herself to death, that woman," her father added.

Brenda found that intending to do more for her mother and *actually doing more* were two very different things. With her father and brothers back out fishing—Tom was determined not to miss one of the last chances at a fishing trip before school resumed—life slipped back into its usual routine. Her mother rose early, retrieved Jasmine, fed her, and changed her diapers downstairs. Brenda got up at the same time as Becky and Millie. After she gave Jasmine her second bottle of the morning, her mother served all of them breakfast and made sure the girls were ready for their day. As soon as they left the house, her mother dove into housecleaning and laundry. Some days she punched bread. Other days, fish had to cut up for the canner or the smokehouse. If her father did not want her mother to work so hard, Brenda thought while making faces at Jazz, why did he bring all that fish home for her? Jasmine was staying awake longer in the mornings now, so Brenda walked her around the house, stopping to play with her on the couch, in the kitchen, even on the porch. By the time her mother was taking her mid-morning tea break, Brenda was ready for one as well.

"Bren, Monica was saying—"

"What does she want now?"

"Nothing much. She was just saying she was coming over this morning sometime. I guess she'll be over soon." Her mother looked at her sternly. "You know, she is trying her best to not upset you."

Brenda could not resist snorting out loud. "Now! Now, she doesn't want to upset me. She was just here the other day. What is she doing—moving back in?"

Her mother did not answer.

Brenda had sincerely hoped that she was done with this roller coaster of emotions. Things were calming down for her, and getting back on more level ground. Apparently, that was not so, or at least not yet. Brenda almost ran upstairs. The last thing she needed was her mother seeing her in tears at the slightest mention of Aunt Monica.

Only a few minutes later, Brenda heard muffled voices downstairs. Opening her bedroom door, she clearly heard Monica's voice. She and her mother were talking and laughing as they had always talked and laughed. Breathing deeply to steady herself, Brenda walked down the stairs. Very deliberately, with her head lifted high and her back straight, she strode into the kitchen. There the sisters were, both of them standing over the crib, both of them cooing over Jasmine.

Ruby and Monica were once again at ease with one another; Brenda had noticed that casual comfort during her aunt's previous visit. It was the same sense of ease that used to include her. She tried to remind herself that Ruby and Monica were extra close to one another because her mother had basically raised Monica after their parents died. She did not know if that helped or not. The sight of her mother treating Monica so well, as though she had done no wrong, still made her fume. Maybe if her mother had lashed out, called Monica to account for the trouble she had caused and was causing; maybe if her mother had yelled and screamed at her younger sister; maybe if her mother had stood up for her own daughter; maybe then some of Brenda's anger would have dissipated.

There was nothing to do but sit in silence and watch the two women handle her baby. The questions Monica asked—about feedings and fussiness and sleep—were all answered by her mother. Brenda did not have to say a word. Instead, she watched the second hand on the stovetop clock and waited for her aunt to leave. She found that she was actually able to ignore both of their voices for short periods if she concentrated hard enough on the ticking hands.

"I don't want to cause trouble," Brenda heard Monica say. That caught her full attention. She could no longer focus on the clock. Anyone saying that they did not want to cause trouble was surely going to do just that. "Michael really wants to see her," Monica announced as she stared down at Jasmine, who was drifting off to sleep in her arms. "Can I bring him over tomorrow?"

Her mother looked at Brenda with a hopeful expression. Brenda even saw her open her mouth to speak, but she could not stand to listen to what was coming. "Sure. Go ahead," Brenda answered. After that, she left the room without another word.

Her father stayed in from fishing. That was momentous in itself. Her dad only took days off when there was something really important happening. Having to see Michael and Monica together was stressful enough, but now she had to cope with whatever her father was going to do or say as well.

It was an excruciatingly long day. Only towards noon did it occur to Brenda that it was a Friday, and Michael was most likely at work. He and Monica would probably not visit until the evening. Brenda had already changed Jasmine's outfit three times that morning; each time she had made the baby girl fussier and fussier. Annoyed with herself, she left her daughter with her mother after lunch and retreated to her bedroom. She already had regurgitated milk on her shirt. She had worn it because it was one of her favourites and she was proud to fit into it again, but not one member of her family had said a word about it. She tried on the yellow blouse that used to look good on her before recalling that she had worn it to visit Michael. The only thing in her closet that looked okay to her at the moment was the new blouse that Monica had given her. Damned if she was going to wear that. In fact, she felt like a fool for even trying to dress up. In private protest, she put on a faded basketball T-shirt that Junior had worn last year.

Monica and Michael arrived just before seven. They had clearly waited until after supper. The sun was still well above the mountains across the harbour, but Brenda was already counting down the hours until she could go to sleep. Her mother served them tea in the living room. Her father sat in his usual reclining chair. Becky and Millie must have been told to play outside; they were nowhere in sight. Junior and Tom were out visiting their friends. Michael and Monica sat together stiffly on the smaller couch. Brenda sat on the matching larger sofa with Jasmine in her arms. *Please, please, please*, she whispered silently to her daughter, *stay asleep*.

Brenda was the first to speak. She just wanted it all over with, and for there to be an end to the painful waiting. "Do you want to hold her?" she asked her aunt.

Monica was up in a split second, carefully lifting Jasmine out of her niece's arms. Brenda retreated back into the couch corner. Monica returned to her seat and then, with Michael at her side, stared at sleeping Jasmine. Brenda could only glance at her father, and then at her mother. They kept their eyes on Monica and Michael and Jasmine.

Jazz's cry cut through the stillness. Brenda instinctively began to rise; her mother made the same movement. However, before either of them could stand, Monica was gently rocking Jasmine and whispering to her. To Brenda's surprise, instead of crying louder as she often did, Jasmine grew quiet. The baby girl looked up at Monica. Ruby brought a bottle from the kitchen. She placed it on the coffee table beside her sister. "She'll probably want that soon."

Brenda wished that she could disappear into the couch. If she stayed perfectly still, if she wished as hard as she could, if she barely breathed, maybe she would just disappear.

"How's fishing?" Michael asked her father. Brenda was looking down at her lap, but she would have recognized that voice anywhere. To her amazement, Martin began telling Michael about the fishing season. He talked at length about the *Pacific Queen* and the salmon openings, and even the recent sockeye runs. She could not believe it; she would not have believed it had she not been sitting right there listening to it. Here was the man who had totally messed up her life, and here was her father casually talking fishing with him.

From the corner of her eye she saw Michael looking down at Jasmine. Brenda heard Monica ask Michael, "You want to hold her?" Her aunt asked the question quietly enough, but her voice filled the room. Michael reached out and gently accepted the baby from Monica. He held her with the utmost care and attention. He held her, Brenda noted, like she was a precious gift. At his side, Monica's adoration seemed to flow unbounded. Brenda could actually feel it from the short distance across the room.

"Hello, little girl," Michael said. Brenda had never heard him speak that softly before. "Hello, Jasmine."

Jasmine did not make a sound. Of all the times for her to be quiet, Brenda thought. She had wanted her to behave well so that they would all see that she was taking good care of her. But now, she wished Jasmine would scream her head off and fling her clenched little fists so that they could also see what Brenda had to deal with regularly. They would soon see there was more for her than just staring at her beautiful baby all day long. Instead, Jasmine's arms moved out of her blankets in what looked like happy excitement. Michael was making faces at her, along with soft humming noises.

When he stopped, Michael cleared his throat and looked up at Brenda. "I owe you an apology," he said quietly. "I'm sorry for hurting you. I'm sorry for what happened."

She could not look fully at his face. She stared at the upper part of his chest and the bottom of his chin instead. She did not dare speak.

"I want to know her," Michael continued, looking down at Jasmine. "Maybe I don't deserve to be in her life, and I know it's completely up to you." Once again, he stared directly at Brenda. "But I would like to. Know her, that is."

Brenda's eyes went to her lap. Maybe some deliverance could be found there. She let herself become hypnotized by her hands grasping and regrasping one another. She knew they were all waiting for her, but she could not answer. If she did open her mouth, she could not rely on what would emerge.

Then Monica broke the silence. "Maybe we could take her for a short visit sometime, Bren. Not for long or anything. Just an hour or two at the most…"

Brenda remained speechless. It was her father who eventually spoke. "Yes, that would be okay."

Michael looked up quickly. Brenda saw him briefly glance at her father, as though to make sure that he was a witness before he looked at her again. "Thank you," he said. "Your kindness means a lot."

Brenda did not know if she had nodded or not.

"Maybe Sunday?" Monica ventured.

They had all ganged up on her. Everyone—even her father—was suddenly on Michael and Monica's side. *The hell with all of them!*

"Sure," Brenda said. She did not recognize her own voice. "Sunday will be fine."

"This is not a war, you know," her mother said after Monica and Michael had left the house and Brenda had re-emerged from the bathroom. "Jasmine has a father. You might not like that very much. You might not think much of him—for good reason—but it's still not fair to keep her away from him. It's about *her*. Jasmine. Not him. She has a father just like she has Grandma Monica. They are her family, too."

Brenda knew that her mother was right, but that did not make it any easier for her to agree. Rather than allow her mother to see how hurt she still was, she went upstairs again. Alone. She seemed to be forever running away. The evening replayed itself over and over again. She could not stop those repeating scenes. Michael and how he had looked holding Jasmine; Michael as a loving father, a proud father. Yes, she had pictured him that way not so long ago. Except, he was not at her side. He was beside Monica. As if Jasmine belonged to them. Brenda was not even in the picture.

He had thanked her. For her kindness, of all things. Like she was some stranger who had given him a ride into town or a cup of hot tea on a cold day. She had wanted to be loved; she had wanted to be desired. Instead, she had garnered his thanks. Even worse, she suspected that she had earned his pity. Her mother could be as philosophical as she liked. Brenda knew very well that she did not always heed her own advice. For that matter, neither did her irreproachable father. They both made mistakes. Big mistakes.

Downstairs, Jasmine was beginning to cry. Within seconds, Brenda was crying too. She loved that little girl beyond reason, beyond anything that had happened or had been said. She wiped her face and went to find her. Jasmine was already contentedly feeding in Ruby's lap, but Brenda signalled that she would take her. Without a word, her mother passed Jasmine and her bottle to Brenda.

The first time that Jazz was gone from the house, Brenda could not stop pacing. The second time, she was still quite nervous. The third time, she found herself starting to relax. After each outing, Monica brought Jasmine back at exactly the time she had promised. The baby was changed and content. Michael stayed in the background. "There is nothing to worry about," her mother assured her.

On the fourth and fifth visit, Jasmine was with Monica from mid-morning until nearly suppertime. One hour had become two; two hours had become an entire half-day. The progression was fast. Brenda was surprised that Monica had the patience. She remembered when Millie and Becky had been babies. Sure, Auntie Monica had held and admired them, but Brenda could not recall her spending all that much time with them. Her taking to Jasmine was different. Unlike Ruby, Brenda remained slightly suspicious.

TWENTY-FIVE

If Monica was amazed at how quickly her attachment to Jasmine grew, she was even more astonished by the connection that was blossoming between Michael and his daughter. Jasmine effortlessly brought out a side of Michael that Monica had never seen before. He seemed to have infinite time to walk and cuddle the little girl when she was fussy; he could have happily spent all day singing silly songs and telling her small stories and rhymes. Monica's feelings for both Michael and Jasmine expanded into a whole new dimension.

One day toward the end of August, Monica picked Jasmine up in the afternoon and promised Ruby that she would have the little girl back home before dark. Michael had been wanting to bring Jasmine over to his Uncle Fred's to introduce her and show her off to his family, but it had been hard to find the right time. Summer was party season in Kitsum and his uncles were often "at it again," as Michael put it. However, Ethel had invited them to come over for supper. Monica was pretty sure that the Clydesdales would not be partying if they had asked them over. Michael was not quite as confident.

"She better not have forgotten," Michael had mumbled while tying his work boots that morning. "I'll check by their place on my way home, and see if it's still a go."

Monica waited with Jasmine. She really had no wish to go to Fred and Ethel's house. When she thought about their last visit she could not help but think of it as slightly depressing. The Clydesdales had so little, and their house all but screamed poverty. Ethel cleaned and tidied the place, but there was really nothing for her to work with. Monica had recognized their kitchen table as one of the old ones from the hall. Similarly, the chairs they had used were the same chairs that people sat on in the community centre. Another pair of seats were merely blocks of wood. As for the couch, it had to be the ugliest, most uncomfortable contraption that Monica had ever sat upon. Why on earth had Fred given Michael the small couch? It was not in great shape, not by a long shot, but it was certainly in better condition than the one he had kept for his own house.

When they had been in Port Hope, Monica had suggested to Michael that they buy a gift for his aunt and uncles—maybe something for their house like a set of coffee mugs or a new sofa cover. Michael had immediately nixed the idea. "They'll only sell it, or trade it for a bottle when they get desperate." Monica had a hard time believing him, especially about Ethel, who had behaved so properly during their last visit.

After fretting all day that the dinner visit would not materialize, Monica was relieved to see Michael smiling in the open doorway. She could see that, even though he was still a little anxious, he was also excited. This was important to him. "We can leave as soon as I wash up and change," he said.

The Clydesdale house was spotless. Ethel had clearly gone to a lot of trouble. Freshly baked bread cooled on the counter. Even with the windows open and the slight breeze, the smell of just-fried fish remained in the air. Murray and Fred looked as though they had just stepped out of the shower. Monica could not help thinking that they looked a bit like fidgety schoolchildren. They were shy and nervous, although they also appeared proud and happy to greet them, and most of all Jasmine. Fred and Murray each held the baby briefly, like men unaccustomed to holding infants, but Ethel relished holding the little girl. She refused to let go of her while they all sat down to eat. Monica swore that Jasmine seemed to know all of them, to recognize the Clydesdales as her relatives.

After the meal, Fred began to speak to Michael. He did so with some difficulty. There were a few rough attempts at starting, but Michael kept his eyes down, sat still, and waited. Monica was almost afraid to breathe.

"Kate came to see us the other day."

Ethel nodded as though to verify what her husband had imparted. There was a long pause. Listening to how the Clydesdales talked, Monica could not believe that she had ever considered conversations with Martin and Ruby slow. Michael shot a quick glance in her direction. She recognized that he was hoping she would not interrupt. She decided to focus on Jasmine, who was snuggling contentedly in Ethel's arms.

"She came to tell us they took Cathy's kids."

Monica knew from Michael that Fred and Ethel's eldest daughter lived in Vancouver with her three children, and that her "husband" had left her a number of years ago. She mostly remembered Cathy from the residential school. She had been a grade behind Monica. When Monica had started staying in Kitsum for school, Cathy had been one of the kids who kept going to Christie. She had lost track of her over the years.

"Kate says that we could take the kids…" There was another long pause. She felt kind of sorry for Fred; she wanted somehow to lighten the weight he was obviously under while trying to relay this information to Michael. "If we quit drinking."

Monica heard Murray snort.

"No one's talking about you, Murray," Fred snapped.

"So anyways, Mike…" Fred stole brief glances at his nephew. His eyes mostly studied his dinner plate or the wall behind Ethel. "We're thinking about it. For the kids, you know." Monica saw Ethel nod while looking down at Jasmine. "You come back tomorrow," Fred said, addressing Michael alone. "I want to talk to you."

Michael and Monica said very little to one another as they walked through Kitsum later that evening to bring Jasmine back to her mother. It was nearly eight o'clock and the sun was just barely above the mountains. Every house door seemed to be open, awaiting some hint of evening coolness before the onslaught of mosquitoes forced them closed again. They walked quickly at first, but their pace slowed gradually as they approached the Joe house. Neither of them wanted to part with the little girl.

Michael was late getting home the next day. She reminded herself not to ask questions when he got back. Michael's family business was exactly *that*—his own business. Maybe she was just a nosy person. Forever having to wait for an appropriate time to find things out was one of the things that had driven her crazy at Ruby and Martin's. Now here she was with Michael, where the same unwritten, unspoken rules applied. Michael believed—presumably like everyone else in Kitsum—that there was a proper time and place for every conversation. How that specific propriety could be determined still remained a mystery to Monica.

Later that evening, Michael told her that Fred and Ethel were indeed serious about quitting drinking. Kate was getting them into a program at a treatment centre. "Six weeks," he told Monica. "They'll be gone for six weeks. Fred's pretty nervous about it. He's never done anything like that before. He says he's been a drunk his whole life.

"But you know what, Monica—I think they just might pull it off. Ten years ago, they wouldn't have even considered a treatment centre, even if there was one around. Kate figures they need to be sober for at least six months for a chance of the court letting them have the kids. But the thing is, Fred and Ethel really want those kids. They can't do anything for Cathy. It's too late for that. But this is like another chance for them to do something right. I don't know," Michael added pensively. "I guess we'll see."

"I hope so," she whispered.

"They're not so bad, my uncle and auntie. They just haven't had many breaks. Uncle Murray, too. You know, I used to stay with him in the summer. He had a place by the river, sort of across from Jimmy's. I don't know if you remember that. It was just me and Murray. I liked it there. Lots of freedom. Murray, he drank a lot, all right, but he still took me fishing in that small boat of his.

He called her *Miss Cindy*. He caught a lot of fish too, enough to make sure that we had grub in the house, and so he could give me money to run over to Jimmy's.

"Then one summer, I got off the freight boat. I was just finished Grade 6, and I got off the boat at the end of June. Nobody was there to meet me, so I walked up to Murray's. Except there was no house there, just the black remains of the foundation. Shit, it had burned down and no one had even told me. My cousin Cathy, she came to get me after a while. She'd come back home early that year but I'm not real sure why. Anyway, I was just standing there stunned, I guess. Cath brought me to their place. Murray was there…and him and Fred were loaded.

"Two days later, Cathy told me what happened. Not my uncles and not my aunt who was drunk and crying all the time. Cathy was the one who told me that Chris had died in the fire. He was Fred and Ethel's youngest son, only four years old. Cathy didn't know the truth at first, but she found out from her mother. Apparently, Chris had gone to spend the night with Uncle Murray and that was when the house had caught fire. Murray had one of those old drum stoves. Lots of people used them back then. I don't know if the stove is what did it. Cath didn't know either. She felt so bad about Chris that she could not ever talk about it much."

Monica saw that it was more than Michael had intended to tell her. He looked at her now with a kind of hostility, an emotion that she found difficult to bear. "I hope they make it. It would be good for them to have the kids," she said.

"Yeah," Michael concluded. "Jasmine can grow up knowing her family."

They sat almost motionless, leaning into one another, staring blankly at the television set. It seemed like hours later when Michael spoke again. He presented the information in a low whisper, almost as an afterthought. "Tonight I asked my uncle who my father was." Louder, with false bravado, he added "You know I always figured I'd ask Uncle Fred when he was half-cut, and I'd coax him into telling me. Then here I go and finally ask him when he's decided to sober up."

"What did he say?"

"He swears he doesn't know. That was the answer I was afraid of getting. My mom refused to tell anyone. She sure never told me. But Fred, he sees now that I want to know for Jasmine. Someday she is going to need to know. He said that he'd ask Murray, but he's pretty sure that Murray doesn't know either. Well, guess who my Uncle Fred figures might know? Of all people?"

"Who?"

"Martin."

"Martin!"

"Yeah. At first, I kind of freaked out. Thinking he meant that Martin…you know. But Fred said no way, just that Martin and Mom were friends when they were young. Friends like brother and sister friends. I guess Martin always kind of looked out for Mom. My uncle said there was a guy around but not from here… from Port Alberni, he thinks. The thing is, that guy disappeared after Martin beat him up."

"Martin beat him up?" This was turning into a strange story.

"I know. I couldn't wrap my head around the idea of Martin beating anybody up either. Though according to Uncle Fred, Martin beat this guy up bad, and no one knew what for. But Fred figures that maybe he'd been the one messing around with Cindy. She was just a kid then, really. Fourteen, maybe fifteen at most. Anyway, my uncle thinks I should ask Martin. When the time is right."

TWENTY-SIX

There were days when fog banks rolled along the mountains and shoreline on the opposite side of the harbour while Kitsum remained in clear August sunshine. That was not the case on this day. Everything was surrounded by wet greyness. The heavy fog and the fact that her mother was still sleeping made Brenda think that it must be very early in the morning. Brenda had gone downstairs already; Jasmine had seemed extra perky after finishing her morning bottle. She had barely put the infant into her crib when there was a soft knock at the door. She had been shocked to see that it was already past eight o'clock, which was nearly lunchtime in the Joe household. Swinging the door open, Brenda found herself face to face with Monica.

After Monica and Michael's visit, Brenda had largely avoided her aunt. That was not hard to do. Mostly, she just made sure that she was in her room when Monica came by to pick up or drop off Jazz. "I'm too early," Monica laughed with her eyes settling on Jasmine, who was kicking away happily in her crib.

Where was her mother? Brenda worried for only an instant. She and Jasmine had both had a decent night's sleep, and she was feeling pretty good. Why let Monica spoil that now? "I'll put on coffee," she said.

Maybe it was the fog that had clouded her brain. For a brief spell that morning, she forgot her animosity towards her aunt. Watching Monica play with Jasmine, her resentment returned, but just as quickly, it also seemed to recede. Her mother was still nowhere in sight. She had no choice but to wait for the coffee pot. She stared out at the thick grey wall. She could not even make out Nona's house across the street.

Once the coffee was poured, Monica began to talk. She talked to Brenda as though there was not a problem in the world, as though things between them had never changed. Brenda found herself being carried along by the conversation and relaxing into a long-familiar setting. Listening to Monica was like slipping on a pair of old comfortable shoes that fit every contour of her feet. For the moment, retaining her anger towards her aunt felt like just too much bother.

Monica talked about finding another place to live. Without saying his name, without even using the word "we," Brenda knew that she meant a place for her and Michael. The two rooms Monica stayed in were nowhere near big or bright enough. The McKays were moving into one of the new houses, Monica explained. She and Michael could have the McKay place for almost nothing if they were willing to fix it up.

"But it's a dump."

Monica chuckled. That was exactly the sort of remark that Brenda might have made a year ago. Monica felt a spark of their old relationship, even if it was just for this rare moment.

"Yeah, well…we're going to fix it up."

Brenda did not think that her aunt even knew how to use a hammer. "But…" she started and stopped herself.

"What about you, Bren? How are you doing?"

Brenda shrugged. She was about to say something about taking care of Jazz, but then she blurted out precisely what she had been avoiding mentioning again to her mother. "I'm thinking of going back to school. In September. That's pretty soon though. I don't know if I'm going to make it."

"Really!" Monica seemed interested. Genuinely enthused, even. "That's good, Brenda. Really good. Yes, you should."

Easy for her to say, Brenda thought.

"I can babysit," Monica continued. "When you're in school. Some days at least. Your mom can probably babysit on other days."

Whether she had heard or not, Brenda's mother made no sign as she entered the kitchen. All that was noticeable was the look of complete embarrassment on her face. "I really slept in," she apologized. "I must have fallen back to sleep after Martin and the boys left this morning."

Her father had undoubtedly left the house, with a sleepy Junior and Thomas in tow, by his usual 4:30 that morning. The night before, he had brought home a tote full of fish that was now waiting for Ruby on the back porch.

"You deserve to sleep in sometimes, Mom," Brenda declared. Monica nodded in agreement.

"Nope. I've got to get that fish done."

"The fish won't swim away, Mom. Plus it's foggy and cool. There's no hurry."

"The girls aren't up yet?"

"It's not even 8:30, Ruby. Have coffee first." Monica set down a steaming cup in front of her.

"They're allowed to be late for summer camp, you know," Brenda piped in. "Most of the other kids don't even get there until after 10:00."

Ruby could not help herself. She smiled broadly at her daughter and her sister and sat in front of the coffee Monica had already poured for her. The three women looked from one to another. It was like old times.

"So Brenda's telling me she wants to go back to school next month," Monica started. That was the old Monica, Brenda thought with a surprising surge of pride, tackling subjects head on and asking the questions that everyone else only hinted at in the vaguest way possible. That was the Monica who Brenda had once so fervently hoped to emulate. "I was just telling Bren that I could help babysit Jasmine here."

"But you work."

"I'll quit," Monica stated simply. "Or I'll work part-time. That'll be better. Gary's been tearing his hair out trying to find room in the school budget to pay me. He'd love for me to only work half-days or half the week."

"Then I could watch Jasmine those times when you're working."

"And her father…" Monica flicked a nervous glance toward Brenda. "He's not going to be working every day in the winter."

"You better ask him first," Brenda cautioned. Maybe he was already getting tired of the father routine. Unlike her, he had the option.

"For sure, Brenda. Definitely. I'll let you know tomorrow."

And just like that, the matter seemed to be settled. Monica had that magic to just make things happen. It was impossible for Brenda not to be swept up in her aunt's plans. A part of her felt like she should not be doing this at all, that it was too soon for her to be returning to school, but another part of her was overwhelmingly eager at the prospect. Anyway, it was too late to back out now. She had started the ball rolling by telling Monica. "I'd really like to try," Brenda said to her mother and Monica. "I could go at the beginning of September and see how it all works out."

Ruby and Monica nodded. The matter was definitely settled.

"I've got to get those kids," her mother announced even as she was already rising to call them.

"I'll be back with Jazz—when?" Monica rose to leave. "I guess you'll be doing fish. I'll keep her till suppertime, if that's okay?"

Brenda smiled in agreement. Then, sitting alone at the kitchen table, she began to think about her future.

TWENTY-SEVEN

Nona did her best to enjoy every bit of the summer days with her son and grandchildren. Charlie, Molly, and young Harry, Jen, and Maureen were visiting for two short weeks. Even so, before anyone else was up, she would gaze out her window and wonder how the Joes were coping with the new baby. Some mornings, she watched Martin and his boy walking down to the boat to go fishing. She did not wave though; there was something about it being so early in the day that made the watching a little too deliberate, almost like spying. Most of her cares and concerns were with her own immediate family. Her house was busy again. She proudly introduced her grandchildren to close and distant relatives every time they went to the beach or the floats or the store. Nona's world was full to bursting.

She had just finished mopping her kitchen floor, and she was chopping potatoes, onions, and carrots for a pot of soup. Molly had insisted on doing the breakfast dishes before she and Charlie and the kids left for the lake. They would be back soon. Intent on preparing lunch, Nona jumped when she heard the rapid tapping on her door. Carolyn stood outside with her own grandchild in her arms. Nona had neither seen nor spoken with her cousin for weeks. She felt obliged to invite her inside for a cup of tea.

At first, Nona assumed that Carolyn was there to show off her grandson. A closer look at the woman's flushed face told a different story. When she offered to take the baby so Carolyn could drink her tea, her cousin thrust the child at her. She spoke in a torrent, her words tumbling into one another. It was a lucky thing that Charlie and Molly had taken the kids out. If they had been home, Nona would have been too distracted to ever piece together Carolyn's latest outpouring.

"Where is Charmayne?" she asked her cousin in frustration.

"She's gone," Carolyn moaned.

"Where?" Nona thought that perhaps Charmayne had gone out visiting or even into Port Hope.

"Gone. Back to Vancouver."

"Without the baby?" Nona had known Charmayne was irresponsible, but to leave her new baby behind would be too much.

Carolyn began to cry in earnest. Her shoulders shook; tears flowed and ran down her cheeks. Nona could not even pass her a tissue because her arms were cradling the sleeping infant. There was nothing for her to do but gently rock the child and wait for Carolyn to calm down.

Between sniffles, Carolyn began to tell Nona what had happened. The telling seemed to stifle her tears, but anger replaced them. Charmayne, it seemed, had come back to Kitsum with her son after a huge fight with her husband in Vancouver. During that fight, Charmayne had admitted to her husband that he was not the baby's father. John—that was his name—had promptly kicked Charmayne and the baby out of their apartment. Then Charmayne had hired a friend to drive her to Kitsum. By the time they had arrived at Carolyn's house, she had decided that she wanted her husband back, and that she would resolve their argument by leaving baby Dwayne with his grandmother.

"Charmayne will change her mind. Come to her senses."

"No…no she won't. She's already gone, Nona. Gone for good."

As near as Nona could make out from the garbled story, her cousin had woken up to the baby's screams early that morning. She had waited in her bed for Charmayne to see to Dwayne, but the baby had kept crying. When she thought that something might be wrong, she went to see for herself. Knocking on Charmayne's door, there was no answer, just Dwayne's gasping cries. Opening the bedroom door, Carolyn found her grandson in the middle of the bed. Charmayne was nowhere to be found. It was already starting to get bright out. Charmayne's friend was not on the couch where he had been sleeping. The car was gone from the road outside the house. Then she saw the note in Charmayne's handwriting on the table. She could not read it right away. Dwayne needed a bottle first.

If Nona understood correctly, during an argument the night before, Carolyn had told her daughter that she would not be able to look after Dwayne while she was still working. Charmayne had yelled at Carolyn that she had no choice. The friend had stepped in and told Charmayne to settle down, and to stop yelling at her mother. Charmayne had taken baby Dwayne to her room and had stayed there for the rest of the night.

After her grandson had calmed down enough to quietly take the bottle — the poor child was famished — Carolyn had read her daughter's letter. It was all about how much she realized that she loved her husband, and how she needed to return to beg his forgiveness. She also admitted to past mistakes and vowed not to repeat them. Carolyn sounded proud of that part, but Nona shook her head sadly. The letter said that Charmayne needed a fresh start with John. That was why she had decided that her mother should keep Dwayne. If she did not want to keep him, she should give him to his real father. That man, according to Charmayne, was Martin Joe. Charmayne had known all along, and she had told her husband because she could not bear to deceive him any longer.

"You see what I have to do?" Carolyn asked, seeking agreement.

Nona did not see at all. She could make little sense out of what Carolyn had just told her. "Take care of the baby," she ventured.

Carolyn looked at Nona like she was stupid. "I want you to come with me," she said. "He's your relative."

"My relative?"

"Martin, of course."

It was only then that Nona realized what Carolyn was up to. There was no way she was taking part.

"Is he home?" Carolyn demanded. "Martin. Is he home?"

"Let's just have another cup of tea," Nona offered feebly. She was still holding Dwayne. To her surprise, Carolyn remained seated and poured herself another cup.

"Is he home?" she asked again.

"Yes, he's home. But wait a minute…what if he's not the father?"

Then Carolyn revealed that Martin already knew he was the baby's father. She had told him so herself only the day before. After Charmayne had first explained the situation to her, Carolyn had waited to see *Pacific Queen* enter the harbour. Then she had gone down to wait on the dock for Martin to come up from the floats. She had waited for over an hour. The man had tried to walk right by her with a brief nod, but she had stopped him right in his tracks with her news.

Carolyn had thought then that Charmayne would be staying in Kitsum with her son. She had thought that she would need help and that Martin should provide for his own child. The man had only stared coldly at her for a moment before making his way home. "There's no way he's told Ruby," Carolyn concluded.

Nona was amazed. Even as upset as her cousin was, she could not resist a poke at Ruby. After all these years, too. There was enough trouble already. "Maybe you should think about this for a few days before going to Martin's," Nona tried. "Maybe Charmayne will be back."

"She's not coming back. I know Charmayne."

Still determined, Carolyn stood up. She bent over Nona and made sure the baby's blankets were wrapped properly. She tossed a diaper bag over her shoulder and took the child. With renewed vigour, she strode out of Nona's kitchen.

Nona could only stare at Carolyn's back as she crossed the street and headed straight for the Joe house. She was inside for less than five minutes. Nona watched in amazement as her cousin nearly ran—without baby Dwayne—out again and past Nona's house down the trail. Nona was not certain, but she could swear that Carolyn had glanced up at her open window with a look of defiance.

It was not long before Charlie, Molly, and their kids piled back into Nona's kitchen. The fish soup was still cooking because she had spent so much of the late morning listening to Carolyn and trying to convince her to alter her plans. Charlie told Harry, Jen, and Maureen that they could play outside near the house for another half hour and out they went. Nona had already let them take a pair of old blankets and the worn bench from her smokehouse to make forts along the trail.

Before she had even begun to tell Charlie about what had gone on that morning, her son asked her if something was wrong. Her dismay must have been that obvious. Charlie would remind her that none of this was her problem, but even so, the events and news had left her feeling stressed, tired, and above all, confused. She could not believe the way Charmayne and Carolyn had acted, or the way they had treated a precious baby. Nor could she believe that Martin was involved. Martin and Ruby had one of the most stable marriages in Kitsum. What was going on with the world?

Nona set her soup pot to simmer and sat down. She related everything she could recall from Carolyn's visit and subsequent actions that morning to Charlie and Molly. It must have made for quite a story because neither of them made a sound or interrupted her flow of words. When Nona had finished talking, it was her son who spoke first.

"Carolyn is nuts. Charmayne too."

Molly shook her head. "How could a mother leave her new baby? Or a grandmother turn away her own grandchild?"

Charlie made a comment about not knowing what a busy neighbourhood his mother lived in. It was not that funny, but they laughed nervously, glad for a break from the tension.

"Did Martin really fool around with Charmayne?" Charlie was serious again.

Nona nodded. "It was early fall, or at least that's what Carolyn told me. It was big gossip around Kitsum for a while. Ruby left for a few days and everything, so I guess it must have been true."

Charlie gave a low whistle. The news surprised him. It certainly had surprised Nona. Then the kids raced back in and Nona set the table. They were nearly finished lunch before Charlie offered her his opinion.

"It's all going to work out, you know. That's how things go. You think everyone in Kitsum is crazy, absolutely haywire, and then all the stuff that seemed impossible, and all the problems that seemed insurmountable, they somehow get resolved. And life goes on slowly, bumpily, but happily enough, as it should. If anyone can overcome problems, it's Martin and Ruby. Next summer, just you wait, Mom — no one will even remember that there was ever trouble."

It was a long speech for Charlie. His children — hearing the gravity in their father's voice but not understanding what he was talking about — stared expectantly at the adults. Nona and Molly remained silent.

TWENTY-EIGHT

Now that Brenda knew that she was going back to school, her life seemed to flow smoothly and quickly. She was getting along well with her mother again. The tension between herself and her aunt had not disappeared — it would be a lie to pretend that it was completely gone — but her feelings of anger and animosity had definitely lost some of their raw power. Even Jasmine seemed to be calmer and more content. The busiest summer fishing was over and her father was often returning home in the early afternoons instead of late at night. Some days the *Queen* did not even leave the float. Her father's plan to bring the whole family to Vancouver for the Pacific National Exhibition, or the PNE, as everyone called it, was causing a whirlwind of excitement. He had already arranged to borrow a van that belonged to his parents so that there would be room for everyone. The kids talked about little else. The entire household was in a good mood.

Everyone was at home that day; they were all eating lunch at the kitchen table. Her father and Junior had been working on the boat. Summer camp was over. School was only a little over a week away. Becky and Millie were in the middle of some ridiculous argument about the breed of a neighbour's old dog. There was a knock at the front door and Junior went to answer it.

"Dad," he called from the next room.

Brenda could not identify the woman's voice. Judging by the puzzled look on her mother's face, Brenda guessed that she did not recognize it at first either. Even the girls fell silent.

"Here," the unknown voice declared. "He's your son."

Brenda saw her mother freeze. Thomas looked from his mother to Brenda as though begging some sort of explanation.

"He's your son," the unknown voice repeated. "Take him."

Brenda saw a flicker of recognition cross her mother's face. "Stay here," Ruby ordered and rose to join Martin.

"What's going on?" Ruby demanded.

"I'm bringing Charmayne's baby. Charmayne and Martin's baby," the voice announced. "It's about time Martin took responsibility."

"Settle down, Carolyn." Her father spoke so hoarsely that his words came out almost like a growl.

Brenda and her brothers and sisters looked apprehensively at one another. They kept quiet, afraid of missing even one word of what was being said in the other room. Then Brenda began to clue in. She had heard the rumours, and she had been able to piece together remarks made by her grandmother and Auntie Kate. There were also the things people had said to her on her walks with Jasmine, and the stuff from Junior's friends who never realized that they could be overheard. Like just about everyone else in Kitsum, she knew that Carolyn's daughter Charmayne was spreading it around that her baby was Martin's child. Brenda was inclined to dismiss the notion as ridiculous, although it had been Charmayne who had fooled around with her father last fall. Yes, that whole "episode" with Charmayne had been the cause of the major fight between her mother and father. No, it really did not seem possible! Everything had blown over and was by now ancient history. How could her father actually be this baby's father?

"I'm leaving him here," Carolyn asserted. "You better take him because I'm going."

"Here." It was their mother's voice. Brenda pictured her stepping forward to accept the mystery baby. Later on, her mother would admit that she had taken the baby because she was afraid that Carolyn would drop him, the way she was flinging him around and shoving him towards Martin.

They heard the front door slam. Brenda and her siblings remained glued to their kitchen chairs. None of them knew what to say or do.

"That woman is insane!" they heard their father roar, and then the cry of an infant. Instinctively, Brenda looked down at Jasmine even as she recognized that the screams were not hers. Becky looked frightened, and Millie appeared close to tears. Brenda waited for her parents to re-enter the kitchen, but no one came.

"You guys should go to your room." Brenda looked at Becky, then at Millie, and finally at Tom, letting each of them know she was absolutely serious. "Please," she added gently. "I'll call you soon."

Junior could contain himself no longer. As soon as the kids had gone upstairs, he let his words out. "What the hell?"

Brenda and her brother could still hear the baby whimpering from the adjoining room. As though the strange sounds were calling to her, Jasmine joined in. Using her daughter almost as a shield, Brenda ventured into the living room. There on the couch, her mother was holding another baby. A baby smaller than Jazz, wrapped in a thin blue blanket. With her free hand, her mom was rummaging through a large white diaper bag. Martin stood in the middle of the room. At that moment, the father Brenda knew, the man who always seemed to be in control of himself and whatever situation he was required to handle, seemed anything but in control. He looked smaller, as though all of the air and energy had been sucked out of him. He did not even seem to see anything. Her mother was the one to find the bottle of formula and begin feeding the now gasping infant.

"I don't even know his name," her mother mumbled. "She didn't even tell us his name."

"Dwayne," her father answered woodenly. "She said his name was Dwayne."

Ruby glared at her husband. "You better tell me what the hell is going on, Martin."

Brenda watched her father sink into his armchair and stare blankly ahead of him. Her mother resumed feeding the baby and waited. Yes, Ruby could wait all day if it came to that. As invisibly as Brenda had entered the living room, she left. She and Junior exchanged puzzled glances. Brother and sister sat at the table looking at one another without uttering a single word. Time passed excruciatingly slowly.

"Junior." Martin's voice broke the stillness that had settled upon the entire household. His voice echoed off the walls. Junior jumped to attention. "Take the kids to visit their grandparents."

Brenda watched her oldest brother go upstairs and come back down with Tom, Becky, and Millie. Not even their youngest sister questioned why they were going or "if they really had to." Brenda considered accompanying them, but decided against it. She was not one of the kids anymore; she was not a child who could be bossed out of the house. Not with Jasmine. Junior did not question her; he just led the kids outside.

The house descended back into silence. Brenda put Jazz into her crib and paced the few steps between the table and the window. She saw old Nona looking over at their house from her porch. She must have seen Carolyn coming over with the baby and then leaving alone. Not much escaped that woman. Now she was probably craning her neck trying to see what would come next. What did she expect? Fireworks?

Jasmine began to fuss. Brenda got her bottle ready. She fed and rocked her daughter gently, hoping that she would sleep. There were still no voices coming from the other room. She did not need to see her parents to know that they were sitting in the same positions as when she had looked in on them. She did not need to see them to know that they were unable to look at one another. It suddenly occurred to Brenda that they might be waiting for her to leave the kitchen and retreat to her bedroom upstairs.

Eventually, she decided to take Jasmine out for a long walk instead. That would give her parents the time they needed. After all, it was a beautiful day. The westerly wind was steady, and just strong enough to keep away the fog and prevent the day from growing too hot. She gathered a few things for Jasmine and was soon ready. She made sure to shut the kitchen door loudly when she left.

Brenda walked with her daughter down the trail alongside Nona's house. Sure, let Nona think they had all been kicked out. What would that matter? She continued on toward the older part of the village; she passed the Band Office and crossed the softball field to reach the shoreline. A few kids were already swimming even though the tide was out. She walked the length of Village Beach. She watched the white-capped waves; it was one of those rare days when the biggest wind stayed offshore for a little while. On the beach, it was perfect weather for a picnic.

She thought of giving Jimmy's store another try. She would buy a juice box or something and sit down by the river. Brenda was already headed in that direction when she realized that she was bound to run into people. Fortunately, everyone she had already seen had been far enough away that she had not needed to stop and chat. People might have already heard about what Carolyn had done. News travelled fast in Kitsum, especially with someone like Carolyn driving it. That woman! No doubt she was already boasting about facing down Martin and forcing him to take "his" baby. Brenda looked back at the length of beach she had just crossed. There were only a few kids there and a couple of dogs. She sat on a log, and kept bouncing her daughter as though she were walking.

Soon, Jasmine began to squirm. Brenda could not sit on the log all day. For about the hundredth time, she wished that Marcie was back home in Kitsum. She would have taken Jazz there in a moment. By now, she would have told Marcie the whole story. Her friend would have done her best to stop her from worrying about the situation too. She would have told her jokes or silly stories to make her laugh. The two of them would have watched Gabriel and Jasmine while imagining the two of them growing up together in Kitsum, just as the two girls had grown up together. Now none of that was going to happen.

Brenda was walking past the school on her way to see her grandparents when she realized it was a weekday. Michael would be at work, and Monica would be alone. Impulsively, she decided to pay her aunt a visit. Besides Marcie, Monica was the one person she could speak with about everything that was going on at home.

It was the first time that Brenda had visited Monica here. Even when her aunt had initially taken the job and the "apartment," Brenda had not gone. She had been too embarrassed then, too acutely aware of her pregnancy to venture out of her own house. She nearly changed her mind when she reached the door, but Jasmine was on the verge of screaming and that strengthened her resolve. She quickly rapped twice. *Maybe she'll be out.* Brenda had scarcely completed the thought when the door opened and Monica's face betrayed its astonishment.

"What's wrong?" Surely Brenda would only have come to see her in the event of an emergency. "Is Ruby all right? The kids?"

"Nothing's wrong. Nothing," Brenda reassured her. "Everyone's okay. We just stopped by to say hello. That's all."

Monica burst into a grin and ushered Brenda and Jasmine inside. "Excuse the stuff all over the place. Sit down anywhere. I'm trying to pack."

Brenda saw that Monica's place really was a mess. It was also even tinier than Monica's descriptions. There were piles of books and papers and assortments of dishes and food in seemingly random locations. For some reason, the disarray relaxed her a little. She cleared off a kitchen chair and passed Jasmine to Monica. Before the tea had even steeped, she had told Monica about the bizarre incident at home.

Monica's eyes grew round. "You're kidding?" She interrupted only twice, and each time, Brenda shook her head before continuing.

"Wow," Monica breathed once Brenda had finished.

Then to make sure that she had understood it all correctly, her aunt asked her to repeat the whole story.

"Holy cow!" Monica was still flabbergasted. "I'm glad you came here."

"Yeah, me too." Brenda realized that she meant it. "I couldn't stay at home. They wouldn't talk until I left."

"No," her aunt agreed. "They wouldn't."

Brenda and Monica both made the same exasperated face. It was the identical expression that they used to make to one another when Monica was in high school and they had shared a bedroom. Brenda had only been young then—she had still been in elementary school—but Monica had always treated her as an equal, and never as a little kid. They began to laugh. Tension evaporated as quickly and completely as summer fog on its way out of the harbour.

"How long do you think I should wait?"

"A month," Monica responded, and they both began laughing all over again. "Seriously, Bren, I don't know, but I'd give them the afternoon anyways."

They ended up enjoying the visit. Brenda and Monica took turns holding Jazz. They also packed piles of stuff into boxes and labelled them. When Brenda looked at the clock—it had been hidden behind a tower of books—she was surprised to see that it was nearly four o'clock. She stiffened involuntarily. As good as the afternoon had been for her and Monica, they no longer lived in the past. Things were different now. "When does he get back?"

Monica almost whispered, "Soon."

"Well, Mom and Dad have had long enough." Brenda rose to leave. Monica began to dissuade her niece from going, but Brenda's sober look stopped her in mid-sentence.

"Hey, why don't you leave Jazz here? I can bring her over later tonight."

That was a good plan. That way, if things were still too weird at home, she could just head back out without worrying about where to take Jasmine. She nodded and murmured her thanks. Her priority for the moment was putting a safe distance between herself and the school before Michael showed up. She had bared enough of her soul for one day.

When Brenda got home, she was surprised to hear her Aunt Kate's voice coming from the living room. There was no sign of her mother or the kids in the kitchen.

"Is that you, Brenda?"

Ruby sounded okay. Perhaps things had been ironed out. She entered the front room.

"Where's Jasmine?"

"With Monica, Mom. She's bringing her back after supper."

"Supper, my God."

"Never mind, Ruby," her father said. Her mother sat back down.

Brenda saw that the baby—Dwayne?—was asleep on the couch beside her mother. Her father was still in the armchair. Aunt Kate sat on the small sofa, and Brenda sat down beside her. She was joining the conversation, whether they all liked it or not.

"So," Kate seemed to pick up where she had previously left off. "I will speak with Carolyn and Charmayne. They can't go tossing a baby around like this. That would be abandonment, by both the mother and the grandmother. But I need to have a very clear answer from you both. Are you willing to keep him here for now?" She looked first to Martin, and then to Ruby.

Brenda watched as her father nodded in the affirmative. Then she heard her mother quietly answer, "Yes, we will keep him."

After that, Kate rose to leave. Brenda sat where she was in stunned silence. This baby was staying. This baby who was her father's child. He was—she had a difficult time with the words, even in her head—her own brother. When her mother and father got up to see Kate out the door, Brenda went to sit beside "Dwayne" on the couch. He was smaller than Jasmine, that was for sure. She stared at his black hair, his little nose, and his one clenched fist that had worked itself out of the blanket. The baby boy slept on, still oblivious of her existence.

TWENTY-NINE

After Monica repeated to him what Brenda had told her, Michael made a hasty remark about people thinking that his family had problems. When Monica glared at him, he dropped the subject and played with Jasmine instead. He was certain that his daughter was already smiling at him.

After they had eaten supper, Monica wrapped Jasmine in her blankets and left for Ruby's. She was so busy going over in her head what had happened that she failed to see Charlie and Molly coming towards her. Usually, she was glad to see Charlie, but this evening she was not in the mood for neighbourly conversation. Charlie said that they were just going for a short walk. He talked about the weather in Kitsum and how much his kids were enjoying visiting their grandmother. Then, out of the blue, he changed the subject.

"Look, my mom feels bad about what Carolyn did. It doesn't help much, I know, but you should know that my mom tried to stop her, to make her see sense and think about what she was doing."

Monica nodded and smiled weakly.

"Yeah, well…in case I don't see you guys before we go, tell Michael I'll stay in touch."

"I'll tell him, and…" She was not sure what to say about Nona talking to Carolyn.

Charlie seemed to understand. He was a genuinely nice guy. She was glad that she had run into him. He had made her less anxious, and had put her in a better frame of mind to see her sister.

Instead of walking right into Ruby's kitchen as she usually did, Monica knocked and called out. She waited for her sister to answer before she entered the house. Martin, Ruby, and Brenda were sitting at the table. It looked like they had just finished eating. The kids were not home yet. She passed Jasmine to Brenda and sat down on a kitchen chair. Charmayne's child lay asleep in Jasmine's crib. Monica could not help but stare.

"Are you hungry?" Ruby asked automatically.

"We already ate."

Brenda smiled over at her. "Thanks for keeping Jazz."

Monica watched her family and waited for someone to speak. There was an air of discomfort in the kitchen, and yet Ruby looked surprisingly in control. Martin mostly kept his eyes down on his plate.

"We'll talk tomorrow, Monica." Ruby gave her a meaningful look.

Monica jumped up at once. "I better get going," she said. No one argued.

She had almost reached the door when she heard Martin's voice. "Monica, tell Michael that I want to have a word with him sometime. No rush. So make sure you tell him that too—there's no big rush."

"Okay." Monica had answered without turning around. She had no idea what Michael had to do with any of this. She brushed aside her burning curiosity and stepped out of the house.

The sun had already gone behind the mountain. It would be dark in half an hour. The summer days were rapidly shrinking. Monica was glad for the walk home. She strolled leisurely, taking a detour along the ocean front to breathe in the salt air. A trace of the afternoon's westerly wind still lingered.

THIRTY

Charlie was leaving Kitsum in less than a week. He reminded his mother about the open invitation for her to return to Hartley Bay. He and Molly, he had repeated firmly, were very serious. They wanted her to stay with them. The kids wanted her. None of them were going to stop asking.

They did not expect her to give up her home in Kitsum. They just wanted her to spend the school year in Hartley Bay. Charlie would bring her back to Kitsum by June, or earlier if she wanted. He made it sound so simple. As though Nona could just pick up and leave everything for nearly an entire year. The whole idea had struck Nona as preposterous. She was sixty years old, for heaven's sake. Why was Charlie being so insistent?

Martin had not been out fishing. Nona knew that the season was winding down, and that it was almost time to put the gillnet drum on the *Pacific Queen* again for fall fishing. She also knew that Carolyn's grandchild had now been at the Joe residence for five full days, and that Kate visited daily. Monica was in and out with Brenda's baby, once with Michael, and the other times by herself. Old Peter and Susan Joe had been over to visit. Ruby and Brenda were often out in the yard, and the kids played around the house frequently. There had been no sign of Carolyn though. No sign at all.

It looked like the baby boy was there to stay. Brenda appeared to be on better terms with her aunt and her baby's father. Martin and Ruby appeared okay. The whole Joe family seemed to be holding together and keeping on as normal, even after everything that had happened.

Maybe Charlie had been right. Things had a way of working out in Kitsum.

Charlie, Molly, Harry, Jen, and Maureen were going back to Hartley Bay. She would have less than a week to get ready. Well, what if she could manage it? Her son and daughter-in-law were right there to help her. The three of them would be able to store away her stuff for the winter. Some of her belongings would be musty when she returned, but those things could be aired out. She could safely leave the key with Martin and Ruby and they would check on the house as often as she wished. Nona really had no excuse to stay home. Still, she hesitated.

The next morning at breakfast, her youngest grandchild asked her a question. "How come you don't want to come home with us, Grandma?"

Nona did not answer. She saw the hurt look on Maureen's face. Still, she said nothing.

The words she wanted to use were stuck inside her mouth. She could not quite get them out. Charlie and Molly stared at her.

"Well, I can't just sit here all day," Nona finally muttered. "There's lots of cleaning and packing to do, on account of our needing to leave so soon."

Charlie stared at her, open-mouthed. Then his smile grew larger and larger.

"Grandma *is* coming to Hartley Bay with us," he told his children.

Nona swore that the smile did not completely leave her son's face for the rest of the week.

ACKNOWLEDGEMENTS

Thank you to Karen Haughian, publisher of Signature Editions. Without your vision and belief in *Through Different Eyes,* this book would not exist.

Thank you to Garry Thomas Morse. Your insights, advice, and solid editing made this a much stronger novel.

Thank you to my husband, Stephen Charleson. The ways of seeing and knowing the world that you have opened up for me continue to keep me amazed and grounded.

Thank you to the beautiful people and loving families of the West Coast. You are truly inspirational.

Thank you also to this place I am honoured to call home: A-yi-saqh, Hesquiat Harbour. I cannot imagine having written from anywhere else.

For so much, *a-tiq-shitls see-hilth* (I am grateful to you all).

ABOUT THE AUTHOR

Through Different Eyes is Karen Charleson's first novel, although she has published three science textbooks with McGraw-Hill Ryerson and has had numerous articles and essays appear in such diverse publications as *Canadian Geographic*, the *Globe and Mail*, the *Vancouver Sun*, and *Canadian Literature*. Karen holds an MA in Integrated Studies from Athabasca University. She is a member through marriage of the House of Kinquashtakumtlth and the Hesquiaht First Nation on the mid-west coast of Vancouver Island. She is a mother of six, as well as a grandmother. Along with her husband, Karen operates Hooksum Outdoor School in the traditional Hesquiaht territories that they call home.

Eco-Audit
Printing this book using Rolland Enviro 100 Book
instead of virgin fibres paper saved the following resources:

Trees	Solid Waste	Water	Air Emissions
2	105 kg	8,536 L	344 kg